Praise for Lauren Baratz-Logsted

"A consistently entertaining read that delivers a genuinely original heroine and frequently hilarious satire." —*Kirkus Reviews*

"Baratz-Logsted fully embraces the . . . fish-out-of-water premise, but those upset over the fates of certain characters in the original will find reason to rejoice in this retelling." —*Publishers Weekly*

"Much of the story's appeal derives from the contrast between this strange new land of Civil War–era New England and Emily's other life as a media-savvy, plugged-in, wisecracking kid trying to navigate adolescent angst in twenty-first-century real time." —*Booklist*

THE
twin's
daughter

"A fast-paced thriller filled with murder and intrigue. . . . This riveting story will keep readers guessing until the very end." —*SLJ*

"Rife with twists and moves swiftly and elegantly." —*Booklist*

"The story offers many absorbing elements of young love, suspense and surprise." —*Kirkus Reviews*

Little Women and Me

Lauren Baratz-Logsted

BLOOMSBURY

NEW YORK   LONDON   NEW DELHI   SYDNEY

First published in the United States of America in November 2011
by Bloomsbury Children's Books
Paperback edition published in July 2013
www.bloomsbury.com

For information about permission to reproduce selections from this book, write to
Permissions, Bloomsbury Children's Books, 1385 Broadway, New York, New York 10018
Bloomsbury books may be purchased for business or promotional use. For information on bulk
purchases please contact Macmillan Corporate and Premium Sales Department at
specialmarkets@macmillan.com

The Library of Congress has cataloged the hardcover edition as follows:
Baratz-Logsted, Lauren.
Little Women and me / by Lauren Baratz-Logsted — 1st U.S. ed.
p.   cm.
Summary: Modern-day teen Emily March turns to Louisa May Alcott's
famous book for a school assignment and finds herself mysteriously transported
to the world of Little Women, where she undergoes surprising changes.
ISBN 978-1-59990-514-3 (hardcover)
[1. Space and time—Fiction. 2. Sisters—Fiction. 3. Family life—New England—Fiction.
4. Conduct of life—Fiction. 5. New England—History—19th century—Fiction.]
I. Alcott, Louisa May, 1832–1888. Little women. II. Title.
PZ7.B22966Lit 2011   [Fic]—dc22   2010038095

ISBN 978-1-61963-033-8 (paperback)

Book design by Regina Flath
Typeset by Westchester Book Composition
Printed and bound in the U.S.A. by Thomson-Shore Inc., Dexter, Michigan
2 4 6 8 10 9 7 5 3 1

All papers used by Bloomsbury Publishing, Inc., are natural, recyclable products
made from wood grown in well-managed forests. The manufacturing processes
conform to the environmental regulations of the country of origin.

FOR MELANIE CECKA,
WITH GREAT THANKS

Little Women and Me

Prologue

"There's no such thing as a perfect book," Mr. Ochocinco says.

Mr. Ochocinco is my English teacher, but that's not his real last name. Or at least it wasn't until last year when my older sister, Charlotte, had him. Back then his name was Mr. Smith, but then when he thought his favorite football team, the Bengals, had a shot at the Super Bowl, he legally changed his last name to that of his favorite player, Chad Ochocinco, who had changed *his* name to match the number on his jersey and whose own real last name before he changed it was Johnson.

This is all by way of saying that Wycroft Academy, the K–12 school where I'm currently a freshman, is an odd place. But then, aren't all schools?

"A writer may *think* his or her book is perfect when completed," Mr. Ochocinco continues, "and pity the poor writer who thinks that! But in reality, there's probably something that the reader would change. Maybe it's just a single extraneous paragraph. Maybe it's a character or an entire plot point! And of course it's possible that no two readers will agree on what that imperfect something is. But no matter how beloved a book, there's usually something."

Blahblahblah.

I normally love English class, which doesn't even feel like school to me, but today I just want him to get on with it. Never mind if some novel needs changing. I've got my own problems, my own things that need changing. Like destroying Charlotte's love life. Well, not for the sake of destroying it, but because—

"Your assignment," Mr. Ochocinco goes on, "is to pick a novel that you have always loved deeply. Then I want you to write a paper telling me three things you love about it and one thing you would change. *Just one.*" Mr. Ochocinco glances at the clock on the wall, sees we're out of time just as the bell rings, and hurries to finish assigning the assignment.

"It's Friday," he says in a rush, raising his voice to be heard over the sounds of students tossing items into backpacks, pushing back chairs, and stampeding toward the door. "I want outlines on my desk Monday morning, finished papers the following Monday. Dismissed."

For a guy who loves football so much, he sure can sound all formal English teachery at times. But who cares? I'm finally sprung!

Now I can get down to what this day should really be about.

Lunch!

Well, no, I'm not really excited about it being lunch because of the food. I mean, normally I would be, because it's pizza day, but that's not it. Plus, I don't even get pizza, because I don't want Jackson to think I'm a pig, so I quickly hit the salad bar, piling a plate high with as much designer lettuce as I can. Then I throw on a few other fresh vegetables and put some fat-free dressing on the side in a little cup. Put the cup of dressing in its neat little slot on the salad plate, add a carton of juice to my other hand, and voilà!

Salad is the one food that even when you pile it into an enormous mound on your plate, like I have done, does not make you look like a pig. On the contrary, the more on your plate, the more you look like an anti-pig.

Which is definitely the image that I want to project when I sit down to eat with Jackson, like I'm about to do right now.

Jackson is an architectural marvel of a boy, the architectural part having to do with the way he's constructed. He's tall, thin, but with wide shoulders—only a sophomore, Jackson's a starter on the varsity football team. He's got a Roman nose, Slavic cheekbones, Scandinavian blond hair, and Mediterranean blue-green eyes. Really, looking at Jackson is like going on a tour of Europe. Right now, though, his cheek is lethargically smushed against a lethargic half fist, his elbow lethargically slouched on the table as he stares at his uneaten pizza.

He comes to life at the sound of me putting my plate and juice carton on the wooden table.

"Emily!" he says, excited to see me.

If only that were really the case.

Yes, he is excited to see me—*in theory*—but the truth of the matter is it's really my sister Charlotte he wishes were seated across from him. How can I be sure of this?

Because Jackson has had a thing for Charlotte all year, but he's too shy to express himself directly to her. You could say I'm his proxy Charlotte. Meanwhile, I've had a thing for Jackson all year, but I haven't let him know, because if he knew, he'd be uncomfortable talking with me about Charlotte and then I would get to spend no time with him whatsoever. I've been biding my time, waiting for him to see that I would make a much better girlfriend than Charlotte would.

True, on the surface, he and Charlotte have more in common, like both being involved with sports, while I tend to be more cerebral; like both being tall and gorgeous, while I am somewhat less than. Still, I know I'm meant for Jackson. And Jackson's meant for me. Sometimes these things don't make sense to other people, but then, sometimes, a girl just *knows*. It's the way I feel when I see him and I don't see how I can feel what I feel without him ever feeling the same way back. Now it's just a matter of getting Charlotte out of the way.

Unfortunately, biding my time has not been working out so well for me thus far. Jackson has yet to realize that Charlotte's all wrong for him and that I'm all right. I mean, who's been metaphorically holding his hand and eating salad while he's been mooning over Charlotte? I'll tell you one thing: it hasn't been Charlotte. It's been *me*, playing the gal pal, the good buddy, the supportive listener.

But as I say, that hasn't been working out, so it's time for me to take matters into my own hands.

"Did you talk to Charlotte last night?" Jackson asks eagerly.

"I did," I say neutrally.

"And?" he asks, still eager.

Here's what I was supposed to be asking Charlotte about: I was supposed to ask her, on Jackson's behalf, if there was any chance she might like him. It was all my idea.

Oh, and who does Charlotte like, if I like Jackson and Jackson likes Charlotte? Why, she likes Jackson, of course. Who wouldn't? After all, he's got that whole architectural-Europe thing going on. But Charlotte doesn't know that Jackson likes her, because she always sees him eating lunch with me, and I certainly haven't told her, nor did I ask her The Question last night.

"I'm sorry," I say now, feigning sadness, "but she said no. As a matter of fact, she likes someone else."

This last inspired tidbit snaps him out of sadness and into surprise.

"Who?" he says. "I never see her hanging with any one particular guy regularly."

"Charlotte likes . . . ," I start, but then I'm stumped. I hadn't planned this far ahead. "Charlotte likes . . ." I scan the dining hall quickly, spot Charlotte standing in line waiting for her pizza, with her perfect long black hair. Right behind Charlotte and her perfect long black hair is Boyd Tarquin. As far as I can tell, they don't even know each other all that well, since he's a senior. Still, I get another inspiration. He's standing really closely behind her, probably eager to get his pizza. This could work.

"Boyd Tarquin," I say. "She likes Boyd Tarquin. And he likes her."

"Boyd Tarquin?" Jackson says in equal parts shock and disgust.

"See?" I say, giving a chin nod toward the waiting pizza line. "There they are together now."

Jackson looks just in time to see Boyd reach across the counter to accept his pizza from the server. As Boyd reaches, his elbow grazes Charlotte's arm and they turn to each other, exchange words we can't hear. He probably said, "Excuse me," and she probably said, "No problem," but it certainly looks intimate from here.

"Huh." Jackson looks deflated. "I never would have guessed." He sighs. "I guess maybe it's time for me to accept the inevitable and move on."

Yes. Yes! He's finally going to turn his attention to me, see what's been right under his nose all this time: *me*. Which is doubly true, because I'm short. So what if it took a little lie or two or three to get me here? I wait, eagerly, for Jackson to come to his senses. I'm sure when he does, it'll be just like a Taylor Swift song.

Jackson brightens suddenly.

Jackson brightening suddenly—that *must* be a good sign!

Jackson speaks.

"What do you think my chances are with Anne?" Jackson says.

"*Anne?*" I'm so thunderstruck, I drop my salad fork. "Who is *Anne?*"

"Your little sister. Anne. I know she's only in eighth grade now, but next year she'll be in Upper School with us. I can wait. I'll be a junior, she'll be a freshman—not too big an age difference. And she's really cute."

I can't believe this. What, is my life a sitcom with me the butt of all the jokes?

I contemplate the idea of my younger sister, Anne, with her pretty blond hair. I could see where a guy would like her, even an older guy.

But never mind that now, because . . .

I've wasted so many lunches eating salad while listening to Jackson moon over Charlotte . . . and now he's going to switch his affections to Anne?

This cannot be happening to me.

When I get home, I go straight to my room.

I cannot believe how much my life stinks.

Immediately, I fish my iPhone out of my backpack and text Kendra. Kendra and I have been best friends for as long as I've been at Wycroft, but our schedules this year are so different, plus I've been wasting all those lunches eating but not eating with Jackson, that sometimes I barely even get to talk to her until after school.

Call me! Call Me!! CALL ME!!! I text madly. *This is 2 big & involved & crisis-worthy 4 texting!*

A minute later my phone rings and for a second I'm happier than I've been all day. There's something to be said for friends you can rely on. Too bad the same thing can't be said about sisters. Or at least not my sisters.

"Yo, dude, what's the emergency?" Kendra says.

I ignore her "yo" and her "dude" and head straight for the emergency.

"Jackson is no longer interested in pursuing Charlotte," I say.

"But that's good news, right?" she says. "Where's the crisis?"

"Where's the crisis? I'll tell you where the crisis is. He's decided to switch his romantic allegiance to Anne."

"Who is *Anne?*" she asks, echoing my question from earlier in the day and giving me a moment of nostalgia as I remember how simple *my* life was before I knew the awful answer.

I tell her who Anne is.

What do I expect when I tell her? I expect outrage. I expect sympathy. Certainly I feel plenty of both of those on my own behalf. But instead I get:

"HA!"

I'm in shock. "You're *laughing?*" I don't believe this!

"Come on," Kendra says. "You've got to admit, it's funny."

"I don't have to admit anything of the kind!"

"It's like that old sitcom *The Brady Bunch.* Have you ever seen it? It's like if Jan liked a boy who liked Marcia only to have him turn his attention to Cindy. You know, 'the youngest one in curls'?" She breaks out laughing even harder.

"Stop this!" I say. "My life is not a sitcom!" It's doubly harsh to hear her imply that it is since I'd had that thought myself earlier. "And Anne isn't some cute little 'youngest one in curls.' She's . . . she's . . . she's some hot little eighth-grade number—a vixen in Justice clothing!—and now somehow she's gotten Jackson to fall for her!"

I'm fuming. Not at Kendra. She's my best friend, meaning she can say anything she wants to me and no matter how outraged I might seem, it's okay. Rather, I'm fuming at the unfairness of it all.

"Emily?"

"Hmm . . . ?" I say vaguely, still fuming.

"Why do you resent Anne so much?"

I can*not* believe she is asking me this.

"Do you *not* remember the Incident of the Shawls?" I say.

"Oh no," I hear her groan, although I'm fairly certain it's a loving groan. "Not the Incident of the Shawls again!"

"Oh yes," I say emphatically. "It's the Incident of the Shawls again. When I was eight, Charlotte was nine, and Anne was seven, Mom went on that two-week trip to Spain with her women's club. She brought back three shawls for us as souvenirs. You wouldn't think a shawl would be a cool thing, but these shawls were *amazing.* They were pure silk and had all this really awesome fringe and each one was a different color. Charlotte got to pick first, which was okay, since she's the oldest. Well, of course she chose the ivory-colored one, which was far and away the prettiest. But that was okay too because the second-prettiest was this orchid purple. With my auburn hair, I figured I could look very dramatic in it. And I was all ready to say that's the one I wanted, but then my mother said—"

"That Anne should pick next," Kendra said, "because she didn't think it was fair for Anne to be last in everything, just because she's the youngest."

"Exactly right. So Anne picked the orchid one and I got stuck with—"

"The puke-green one."

"Yes! Green in general is my favorite color and nearly every green in the universe is cool, except this one shade that looks like what people throw up when they puke in horror films. So what did I look like in it? I looked like a Christmas tree that someone had upchucked."

"Totally gross image."

"You're telling me! And that's exactly what my entire life has been like. Charlotte or Anne gets first in everything because they're the oldest and the youngest, and then the other gets second because the oldest or the youngest can't possibly be last in any-thing, while I'm always stuck with—"

"Why do you like Jackson so much?" Kendra asks, cutting me off.

"Hel-*lo!*" I say. "Because he's gorgeous? Because he's nice?"

"How is Jackson nice to you?"

I open my mouth to answer, but nothing comes out. Why *do* I like Jackson?

"And why did you like Kurt so much last year?" Kendra presses.

"Or Michael the year before that? Or Dale when we were in sixth grade?"

"I don't know!" I say, exasperated. "Because they're all hot! Because they're nice or funny or smart or something like that. A person can't always *explain* why they like who they like!" I pause as something hits me. "Wait a second. Are you saying that I'm . . . *shallow?*"

Kendra sighs. "No. I would never say that. I wouldn't even think it! But sometimes, you go after things or people without thinking everything through first."

Huh.

That's a lot to think about. Only problem is, I don't want to think about it right now. I've got to figure out how to fix things so Jackson doesn't become Anne's orchid shawl.

"I gotta go," I say. "I've got a ton of homework, plus Mr. O. gave us this big English assignment."

"You're not mad at me, are you?" she says hesitantly. "For laughing before and because of the things I said?"

"Are you kidding me?" I say. "Sometimes I wish I could laugh at myself. Don't worry, we're good—bests forever."

"Good." She sounds relieved. "Meet you in the lunchroom for doughnuts before school on Monday?"

"I'm totally there," I say, and snap my phone shut.

I decide to be true to what I told Kendra and get my homework done first. True, it's a lame way to spend Friday afternoon and evening, but once that's out of the way I can devote the rest of the weekend to plotting a new strategy for Jackson.

Not that I know what that is yet.

I work through my assignments from least favorite class to most favorite, which means moving through biology, algebra, and history before I come finally to English.

What was that assignment Mr. Ochocinco gave us?

Oh, right.

We're supposed to take a book we feel is nearly perfect, give three things we love about it and one thing we'd change; outline due Monday.

This should be easy enough.

But which book to choose?

I go to my bookshelves. I have a *lot* of books. You could practically say I live in them.

Something modern like *Harry Potter* or *Twilight*? No. Teachers are never impressed with anything modern. They like the older stuff.

Maybe Judy Blume? But what would I change? Turn it into *Are You There, God? It's Me, Marcus*? Nah, that wouldn't work. Besides, to impress teachers, you need to go for the really old stuff.

Which is fine, because I like some of the really old stuff too.

A Separate Peace? No. Even though the ending always makes me cry, I wouldn't change a thing. It's a perfect example of how jealousy corrodes love. People really should be careful about that.

Wuthering Heights? No. There's too much I'd want to change there.

Winnie-the-Pooh? It does qualify as "old stuff," so you'd think it would have the potential to impress, but how would I change it for the better? Add conflict by making Eeyore a depressed serial killer?

Little Women.

Huh.

For the first time, I pull one of the books from the shelf. As I tug the volume loose from the bookcase, my fingers tingle as though zapped by electricity.

Weird.

I hold the red cloth-covered volume in my hands. I *loved* this book when I was younger, but I haven't read it once in the last four years. How much do I still remember of it? Enough to do the assignment without rereading? After all, I've read a lot of books in the years in between. Still . . .

I go to my desk holding the book in one hand, sit down in front of the computer, and think about what to put in the outline. Hmm . . . Three things I loved about the book . . .

One. The first is easy. The name of the family: March. You'd think that with daughters named Charlotte, Emily, and Anne, my parents' last name might be Brontë. But no. Our last name is March, which is something I loved about *Little Women*. It may sound superficial, but the characters having the same last name as me always made me identify with them, kind of like Mr. O.'s ability to identify with a football player now that they share the same last name.

Two. Jo March is a writer. I've always loved writing, even more than I love reading, and a lot of that can be traced back to Jo March. What girl doesn't want to be Jo March after reading about her writing stories in her garret while chomping on crisp apples? Chomping apples may not seem like the definition of cool, but the way Jo did it, it just set her apart from everyone else, and in a good way, like it was somehow a sign of her independent spirit. Jo is the March girl every reader wants to be.

Three. The amazing relationship between the four sisters: Meg, Jo, Beth, and Amy. They were all so different, yet even when they argued—unlike with Charlotte or Anne and me—they always managed to love and eventually support one another. They actually made having siblings seem like a good idea. Girls without any sisters want to have sisters like them. And girls like me, ones with sisters who always make you feel like the least important people in your own families—those girls *really* wanted to have sisters like them!

This is good. My outline is practically writing itself.

Now for the second part. What's the one thing I would change to make *Little Women* a perfect book?

Hmm . . .

I open the book, figuring maybe reading a little bit will help me decide, flip past the first woodcut illustration to the first chapter and the first line:

"Christmas won't be Christmas without any presents," grumbled Jo, lying on the rug.

Having read the first line, I read another, and then another. Before I know it, I'm caught up in the story. This surprises me, given how often I've read it before. And what further surprises me is that even though I have read it many times already, there's so much of the story that feels new, things I don't remember reading before. Is that because it's been four years since I last read it? Or is it because I'm different now, older?

I stare at the pages, still stuck with trying out what should be changed about the book.

Maybe the thing that happens to Beth? I always hated that. But wait a second. What about how things end up for Jo and Amy with the boy next door, Laurie? That has to be the most frustrating romantic outcome in any book ever.

But which to change?

The thing with Beth? The thing with Jo and Amy and Laurie? The—

V-ROOM!

What's that sound? Is that Charlotte vacuuming in the hopes of getting our mother to think her even more wonderful than she already thinks her to be?

I cross the room, bang my copy of *Little Women* against the closed door. Rude, I know. But still.

The sound doesn't stop, however. Instead, it grows in volume and suddenly I feel myself spinning in circles rapidly, spinning and spinning until . . .

WHOOSH!

Talk about being sucked into a book.

One

"*Christmas won't be Christmas without any presents,*" *grumbled the girl, lying on the rug.*

I looked at the girl sprawled out in front of the crackling fire. She was my age or maybe just a bit older—tall, thin, large nose, gray eyes, chestnut hair piled into a messy bun, long gray dress. I *knew* her. Oh, not from school or town. No, I knew her from the woodcut illustrations—yeah, the ones in my book. And I knew the words she'd spoken, which were the opening lines, of course.

Jo March!

I blinked my eyes hard at the impossible vision—what was going on?—only to snap them open again at the sound of other girl voices.

It was so strange, coming in on the middle of the conversation. What were they talking about? Something about missing Papa? Something about the war?

I followed the voices to the speakers. They all wore long dresses, seriously ugly boots peeking out from beneath the hems. The oldest looking of the girls had soft brown hair tied up in some kind of funky 'do. She looked like a size 16 and she kept studying her hands as though she thought they were the coolest thing ever. *Whoa! That's Meg March*, I thought.

The girl next to her looked the youngest, a skinny chick with long, curly blond hair. Her eyes were a startling blue. *Amy*.

So where was . . . ?

I heard a soft voice say something about not minding about the money. That's when I saw her, almost hidden like a mouse, as she knitted away in the corner. The rosy cheeks, the flat hair, the bright eyes, and the peaceful expression. Check. Had to be *Beth*.

As I looked around the room, and took in the old-fashioned furniture and stuff, I tried to figure out what had happened. The last thing I remembered was opening my copy of *Little Women* and reading the first line, then reading more and thinking about things, and then . . . *WHOOSH!*

Had I turned on the TV while doing my homework and stumbled on an old movie version? But no, *this* Jo March didn't look like an actress playing Jo March. She looked like, well, Jo March! Maybe I'd eaten a contaminated lettuce leaf at lunch and was hallucinating or someone had poisoned me? Or maybe the answer was simpler: I fell asleep while reading, and this was just a dream?

I pinched myself, hard, but after the pinch I was still in the room. In a dream, can you give yourself a specific direction like that and actually have the dream-you do the thing?

"Emily." I jumped in my chair as Jo kicked me in the foot.

As I looked down at where she'd tapped me, I saw for the first time that I had the same seriously ugly boots on my feet as the rest of them: they were brown leather, heavily creased, and laced from the toes to a few inches above the ankle. I also took in my long brown dress, and felt something thick and binding across my midsection. My hand moved to my waist. At the feel of the narrow bonelike strips, a bizarre thought occurred to me—was I wearing a *corset*? This was worse than a bra! And my underpants felt . . . loose. Not like panties at all. They felt bloomerish! All of it—the boots, the long dress, whatever bizarre garments lay underneath the dress—felt incredibly heavy, like I would lose weight just by walking around and sweating in this stuff all day long. My hand traveled up to my head only to find my auburn hair pulled up into a loose bun with . . . pins? I had pins in my hair? That's when I jumped in my chair for the second time in as many minutes. What the heck had happened to my own clothes? Why was my hair like this? What was going on???

"Emily," Jo said again. "Why must you always daydream when we're trying to have an important discussion?"

And how did she know my name?

It had felt real enough when she nudged my foot hard, and I suddenly needed to touch her, to see if *she* felt real. But as I reached, half tempted to tap her on the shoulder as hard as she'd tapped my foot, I saw my own hand. It was no longer the hand I knew. Gone were the longish nails, painted near black, and the ringed fingers I'd used to hold my salad fork while talking to Jackson. In its place was a hand that looked rougher than mine, like it had been doing some sort of work, the nails very short and very clean.

I jumped to my feet. Not seeing any mirrors in the room,

I rushed to a set of windows and glimpsed what I could of my reflection in one of the panes, the night black beyond the glass. I looked like me, I saw, and yet not at all like me. Where was my makeup? My eyebrows were no longer tweezed! Suddenly I had to wonder: If I took off all these clothes—obviously not in front of everyone else, of course—would I discover unshaved armpits and hairy legs? Gross!

On a small table next to the set of windows stood a small lamp, the light glowing through a cloudy glass globe attached to the silver base. I couldn't see any wires attached to the base, so I glanced inside the globe, saw a flame burning from a thick wick. I sniffed: oil.

First, I was hearing things from *Little Women*. Then I was seeing things. Now I was *smelling* things? What was going on?

It's just a dream, Emily, I muttered to myself repeatedly, closing my eyes on all the confusing things, *just a dream, just a dream . . .*

"Really, Emily," Meg said sternly.

My eyes snapped open again. I was myself and not myself, and not only could I hear these four girls talking to one another, but they were talking to me too, even using my name. This was some dream!

And if I could see and hear them, then maybe they could hear me too?

I opened my mouth to speak, not taking the time first to think of what to say. What came out was:

"What year is this?"

"It's 1861," Amy said with a smirk, then for good measure she rolled her eyes.

1861? Wow. Radical.

"If I ever asked a question like that," Amy continued, "Jo'd tease me forever."

I ignored her.

"And how old am I?"

"You're fourteen, you goose," Jo said, adding in an exasperated singsong, "and Meg is sixteen, I am fifteen, Beth is thirteen, and Amy is twelve."

"And that makes me . . . ," I started to say.

"The middle sister"—Jo's tone remained exasperated—"just like you've always been. Now do try to stop being so silly, if you possibly can. We're trying to figure out what we shall each get for Marmee."

I must have looked confused, because Beth piped up in a nice way, "You know, Emily, how we decided it wouldn't be right to spend money on our own pleasures when the men are in the army? So we decided instead to take the dollar each of us has received and spend it instead on Marmee?"

"And now," Jo said pointedly to me, "we are wondering what *you* plan to get her."

Was she for real? No, of course she wasn't. She was just a dream, which was why I burst out laughing and then said, "What can you possibly buy someone for just one dollar?"

Now it was the four others' turn to look puzzled as they stared at me for a long moment.

Meg finally spoke. "Actually, you can get quite a lot. I plan on buying Marmee gloves when we all go shopping tomorrow."

"I had been planning on buying myself a new book," Jo said, adding with an insane level of seriousness, "but now I am going to buy Marmee army shoes."

"I was going to buy myself some music," Beth said, "but I'll be much happier getting her handkerchiefs, and I even plan to embroider her name onto them."

"I had so wanted some drawing pencils," sighed Amy. "But

I suppose now I shall get her cologne. Although if I get only a smallish bottle—"

"What about you?" Jo cut Amy off as she turned to me. "What shall you buy for Marmee with your dollar when we go shopping tomorrow?"

They'd just listed four things they apparently thought they could buy for a buck each, but how should I know what you could buy in the stores around here? Besides, I wouldn't even be here tomorrow. I'd be awake, since this was all a dream!

"I don't know what I shall get," I answered. Did they have any dollar stores around here?

Wait a second, I thought. *I just said* shall. It was so weird, like being around Brazilian people and suddenly thinking I could understand Portuguese!

Whatever, I told myself. *Just go with it, Emily. You'll be out of here soon enough.*

"I don't know," I repeated, feeling the others stare at me. "I guess I'll just get her one of those things like the things you all are going to get her."

Meg felt my forehead. "Are you feeling unwell?"

"Emily is behaving peculiarly," Jo said, adding wryly, "even for her."

"I'm fine." I waved Meg's hand away. "It's just that sometimes things get . . . confusing around here."

Confusing? Ha! I had no idea what was going on! Maybe I'd been kidnapped and brought to some historical re-creationist cult run by those old dudes who like to put on war uniforms from World War II or the Civil War?

"I don't under—" Meg started to say, but Jo cut her off.

"Didn't you hear her say she's fine? Besides, we really should practice the play I wrote for Christmas before Marmee comes home. We don't want to spoil the surprise by having her see it before we're ready."

"Yes, of course," Meg agreed. "But perhaps Emily should just observe while we rehearse? She really doesn't seem herself."

"Fine," Jo grumbled.

It was a good thing Meg had given me an out. I was having a hard-enough time keeping up with all the conversations in this confusingly elaborate dream—because that's what I decided this *had* to be—and it would have been impossible to rehearse for a play I knew nothing about.

As I watched the other four working and playing together, I thought about how their personalities in my dream matched what I remembered about them.

Meg was the prig.

Jo was the rebel.

Beth was the least cool of the four, but she was so sweet and kind, it would be impossible to make fun of her.

Amy was totally into herself, a blond Bratz doll.

But where did I fit into all this? I wondered. Where was my place? Jo had said I was the middle sister, but what exactly did that mean here?

Not that it mattered. I wouldn't be here much longer. I was bound to wake up any second.

Except I didn't wake up.

I didn't wake up during the long rehearsal, which was confusing—put it this way: it was no episode of *Glee*.

I didn't wake up when Marmee came home. She was on the shrimpy side when compared with her older daughters and she had some kind of a cloak thing on plus a bonnet. I mean, come on.

A bonnet? Still, in spite of her uncool appearance, when she entered the house the others acted like they'd seen the sun rise indoors.

I didn't wake up when we had our dinner, which they kept calling "tea," with bread and butter; or when we all gathered around Marmee in front of the fire as she read a letter from "Papa," who, it turned out, was a priest or pastor or something in the American Civil War. I always thought old people didn't have to serve, but the letter said he would be gone for a year. It also contained messages for each of his "little women." And here's the weirdest part—my dream was *so* detailed, there was even a direct message from him to me in the letter:

> *Emily, my middle March, know that even when you feel there is no clear place for you, there is always in my heart.*

Not that the message made a lot of sense, but it felt kind of nice to be treated like one of the in-crowd around here.

As the night went on, in order to keep that feeling of fitting in, I pretty much followed along with whatever they did, mirroring their every move, trying to speak like them the few times I opened my mouth. It got a little easier, I guess, but those *shall*s were still coming hard to me.

We sewed until nine at night; or I should say, they sewed. I'd never sewn a stitch in my life! I was relieved to see each sister take one corner of a quilt. All I had to do was pass them supplies as they worked. Then there was some singing around the old piano while Beth played, followed by getting ready for bed; I didn't wake up during any of it, though I kept expecting to, any moment now.

I didn't even wake up when Beth and Amy went to one bedroom while I followed Meg and Jo into a connecting bedroom.

There was a white linen granny nightgown and there was even a bed for me in my Dream March House! Eventually, Marmee came up and sang us lullabies in the most beautiful voice imaginable, before giving us each a kiss on our cheeks.

At that point feeling a part of things, I didn't want to wake up.

Two

But the next morning when I became aware that the bedroom was freezing cold, OMG, I certainly wanted to wake up!

I don't know everything about every subject in the world, but I'd had enough dreams in my life to know that dreams don't just go on and on like this. Unless . . .

Wait a second here. Was I in a *coma?*

But I must have been in some sort of an accident to be in a coma. And I didn't remember any accident, only opening up that darned book and reading the first line.

No, I told myself. It wasn't a coma because I could *feel* the cold. I'd simply dreamed that I'd somehow landed myself in the March household in 1861. But as hard as I tried to shake myself awake, the evidence before my eyes wouldn't go away. There was Meg, still sleeping. There was Jo, still sleeping.

So, not a dream. Not a coma.

I tried the pinching thing again but all I got for it was a red mark on my hand. I was going to have to stop doing that to myself.

But, if not a coma, then what?

Had I found some way to bust through the space-time continuum?

That didn't make any sense either. As far as I could remember, the March family had never been real. They were merely a figment of Louisa May Alcott's imagination.

Then what? What exactly had happened to me? All I knew was that I had to get out of here. I had to get back to my normal life—the one where there were no granny nightgowns in my wardrobe and people didn't say "shall."

But how? How?

Then it struck me. Ever since this "dream" had started, I'd been inside the house. *Inside* the house. That was it! If I could only get *outside* again, things would reset and I'd wake up.

I threw off the sheets and blankets, not minding a bit about the cold in spite of my thin white granny nightgown and hairy legs—I'd peeked the night before as I'd climbed into bed.

I heard a woman humming and followed the sound to an old-fashioned-looking kitchen. It reminded me of a class trip we'd taken to Sturbridge Village, what with all the antiques, like a barrel with a wooden paddle thingy sticking up through the middle—a butter churn, maybe? Standing at a table was a woman I didn't recognize. Well, that wasn't a huge shock. I hadn't known any of these people until just recently!

Ignoring the woman, even when she shouted "Emily!" after me, I raced for the back door. Once there, I threw it open and stepped out into . . .

Fresh snow! I instantly felt the coldness on my bare skin as my feet sank into it. I looked around me and saw real winter just like on an old New England postcard.

But never mind that now . . . I was free!

I experienced a head-rush of excitement at having left the March household behind me. Somehow, I would find my way home! But when I turned around, the house was still there—a house without a satellite dish or a paved driveway. And looking at the landscape around me? It was all equally unfamiliar. I saw a horse and carriage traveling by on the dirt road. The horse and carriage might have fit into any country road back home, but the driver with his odd clothes wouldn't. Was he wearing *knee pants with stockings*? Had I escaped or hadn't I?

Barely thinking about what I was doing, I leaped back over the doorstep, then outside again, then back and forth. Maybe I had to build up speed to trigger the trip back to the future.

Mixed feelings filled me as I leaped back and forth. What was I going to do? How was I ever going to get out of here? But then the other part of me felt something different, something the opposite of panic. I felt a sense of calm as I realized that no amount of jumping out the back door was going to work. I was stuck, with no choice but to just deal with things until some other solution came along.

I'd always been known to be, well, a little excitable about things. In fact, Charlotte used to call me "emo" until Anne pointed out that nobody said "emo" anymore. So how could overreacting me be so accepting of this situation now? Maybe because I knew there weren't going to be any handbooks lying around on *How to Get Out of a Strange Time Period When You've Accidentally Slipped into One*. But it was something else too. I was experiencing something completely original. Had anyone ever had anything like this happen to them before?

"Hannah, what *is* Emily doing?" I heard what I now recognized as Jo's irritable voice and I realized who the woman in the kitchen was: Hannah, who was more of a friend than a live-in servant, even though that's what she technically was to the March family.

I couldn't exactly tell Jo that I'd been searching for the seam that separated her fictional world from my real one.

Even I wasn't crazy enough to try that!

"I was just . . . enjoying the snow," I said instead with an awkward laugh to Jo as I leaped back inside again. I'd work out my escape later. That seam, the way in and back—it had to be here somewhere . . .

"Silly goose." Jo gazed down at my red feet. "You'll catch your death of cold." Then she shook her horse's mane of hair as she grabbed my hand. "But never mind that now. Marmee has left presents for all of us under our pillows."

I followed obediently as she tugged me along, feeling grateful that thanks to her I hadn't had to embarrass myself even more by asking who Hannah was.

Marmee had indeed left presents for us. Oh, yay, whoopee.

There were copies of *Pilgrim's Progress* for each of us: crimson for Jo, green for Meg, gray for Beth, blue for Amy. As for mine? It was brown.

Brown? It was the Incident of the Shawls all over again!

"I'm so sorry," Marmee explained, "but it was the only color left."

As for the inscription?

Wherever you go, dearest Emily, there you are.

I felt a rush of frustration. Was this some kind of joke?

Hurriedly, I sneaked glances at the inscriptions in my . . . *sisters'* books. But theirs were all inspirational, biblical even. Whereas mine was . . .

Wherever you go, dearest Emily, there you are.

They were taunting me! I was on the point of saying something, but then I glanced over at Marmee and saw the sweet look on her face.

"It's . . . lovely," I finally lied through my teeth. Then, thinking it would be smarter to talk like the rest of them in order to avoid detection, I added, "I shall rely on these wise words and, um, let them guide me like a beacon through life, always."

Marmee beamed.

"Well," Amy said, with an uncharacteristic snort in my general direction, "don't overdo it."

Jo was going on and on about the army shoes she'd given Marmee for a Christmas present.

And what had I bought Marmee, to go along with Jo's army shoes, Meg's gloves, Beth's handkerchiefs, and Amy's—as it turned out—big bottle of cologne? Well, even though I couldn't remember going shopping with them, even though I'd somehow leaped from that first night in front of the fireplace to this Christmas morning, somehow bypassing the mall crawl altogether, I'd managed to buy Marmee a dollar's worth of paper so she could write to Papa. It was nice to know I was thoughtful if hardly original.

The way Jo blathered on about how she wished she were a boy so she could fight with the men, side by side with our chaplain papa—honestly, I'd only been here a short time, but already I was sick of it.

Someone needed to set her straight about war! After all, I'd watched the news and gone to history class! However necessary the American Civil War might have been, there was nothing nice about young guys getting killed.

"Iraq!" I burst out with it. "Afghanistan!" I went on hastily when they all stared at me. "And by the way," I mumbled, hoping to distract them from my outburst, "I'm hungry. When's breakfast around here?"

I stared back, returning their stunned looks with what I hoped looked like firmness. Of course, they didn't have a clue about Iraq and Afghanistan! For a moment, fear grabbed me, fear of being discovered as the . . . *March impostor* that I was. If they discovered that, they might throw me out on the streets. And then not only would I be stuck in the wrong time period, I'd be a homeless person stuck in the wrong time period. But then again, they already seemed to have accepted me as one of them. *So I'd be the eccentric March*, I thought with near-manic glee—I'd found my place!

"Never mind whatever it is you're going on about, Emily," Jo said. "Didn't you just hear Marmee say that there's a poor German woman living nearby with a newborn baby and six children all freezing in one bed because they have no fire and nothing to eat and that we should give them our Christmas breakfast?"

Um, no, I thought. *Somehow, I'd missed that.* On top of everything else, was I now suffering from story amnesia? It was like there were things that happened that the others seemed to know but I didn't. And there were also things I didn't remember from my many times reading the book.

"We will have bread and milk for our own breakfast," Meg said, tying a totally ugly bonnet on her head.

"Yes, Marmee says we will make it up at dinner, so what does it matter if we starve a little now?" Amy's words were brave considering she was, well, *Amy*, but I got the impression that if her sisters hadn't been pressuring her, she'd have loved to do the wrong thing.

And so would I. What were these people, nuts? They planned to go from a breakfast of bread and milk straight to dinner with nothing in between. I couldn't live that way. It was worse than eating lettuce every day to impress a guy!

"I'm not going." I crossed my arms in front of my chest.

"Aren't you feeling well?" Meg asked, placing a hand on my forehead.

"Would you stop doing that all the time?" I said, annoyed, as I swatted her hand away. "I just don't see any point in giving away a perfectly good breakfast."

The others gaped at me.

"What?" I said, feeling self-conscious and indignant at the same time. So what if the others thought me selfish—I was hungry! "Honestly, what difference does it make?" I went on. "So we make the big gesture of giving them our breakfast now, but what next? Do we give them our dinner too? Our breakfast again in the morning? Of course not! We can't do that, or eventually *we* starve. So, please tell me, what is the point in doing something that will only help these poor people for a few hours but, in the long run, the larger problem will still be there?"

Beth stepped forward and stood in front of me. For a strange moment, I thought she might say something harsh, the sort of thing I expected from Jo. But when she did speak, her words were gentle, her expression sad.

"It is Christmas morning," Beth said, taking my hand in hers. "I admit, it is hard to give away our feast, and I shall be hungry all day. But think of how much harder it is to go daily without, as the Hummels do."

The Hummels—that must be the name of the German family.

"Yes," Beth went on, "tomorrow the Hummels will have to go back to starving to death, but should we not give them this one happy moment, on Christmas morning of all days? I, for one, should be happy to go hungry all day. Indeed, I wish we could do this for them every day."

Oh God, I groaned inwardly at her sincerity. *How had I landed myself here? And who did Beth think she was—Oprah?*

Still, the combination of sincerity and serenity in her expression got to me. Somehow, I could stand to have the others think I was selfish, but not Beth.

"Oh, *whatever*," I conceded sourly. "Let's go give our breakfast away."

The Hummels turned out to be exactly as described: a poor mother with a newborn and six children freezing in one bed with no fire and nothing to eat.

Now they had fire, at least for the morning, because Jo had hauled some of our own firewood over. And they had food, at least for the morning, because we'd brought *our* Christmas breakfast.

In spite of the grumbles in my stomach, as I looked around at those six little faces, happily eating the fresh muffins and pudding I wished I were eating, I *was* glad I'd been a part of this, this giving. But then I saw Beth seated in front of the fireplace, the Hummel woman's baby cradled in her lap, and I felt a chill go up my spine. I didn't know where it came from, but I knew there was something I should be remembering right now and yet couldn't.

"Hey, Beth," I tried to urge her. "Give the baby back to its mother and come over here."

But she was so caught up in that baby, it was as though she never heard me.

The bread we had for our breakfast was the warmest, most awesome-smelling bread I'd ever eaten—even better than Panera! "Are you going to sniff that bread or eat it?" Jo said at one point. Well, I guess I did have my nose pressed a little too closely. As for the strangely yellowish milk, it didn't necessarily look bad, just different. "Aren't you going to pour the cream off the top and then shake yours?" Jo said at another point as I raised the glass toward my lips. Oh. Right. I poured. I shook. Then I raised the glass again hoping to drink a bit before any more nasty comments were flung my way, but as the glass got nearer, I wrinkled my nose as it struck me: yuck! Unpasteurized. Still, in spite of the wonderful newness of the one and the strange newness of the other, bread and milk for breakfast wasn't exactly exciting. But as I went through the rest of the day, feeling hunger grow in my stomach, I felt good about that hunger, virtuous even. We had done a good thing and, as the others pointed out, it was just for one day. Tomorrow we'd be back on regular rations.

As it got dark, Meg announced that it was time for the Christmas play I'd seen the others rehearsing. I watched carefully to see if I was supposed to do anything, but it didn't seem like it. As far as I could tell, I was just supposed to be an observer.

A part of me was relieved—how could I have performed in a play when I hadn't learned the script?—but a part of me felt PO'd. Why didn't I, the middle March, have a part in the play? Did I have stage fright? Was I a bad actress?

Meg and Jo put on their costumes on a cot bed they referred to as "the dress circle," while Beth and Amy helped. Then, as the audience—in other words, Marmee and Hannah and me—took their seats, a blue-and-yellow chintz curtain was raised.

The play, which was mostly confusing, was also mostly Jo. She played all the male parts, wearing leather boots and an old sword and a slashed doublet that she obviously loved. Meg played the female—no big stretch.

I was relieved when it was over, because I hadn't been able to figure out what was going on in the play. Besides, it was finally time to eat again.

Pink and white ice cream, cake and fruit, French bonbons, and a bouquet of flowers for each of us. Whoa! It was way better munchies than I'd been expecting. Marmee said that Mr. Laurence—the grandfather of the Laurence boy, whom Meg swore we didn't know—sent it. Marmee said he had sent it because he heard about us giving our own breakfast away.

Ah, the rewards of virtue! I thought happily, reaching for another bonbon and dropping it on top of a spoonful of pink ice cream before popping it all into my mouth. The pink ice cream was so good.

I had a sudden inspiration.

"Hey, do we still have any of that thick milk from this morning?" I asked.

"Of course, why?" Marmee said.

"Can I have a glass?" I asked.

Hannah brought me one—I had to admit, the servant thing was easy to get used to—and I scooped up the rest of the ice cream, dumped it into the glass of milk, and swirled the two things together. I was going to ask for a straw but stopped myself. Did the 1860s even have plastic yet? Shrugging, I sipped from the glass. Oh, yum.

"What *are* you doing, Emily?" Jo demanded.

"Hmm?" I said, wiping with the back of my hand at the milk mustache I could feel on my upper lip.

"That thing," Jo said, pointing at my glass.

"Oh," I said. "Here. Try it."

Jo took a cautious sip and then a smile broke across her face. Before I knew it, she passed the glass to Meg, who had the same reaction, and so on through the sisters and finally to Marmee. Then they all asked Hannah for glasses of milk, adding their own pink ice cream and swirling.

Hey! It struck me. Had I just invented milk shakes?

"Well, *I've* spoken to him before," Jo said importantly. "The Laurence boy, I mean."

Then, as the others listened closely, she told us how she talked to him once over the fence about cricket, whatever that was, until Meg came along and spoiled the fun. Jo added that he seemed shy and in need of a good time. Ha! I could tell Jo thought she was *just* the person to provide it.

With the exception of the spectral figure of Papa in his letters and perhaps a few of the Hummel children, it had just been women, women, women since I'd arrived. But now things were changing. A boy was being introduced into the story!

There's always trouble when a boy enters the picture—hel-*lo*! Jackson, anybody?—and I did try to warn the others.

But, just like with Beth and the Hummel baby, no one would listen to me.

Beth and the baby . . .

Suddenly it hit me. In the original *Little Women*, Beth and that baby was really the beginning of the end for Beth, even though the reader had no clue at the time. And then it further hit me: Mr. Ochocinco's assignment, back in my real world. We were supposed to pick one thing we'd change about a favorite book to make it perfect. I'd been going back and forth about changing what happens to Beth or fixing things between Jo and Amy and the boy next door to make the book more romantically satisfying. But now . . . now that I *knew* Beth, the choice was obvious. I'd save Beth's life. To heck with who wound up with the boy.

So maybe that was my purpose in being here? The thing that would get me home again?

I'd been sent into the story to keep Beth from dying!

Three

But before I could save Beth's life, I needed to find my way in this strange new world for as long as I was in it. So, after placing my hand on Beth's forehead and not feeling anything that felt like a fever, and after promising myself to always keep a close eye on her so I could prevent her original fate from happening, I got back to the business of doing just that: finding my way.

And what a random way it was! If someone had asked me before I got here if *Little Women* was a normal novel, with a regular plot like any other, I'd have said yes. But now that I was living it, I saw for the first time how episodic it was. Talk about people being random!

Every girl who has grown up in the last hundred years or so wanting to be a writer, including me, has Jo March to blame. An overstatement? Maybe. But still.

Meg reported finding Jo in the garret, her favorite escape,

wrapped in a comforter on the three-legged sofa by the sunny window with her pet rat named Scrabble not far away. Meg reported that Jo had been eating apples and crying over a book. That's when it hit home: my memories of Jo March from that *other* book. How obsessed with books and her own writing she had been. How whenever I read about her in that garret, I'd wanted to *be* her. How, whenever she'd been writing something in the book, I wanted to be a writer *like* her. How, in spite of the various charms of the other three sisters, it was Jo who really rocked.

But now that I'd started getting to know her, she was proving to be a regular P.I.T.A.

"Of course you're not invited to the party, silly goose!" Jo laughed in my face now.

My fingers itched to slap her as I repeatedly clenched and unclenched my fists at my sides. I swore, if she called me "silly goose" just one more time . . .

"You are only fourteen!" she said, laughing some more.

"Oh, right," I said. "And you're so much older at—what is it again? *Fif*teen?"

"Even if you were older," Meg soothed, "you must be reasonable, Emily. Look at the invitation. It says that *Miss March* and *Miss Josephine* are invited to a little dance on New Year's Eve at the home of the Misses Gardiner. It doesn't say a thing about Miss Emily. Surely, you must realize how wrong it would be to show up at a party when you haven't been invited."

Well, I thought unreasonably, *I hadn't exactly been invited to this book either, yet here I am!*

"See, Emily?" Meg thrust the invitation at me again. She could be so . . . *teachery* at times. I supposed that was the teacher in her. "Your name doesn't appear—"

"Yes, yes." I swatted the folded note away. "I've already seen the stupid invitation, thank you very much."

"Emily!" Meg looked scandalized. "Your language!"

"Oh, who can blame her?" Amy said with a self-pitying groan. "I cannot *wait* until *I* am old enough to go to parties and dances and balls. But of course, when *I* am old enough, I will wear perfectly beautiful gowns that will not be at all like the dreadful poplin Jo must wear tonight. That is, the one with the tear and the burn mark in the back because she always stands too close to the fire. And *that* means that she will have to stand with her back to the wall all night, never even joining in the dancing. Nor will my gloves have lemonade stains on them like Jo's do. Meg and Jo will have to share gloves tonight, each wearing one of Meg's good ones while carrying one of Jo's soiled ones in their other hands. And when *I* am old enough—"

"Which you will not be for a very long time," Jo said sternly, "since you are only twelve now."

"Yes, yes," I said. "And Meg's sixteen, you're fifteen, Beth's thirteen, and I'm fourteen. We all know how old we are." I yawned, overacting like a character in one of *her* plays. "Is there some reason you feel the need to keep reminding us?"

"Don't be irritable," Beth said gently, grabbing on to my hand. "We will have our own fun here at home tonight. First, we will have the excitement of helping Meg and Jo get ready. Then we will sit around in our nightcaps, sewing and singing, all the while imagining the fun they are having. And then, finally, they will come home and tell us all about it!"

Beth was so good, it was hard to be grumpy around her. Still, Meg and even *Jo* were going to a dance while I had to stay at home, sewing and singing? *I* wanted to get out of the house for a change! *I* wanted to go to a dance! I was sure there would be *boys* there!

I couldn't completely prevent the sourness as I forced myself to smile at Beth and respond, "Sounds great."

Actually, it turned out it was fun helping someone else get ready for a party you weren't invited to.

It was fun when Jo accidentally burned Meg's hair when she tried to curl it with a pair of hot tongs.

And it was fun watching Jo try not to itch her head after Meg put nineteen pins in her hair.

And it was really fun hearing someone other than me get "admonished" for a change as Meg gave Jo a lengthy list of don'ts, which included:

Don't say "Christopher Columbus" or wink.

Don't dawdle when Hannah comes to collect us at eleven.

Don't eat much supper.

Don't shake hands.

Apparently, in the 1860s, girls weren't supposed to have any fun, punctuality counted, they were laying the groundwork for female eating disorders, and they were scared to touch other people.

"Now remember, when we get to the party," Meg gave Jo one last warning, "if I lift my eyebrows at you, it means you are doing something wrong and you must stop it at once, while if I nod my head it means you are behaving correctly, at least at that moment. Have you got all that?"

"Yes," Jo said with a sigh that made it clear she was no longer excited about the party.

It was very satisfying, seeing Jo looking less alpha girl for once. Nearly on the verge of laughing out loud at the situation, I caught myself. What exactly was my problem with Jo? Well, outside of the fact that she was completely full of herself. But really, what was my problem? I shook the feeling away, promising myself I'd get back to it. Right now I was too busy helping Beth and Amy wave Meg and Jo off.

There stood Meg, wearing a silvery poplin gown, her singed hair carefully camouflaged by some thingy that reminded me of the hairnets the kitchen workers wore at school, only nicer because it was blue velvet. There were lace frills here and there, a white chrysanthemum attached to her shoulder, and she tottered back and forth in heels she obviously wasn't used to wearing.

And there stood Jo, with her nineteen pins in her hair.

"Good-bye!" "Good-bye!" they shouted back at us as they bobbed their way out the door and into the night. The way they bobbed—they kind of reminded me of bobbleheads.

"So what shall we do first?" Beth asked with timid eagerness as soon as the door had shut on the others. "Shall we sing first? Or sew maybe?"

"I have a headache," I said, feeling the sudden need to be alone. "I think I'll just lie down for a few minutes."

"Oh, not a headache!" Beth said.

"I hope you don't die from it," Amy added.

"Of course I won't—" I started to say; then, "*What?*"

"I'm sure Amy didn't mean to upset you." Beth blushed. "But you do know, when people get headaches, sometimes it does lead to . . . *other things.*"

"I'll be fine," I said impatiently.

Honestly, no matter how often Jo reminded me that I was fourteen, I couldn't help but feel like I was surrounded by a group of people much younger than me, less sophisticated. Well, maybe because I *was*. If only these people could see YouTube, they'd probably have heart attacks.

"I just need a few minutes of peace and quiet," I added, "but I promise you, I'm not going to *die* from it."

And that really was all it was, I thought as I entered the bedroom I shared with Meg and Jo, for once having the whole room to myself: *I just needed a few moments alone.*

You'd assume that without the endless noise of the life I was used to—there were no TVs or computers or iPods here or cell phones ringing with Justin Bieber, barf—it would be quieter. The kind of place that would offer a girl opportunities for silent thought. And maybe there were, in other parts of this Brave New World. But here? I could barely hear myself think.

And I had so many things to think about!

Like the color of my hair.

Okay, I do realize that sounds lame, but the other girls all had hair ranging from the various browns of Meg, Jo, and Beth to Amy's yellow, while mine was auburn. Didn't the others notice how different I looked compared to them? What did our father, the vaunted Papa, look like? Had I gotten my coloring from him? Perhaps dearly beloved Marmee had had an illegitimate child on the side—me! But I could hardly ask the others about all that, could I? "Oh, by the way, what is Papa's hair color?" They'd lock me away!

Didn't the others notice, given my looks and the odd things I tended to say, that I didn't fit in? And yet, no one seemed to think that at all.

On the contrary. On returning to this bedroom after my

barefooted attempt in the snow to break the seam between this world and my real one, I'd discovered a wardrobe where some of the clothes were supposed to be mine. (Well, I discovered which ones were mine after first mistakenly trying to put on one of Jo's things—she quickly put an end to *that!*) With two older sisters to provide me with hand-me-downs, I had more clothes here than I had back home! Yes, I had clothes here, and a family—a family who seemed to have memories of everything I'd done for the last fourteen years, going back to when I was first born into this house, as if the story had been preadapted for my entrance, and yet they were memories that I had no knowledge of. What *were* those memories? What did they all *know* about me? What had I been like at age two? At ten? And what about their lives—what did I need to know about them?

Again, more questions I couldn't ask.

Was I a different person in this world than in my own world?

My own world!

Ever since arriving here, I'd been in defensive mode, only really able to react to all the newness of the strange life surrounding me, so I'd had little time to think about what was going on back there.

What *was* I supposed to have been doing back home today? Or tomorrow? Had I been invited to any New Year's Eve parties? Was I at one right now with Kendra and even having a good time there? Did I still exist back home, living on two planes at once, or did I just live here? And if only here, there must be things I had to get back there for. School. Homework assignments. Parties—*real* parties, not like this silly cookies-and-punch gig that Meg and Jo were going to. Wouldn't people miss me and start looking for me?

But wait a second. *Did* life still go on out there? Did the clock still go on ticking in my real life even while I was in here?

I. Had. No. Idea.

"So, tell me about the Laurence boy," I said. "Jo made such a big deal about speaking to him over the fence. Have either of you ever seen him?"

In spite of my initial reluctance to stay at home with my . . . *younger sisters* while the older two went off to the dance without us, it was turning out to be a bizarrely fun evening, just as Beth had promised.

Without the other two around to boss us, we were free to act like, well, silly gooses if we wanted to. We'd already found some munchies and had laughed over how Jo was dealing with her nineteen pins as we huddled in our white nightshirts and night-caps in front of the fire.

I caught sight of my image in a reflective surface. Huh. Not bad. The nightcap looked kind of cool on me, sort of like a floppy French beret. Maybe I'd start a trend when I got back home?

Of course, being the oldest of us, *I* was the first to bring up the topic of boys. It was satisfying for a moment to have them look at me as though I were worldly on the subject. In my whole life, no one had ever pegged me as being worldly on the topic of boys! But these girls? Except for Papa, it was as though boys were aliens to them.

"I did see him once," Amy said, seeming oddly shy for her. Well, I guessed, guys could have that effect on some girls. Me, I certainly hadn't been shy when I tried to hijack Jackson's attentions from Charlotte. Darn, I hoped he hadn't already made a play for Anne!

"That same day Jo spoke to him over the fence," Amy went on, "I guess you could say I was spying on them . . . but only for a minute!"

"Amy!" Beth was shocked. Then, with a voice dripping with wistful curiosity: "What did he look like?"

"Oh, he was very fine." Amy, all amped up to know something we didn't, was full of self-confidence and excitement now. "He had big black eyes, curly black hair, brown skin like he'd been riding his horse in the sun, a longish nose, nice teeth, curiously small hands and feet. Oh, and he was easily as tall as Jo and seemed awfully polite and jolly."

"That must've been some long minute for you to have seen so much," I said. Then: "Wait a second. Did you say 'small hands and feet'? Combine that with some of his other features, and your description could fit Jo's rat, Scrabble!"

"Oh no," Amy insisted as her yellow curls shook in vehemence. "He was very fine indeed. I only mentioned the small hands and feet because they impressed me as being so much more refined than, you know, the usual galumphing hands and feet you see on other boys."

I sniffed, a rather Jo-like sniff. Amy suddenly made it sound as though she knew a lot about boys. Still . . .

"So, the Laurence boy is hot, then?" I wanted to know.

"Oh no," Amy said, looking puzzled. "I am most certain that when I saw him he did *not* have a fever."

"I wonder what they are doing at the dance now?" Beth cradled her cheek in her palm, a dreamy expression on her face. "I would bet anything that the Gardiners have the finest piano—"

"Yes," Amy cut her sister off, "but there are six girls in that family, including Sallie, so you'd hardly ever get a chance to play."

"Well, there are five girls in this house," I said, "and Beth gets to play that wretched piano all the time, so I don't see how much difference one more sister could make."

Beth looked on the verge of tears.

"Honestly, Emily," Amy said, "sometimes I think you're as bad as Jo."

As bad as . . . ?

My hands went straight to my hips.

"Wait a second here," I half shouted. "What did *I* do?"

Amy nodded smugly as she gave me the once-over from head to toe. "Well, *that* for one." She imitated the way I was standing. "And you hurt Beth's feelings, even if you didn't mean to. You know how she loves her music."

"I'm sorry, Beth." I could feel my cheeks redden. "I never meant to say your piano is . . . wretched." (Except it was.) "It's a . . . lovely piano and you play it . . . splendidly." (Well, as well as anyone could play a wretched piano.) "Certainly you play it better than I could." (This was no lie. I couldn't play at all.)

"I guess," I went on, "I was just still feeling nasty about not getting to go to the party."

Just like Jo made me feel annoyed, Beth could make me feel ashamed of myself. Of course, of all the girls, Beth also had the greatest capacity for making me feel better after one of my screwups.

"Oh, I know *exactly* what you mean," Beth said, smiling now. "I don't think there is anything more confusing in this life than life."

"Well, I haven't figured it out yet," Amy said with a very

Jo-like snort of her own. "Life—it's just one great big muddle to me." Then she laughed. "Except for boys."

"Boys, boys, boys!" I laughed back, tickling her. "Is that all you ever think about, Amy March?"

And then we were all laughing and tickling.

When we had had enough and were back again before the fire . . .

"I wonder what they're doing," I said aloud, "right this minute?"

"I'll bet," Amy said, her face lighting up, "that the boys will be talking about skating, since it is winter, and Jo will want to join in the conversation."

"But Meg will lift her eyebrows at Jo before she can," Beth said with a sigh. It was impossible to picture Beth approaching a group of guys about anything, let alone something like skating, but maybe she sighed at the idea of Jo's wings being clipped. Beth may not have had much boldness in her, but it was obvious how much she admired that quality in Jo.

"Jo will not be able to dance because of the burn at the back of her dress," Amy reminded us.

"But," Beth added brightly, getting excited now, "she can still tap her foot smartly whenever a lively tune is being played."

"Except," Amy put in, "she will probably be standing in front of another fireplace while she is doing so . . . and she will burn her dress all over again!"

Amy laughed as Beth tried to look serious but instead started laughing herself.

"I know," I said excitedly, wanting to join in, "and if that Laurence boy is there, Jo'll think of a way to get him alone so she can get to know him better."

The other two stopped laughing and just stared at me.

"Oh no," Amy said way too seriously as Beth gazed on. "I am quite certain that even Jo would never do *that*."

It was all I could do to keep from snorting aloud, because if memory served me correctly—

But then our two older sisters were there again, bobbing back in like bobbleheads, only bobbing a little more slowly this time because Meg had her arms draped around Jo's and Hannah's shoulders as she hopped on one foot.

"What happened?" Beth said, alarmed.

"Meg sprained her ankle in those ridiculous heels," Jo said.

"That Laurence boy offered us the use of his grandfather's carriage," Hannah put in. "He rode all the way here on the box, even though it was cold out, so that Meg could put her foot up on the seat inside."

And then Marmee was there, all capable movements.

Where had Marmee been hiding herself all this time?

But there was no time to ask about that now as she settled Meg in her own best seat beside the fire, propping Meg's foot on a low stool and sending Hannah for a warm towel to wrap around Meg's ankle.

The invalid comfortably settled, Meg and Jo began chattering about their evening.

"I was trying to escape a redheaded boy," Jo said, "who wanted to dance with me."

This sounded familiar. *A redheaded boy,* I wondered. *Should I know that redheaded boy?*

"He was a fine boy," Meg said, "and a marvelous dancer. I know, because I danced with him."

"I'm sure that's all true," Jo said. "But I couldn't dance in front of the others in this dress and let them see the burn on the back, could I?"

Meg grudgingly agreed that this was true.

"So I slipped into a curtained recess," Jo went on, "where I just happened to bump into the Laurence boy."

I knew it!

"He is called Laurie," Jo went on as though this was the most exciting detail ever, as if the whole world didn't know the boy next door to the Marches was called this. "His real name is Theodore, but he doesn't like it because some of the boys at school called him Dora, for which he thrashed them, making them call him Laurie instead."

Laurie was an improvement on *Dora*?

"*And,*" Jo rushed on breathlessly, "he has been to school at Vevey—that's in the Swiss Alps—and he will be sixteen next month, talks a lot about going to college, and longs to live in Italy. Oh, and he dances marvelously too, no doubt far better than that redheaded boy."

Amy's blue eyes went wide. "So you danced with the Laurence boy?"

"In that dress?" Beth added.

"Well," Jo said, barely blushing, "at first he asked me and I said no, showing him the burn mark at the back of my dress—"

"Josephine!" Now even Marmee was scandalized.

"But Laurie found a long hallway that was deserted and where no one would see us," Jo went on, as though there'd been no interruption, "and we romped up and down the length of it. It was wonderful because, as I explained to him, there was plenty of room and nothing for me to harm as I am normally so likely to do in my usual galumphing way."

"Jo!" the three other sisters shouted at her.

"What?" Jo said, all innocent confusion.

While all I could think was:

Boys, boys, boys.

Earlier, I'd been excited that there was finally at least the *idea* of a boy in the story. But maybe that wouldn't be such a good thing. Sure, they were all "scandalized" by Jo's behavior now. But before long, they'd mostly all be fighting and falling all over each other to get to this Laurie character. That's what happens when a cute guy comes into the picture, even if he does have some features in common with Scrabble the rat.

"Let's make a pact," I said impulsively.

The others stared at me, puzzled.

"It just seems to me," I said, "that we all get along well. But now that this . . . *Laurie* boy has been introduced into the picture, we'll probably all start acting ridiculous, fighting with one another and competing for his attentions. I don't want that to happen to us."

It was true, I didn't. The one thing this world had going for it was that here my sisters all mostly got along together, not like back home with Charlotte and Anne. I didn't want to see that all messed up.

"I'd *never* do that," Beth said, obviously horrified by the idea of girls competing for a boy, while Amy instantly looked guilty.

"He's too young for my tastes," Meg said. "I think I favor a more mature man."

"This is the most ridiculous thing I've heard from you yet, Emily," Jo said. "The very idea . . . that we'd fight over a boy!"

"If you think it's so ridiculous," I countered, "then it should be easy for you to agree to a pact, not to let Laurie come between us."

"Fine," Jo said grudgingly. Then she added, "But I'll bet you buttons to bows, if one of us should break that pact, that person will be you."

Buttons to bows? What a bizarre thing to say! Still . . .

"Fine," I said.

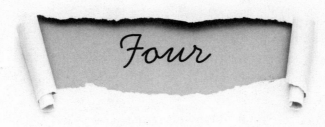

Four

How I missed Facebook!

If only there were a computer around here somewhere and I could log on to say, **Emily March** *opened a book to do an English assignment and got sucked into a whole different time period—WHOOSH!* My friends would comment with "LOL!" and "OMG!" and a few dozen people would simply hit the "like" button, and I'd feel like my day was off to a regular start.

But no.

The holidays were over and it was time to get back to normal life, which for me meant first having to figure out just what my normal life around here was supposed to be.

But first I had to deal with . . .

My period!

I'd never had to suffer through it in 1862!

I lay in my bed, sheets pulled up to my chin. What was I

supposed to do? I was pretty sure there weren't any tampons in this house!

"Get up, lazybones!" Jo cried, somehow making her words sound both cheery and admonishing all at once as she tried to rip the sheets off of me.

I clung tighter to them.

She pulled harder.

"It is time to get back to our regular lives," she said with another tug of the sheets. "Life can't be all plays and dances all the time."

Ex*cuse* me? I felt like pointing out. *I* never got to be in the play. *I* never got to dance at the Gardiners' New Year's Eve party—that was you!

"I'm not feeling well today," I said instead, clinging even tighter to the sheets. "I think maybe I'll just stay home today."

"Come on, Emily, you know the rules. Unless one is literally *dying*, no one gets to take a day off from their duties around here."

"'Unless one of us is dying'?" I echoed. "Well, that's a little overdramatic, don't you think? Why do you always have to be so—"

"Do you have a fever?" she cut me off, placing both hands on my forehead.

"What are you doing?" I cried, swatting her hands away. "You're worse than Meg!"

"HA!" she laughed. "I saw you do that swatting thing to Meg and I just knew you'd do it to me too." Then she reached for the sheets again, which, now that I'd removed my hands in order to swat at her, she was able to rip from my body.

"You give those back!" I lunged at her.

"No!" She laughed again, darting out of my reach. But then her expression changed, becoming a sober combination of wistful and sweet. "Oh, Emily. Your first bleeding!"

My *first*...? I wanted to point out that I'd been getting my period for over two years now, thank you very much, but then I realized how lucky I was. At least now I wasn't going to have to explain why I didn't know how to take care of my own period in 1862.

"Here," Jo said, taking me by the hand, "let me show you what to do."

A few moments later, it occurred to me that what was going on between us was kind of nice: Jo and I were having a real bonding moment!

"Yes, you are a woman now," Jo said, "and now I must tell you all about the making of babies and such."

Darn! Just when things were going so well. Sometimes she was worse than Meg.

"I don't think that's really necessary," I started to say, but she just blathered on.

I listened in horror as she gave some long and yet vague explanation that had dogs and horses and, I'm fairly certain, chickens in it.

Was this really the 1862 view of sex?

"Here." Jo handed me my nightgown. "Here." Jo stripped the sheets from my bed, shoved them into my arms.

"What?" she asked, when I only gaped at her, stunned. "Well, you can't very well expect Beth to do your laundry, can you? Honestly, Emily!"

So much for our bonding moment.

I swore, if I ever made it back to my real life, if I ever heard anyone yak about the "good old days" again, I'd punch them. On the surface, things may have been sweeter and simpler in 1862, but doing laundry by hand sucked.

The holidays over *and* my first period attended to, now it really was time to get back to normal life around here.

Amy was doing math or something on a slate while Beth lay on the sofa, the cat and three kittens around her.

"Hurry along, Amy," Meg said briskly. "Mustn't be late for your first day back at school."

"Are you sure it's just a headache?" Jo said, placing a hand on Beth's forehead. "You do feel a little warm."

While the sisters did many things together as a group and some activities were split into the two youngest and two oldest, with me roving between the two duos, Meg was Amy's confidante, while Jo was Beth's.

So where did the middle March fit into all this? Seemed to me, I was odd man out here. Or at least odd girl out.

"Come on, muffs are getting cold," Hannah called to us from the kitchen as Meg and Jo and Amy hurried into their outdoor clothes: cape-like cloaks, a bonnet for Meg, a wide-brimmed hat for Jo, and no hat for Amy, who simply took a few strands of hair from each side of her face and tied them neatly in the back with a blue ribbon.

What Hannah had called "muffs" turned out to be turnovers fresh from the oven. There were four of them, and since Beth was still on the sofa, I assumed I was supposed to go out with the others and that one of these turnovers was for me.

Suddenly I realized how hungry I was. Bringing the turnover

to my mouth, I was about to take a bite when Jo shrieked, "What *are* you doing, Emily?"

I raised my eyebrows at her. "Eating?"

"You can't eat your muff now!" she said to me with scorn.

"I can't?"

"If you do," Amy said, "how will you keep your hands warm on the long walk?" She laughed. "Sometimes, it's as though you don't know anything about how we do things around here."

Oh no! Was Amy on to me?

"Oh, right," I said with a nervous laugh, "the long walk. What was I thinking?"

Then I hurried into my own cape-like cloak and followed the others out the door, muff in hand.

I was happy the muff was so warm as we walked—stupid cold New England winters!

But where were we going? I wondered as we looked back at the house one last time to see Marmee at the window—nodding and smiling and waving at us, reminding me of a creaky mechanical toy or the queen of England—before we turned the corner.

"Oh, I do wish we could live lives of leisure as other girls do," Meg said with a put-upon sigh.

"And we don't *because* . . . ?" I asked the leading question.

"Why, because we don't have enough money, you know that," Meg said. Another sigh. "Of course, we once had money."

"And we lost that . . . ?"

"Why, Papa lost the money trying to help an unfortunate friend, which is why we older girls have to work."

Was I included in that "older" too? Did I work in some sort of factory? Was I a salesgirl in a shop? I'd bet anything if I *was* a salesgirl, I was a really rude one.

"You know all this, Emily." Meg sounded exasperated, but then her tone softened as she looked self-pitying again, a faraway look in her eyes. "Or maybe you don't remember what it was like when we had money. I suppose that *I* am the only one who remembers what things used to be like because *I* am the oldest and therefore *I* am the only one who ever—"

Jo yawned with such deliberate loudness, she snapped Meg right out of her self-pity party.

"I know you like to go on and on about being older than the rest of us," Jo said to Meg, "but you are only one year older than me and *I* remember a few things too."

I felt the frigid cold around me intensify as the muff turned cooler in my hands. Suddenly I wanted to be back at the cozy house with Beth. I may have had to do my own laundry, but at least there were fireplaces.

"So, um," I said, "just where exactly are we going?"

The other three stopped in the snow and turned to look at me as though I'd just landed from another planet, which, essentially, I had.

"I'm going to the King house," Meg said. "You know—where I'm nursery governess to their four spoiled children?"

"It's Aunt March's house for me," Jo said with a wrinkle of the nose.

"Josy-phine!" Meg said in a loud old-lady voice, and I remembered that this was how Aunt March spoke to Jo.

"At least I get to read in her large library whenever she's

napping," Jo said, "although that's hardly compensation for when she's awake."

"And I am off to school," Amy said with a heavy sigh. "Oh, I do wish Beth weren't so bashful, for then at least she could accompany me. What a wonderful life Beth has! All Beth has to do all day is play with her imaginary friends—those wretched six dolls she dresses every day, tending to them when they are sick—and take care of stray animals and practice on her piano with the yellow keys. Oh, and all the housework that Hannah doesn't do—that's Beth's job too."

I'd seen one of Beth's dolls: a castoff of Jo's, the thing was limbless and had no head.

"And what am I supposed to be doing?" I asked.

Meg narrowed her eyes at me as though wondering why I would be asking about what I should already know.

"Why, you are our jack-of-all-trades."

"Your what?" She had to be joking. This sounded like it might be as bad as Marmee's *Wherever you go, dearest Emily, there you are* inscription in my brown copy of *Pilgrim's Progress*.

"You do a bit of everything," Meg said. "On Mondays you go and help me at the Kings'."

"On Tuesdays," Jo said, "you help me with Aunt March."

"On Wednesdays," Meg said, "you stay home and help Beth and Hannah around the house."

"And I suppose on Thursdays I go to school with Amy?" I said, finally catching on and not liking what I was hearing at all. What kind of family role was "jack-of-all-trades"? I knew what that meant. It meant I was a master of none. Worse, it meant I fit in nowhere. Just like at my real home.

"No," Amy said, looking at me like I'd gone insane. "You

don't go to *school* with me. What sort of sense would that make, to go for just one day? And you being two years older?"

I shrugged. I had no idea. Seriously, very little of this made any sense to me.

"On *Thursdays*," Amy said, sounding an awful lot like Jo at this point, "you walk me all the way to school, you meet me there afterward, and you help me with my homework and any problems that might arise, which is basically what Meg does on the other four days of the week."

So . . . at fourteen years old, I never had to go to school again? At least not here? Cool!

"And on Fridays?" I wondered aloud. "What do I do on Fridays?"

Now it was their turn to look puzzled.

"Huh," Meg said at last. "I don't think any of us know."

"What *do* you do on Fridays?" Amy asked.

"Never mind that now!" Jo said, using one hand to hold her hat to her head as a strong gust of wind threatened to blow it away. "Don't you two realize what Emily's been doing?" she said to Meg and Amy.

"What *have* I been doing?" I asked, wanting to hear this as well.

"Emily," Jo accused, "you've been asking all these silly questions because it is Monday and you do not want to go to the Kings' with Meg."

"Oh, right." I laughed nervously. "I guess you caught me, didn't you?"

"Come along, Emily," Meg said as the four of us reached a fork in the road and she pulled me toward the left.

"I do wish you hadn't dropped me into the cold hod when I

was a baby," I heard Amy mutter at Jo as they veered off to the right. "It is all *your* fault my nose looks like this . . ."

Anyone who tells you that it's easier not to have to go to school never had to baby-sit the King children, I thought, rubbing my feet by the fire that night. I'd somehow managed to get through my first day as a function-ing, *working* member of the March family, subsisting on just that one turnover the entire day. I was sore. I was tired. And those King children—they were monsters!

While sewing after dinner that night, each sister recapped her day. Meg complained about ours and told the others about the oldest King boy being sent away for doing something "dreadful"—neither of us had been able to worm out of the other monster King children what that dreadful something was, but I had my suspicions, even if Meg didn't. Jo complained about her day with Aunt March. ("Josy-phine!") Amy complained about the teacher humiliating some chick at school. Beth didn't complain about anything, instead telling us of seeing Mr. Laurence give a fish to some beggar woman at the market who'd been about to be turned away by the shopkeeper.

That's when Marmee told all of us a fable about four—no, make that *five* girls who always complained, always saying "If only we could do this or have that," until an old woman cast a spell over them so that in the future, whenever they became discontented, they would think over their blessings and be grateful . . . or they'd lose whatever good things they had.

I was sure there must be a moral in there somewhere, but for the life of me, I could not care less.

I was too busy trying to sew—*when would I learn how to sew as well as the others?* I wondered, pricking myself with the needle; not that I cared about sewing, but I was sick of having marks all over my hands—and my feet were still sore, my temper fried from dealing with the wretched King children.

And tomorrow I'd have to go with Jo to Aunt March's.

Five

I settled in to my first week as the jack-of-all-trades.

On Tuesday I went to Aunt March's with Jo. For once, Jo hadn't exaggerated. Aunt March was as obnoxious as Jo said she was. And while whenever she bellowed "Josy-phine!" I laughed, it was substantially less amusing when she started bellowing "Emi-ly!" As my own mom used to say: "It's always funny until it happens to you." Still, Aunt March did nap often, and when she did, I followed Jo to the most amazing private library, where Jo showed me the one thing we really had in common: books. All those books made me itch to get back to writing.

Wednesday turned out to be the best day of the week, being at home with Beth. Yes, doing the housework was hard. There were no vacuum cleaners, no dishwashers or dryers, no laundry machines, no Dustbusters—everything had to be done by hand. My beautiful hands—honestly, I grumbled to myself, someone should have invented rubber gloves by now. And if doing the housework was hard, watching Beth play with her six dolls could be a little odd too. That limbless castoff she'd gotten from Jo, the one with no head—it was creepy! But that was Beth: she was capable of loving anything and everything, even the most loveless creatures, even me. And that was why it was the best day of the week, even if it was the hardest work and there were those creepy dolls: because a person couldn't be around Beth and not feel a little more peaceful, a person couldn't be around Beth and not feel inspired to be just a little better than the person they normally were.

You'd think that Thursdays with Amy would be the easiest of my jack-of-all-trades days since all I had to really do was walk her to school and then I was free until I had to pick her up later, and help her with her homework if necessary. But you'd be wrong. Thursday wound up being a loose-ends day for me, with me spending a good deal of it staring over the low hedge at the Laurence estate—a McMansion compared to the little brown March house—and wondering what went on inside there.

As for Friday . . . the others had grilled me on what I did on my free Fridays, but I still wasn't saying, in large part because I hadn't figured it out yet!

But then Saturday finally came and everyone was home again with lots to do.

At least, there *should* have been lots to do, except there wasn't, because it turned out to be a blustery and snowy Saturday, leaving the others happy to do totally exciting activities, like reading and sewing.

All except for Jo, of course.

Meg was lying on the sofa reading *Ivanhoe*, of all things— *bo*-ring!—while Beth played with her kittens, Amy drew pictures, and I tried to figure out how to sew a straighter stitch. That was when Jo entered wearing rubber boots and an old sack and hood. In her hands, she carried a broom and shovel.

One thing you had to give Jo: she never cared how she looked or what anyone else thought. You'd never catch her wearing skinny jeans or eating salad just to impress a boy.

"Where are you going dressed so abominably?" Amy asked lazily. "I hope no one recognizes you as my sister."

"I'm going to get some exercise," Jo announced.

"But you've gone for two walks already today," Beth pointed out.

Beth was right. Honestly, was there ever anyone so hardy as Jo March? It was annoying.

"Beth's right," Meg said, laying aside her book with an air I now knew signaled an older-sister lecture. "I would advise you—"

"Never take advice," Jo cut her off.

That suddenly sounded so familiar, the idea of Jo being the sort of person who never took advice. No, of course *she* wouldn't.

"Anyone want to go with me?" Jo asked brusquely, giving none of us any time to answer as she hurried on with, "No, of course you don't, so I guess I'll just—"

"I'll go with you," I said, getting up so fast my sewing got dumped on the floor, which was fine: I was a lousy sewer.

I don't know why I did it. I hated being cold, would never volunteer to go outside when I could remain in here, even if *in here* was slightly boring today. But there was something suspicious about Jo's attitude. I got the sense she didn't want any of us to go with her.

"No, you won't," Jo insisted. "You'll hate it out there."

"I can assure you, I'll love it," I said brightly.

"No, you won't," she insisted again. "You hate the cold and all you'll do is complain of it all the time."

I *knew* it! For some reason Jo didn't want anyone to go with her.

"I'll be a perfect soldier about the cold," I said, still brightly. "And if I'm not? You can always send me back. Now, wait here"—I paused to check out her ridiculous outfit—"while I hunt down a pair of rubber boots. And an old sack and hood. And a broom and shovel."

Gee, Emily, you really showed her, I grumbled internally as I proceeded to sweep and shovel the walkway with my hardy sister. *And to think, you could have been comfortably inside, seated by the fire, even if you had to do something stupid like sewing. But instead you had to insist on accompanying her outside. You couldn't leave well enough alone. You were so certain that Jo was up to no good, or at least up to something interesting, when in fact all it was is that Jo March is the most annoyingly hardy person who ever lived!*

WHAP!

I felt the wetness penetrate my hood, soaking my neck beneath the fabric, before it occurred to me: I'd been struck by a snowball!

"Why, you little—" I whirled on Jo, who was holding her sides, she was laughing so hard at my outrage.

I thought for sure she'd stop laughing when I scooped up twin handfuls of snow, packed it into a tight ball, and hurled it at her head. But she only laughed harder.

Seeing her laughing, in spite of the cold her big nose must be feeling with the snow dripping off it, I began to laugh too.

Suddenly, we were laughing together, scooping up snow and flinging it at each other, using our brooms to sweep even more snow at each other. I couldn't believe it, but I was actually having fun.

Now, *this* was a Jo March I could get along with: impulsive, vibrant, full of life, *zingy*.

Of course I'd been wrong to suspect she had something up her sleeve because she wanted to go outside by herself for the third time on a blustery and snowy day. She was merely a spirit too big to be caged indoors. There was nothing underhanded about her behavior, nothing nefarious—ooh! good PSAT word!—about it.

I'd just thrown a snowball at her and she was bending down to scoop up some snow to return the favor when she saw something that brought her up short. "Oh, look," she said.

I followed her gaze across the expanse of snow separating our house from the Laurence estate.

Of course, I thought.

"Mr. Laurence is driving away," Jo went on, as though she couldn't stop herself. "And look, Laurie is up there in that window."

She turned to me, as though snapping out of her trance. "You can go back into the house, Emily," she said hurriedly.

"Not on your life," I said.

"But you always hate the cold," she objected, "and we've already been out in it so long."

"I've changed my mind." I laughed. "Now I love the cold!"

"Do not."

"Do so."

"Do—" She shook her head in exasperation. "Never mind

that now." Then she raised her old sack and, vaulting the low hedge that separated our property from our neighbors', began trudging as quickly as she could through the snow toward the Laurence house.

"Hey!" I shouted after her. "Wait for me!" Then I raised my own sack and began to run too.

That low hedge turned out to be higher than it looked.

"You can't just throw snow at his window," I started to say. Now it was my turn to be exasperated, five minutes later, as we stood beneath Laurie's window.

I had to hand it to Jo, though: she had one heck of an arm. And her snow-throwing thing had worked because a guy had appeared in the window.

This was the first time I was seeing Laurie in person, even if it was only through a window. Before I'd only ever heard him described by Jo or Amy or the book.

Woo-hoo! He was a hottie.

"I've been sick for a week with a cold," he shouted down to her, having finally forced the window open. The way he talked to only her, it was as though I wasn't even there. "I can't go out," he added, "and it's awfully boring in here with no one to read to me or amuse me. I can't, after all, be asking Brooke all the time."

In the time it took me to puzzle over who Brooke might be, and failing to remember, due to my problems with story amnesia, Jo shouted up to Laurie, "I can take care of that."

"*We'll* take care of that," I muttered under my breath, hurrying to keep up with her as she raced for the front door.

"Remember your pact," she reminded me.

Did she mean that time I made her swear that we wouldn't let that "Laurie boy" come between us March girls?

Just when I'd seen what a hottie he was, she had to remind me of that *now*?

She's got nerve, I thought, watching as she waltzed into the unfamiliar house as if she owned the place.

"You must be Miss Emily," Laurie said to me as I entered, leaving me surprised.

How did he . . . ?

"I realize we've never been formally introduced," he went on, his cheeks coloring, "but I hear you all call to one another. And at night sometimes, when you forget to draw the curtains, I can see you."

Okay, I thought, *that's just a little creepy*.

"If you enjoy watching us," Jo said cheerfully, "if it entertains you, then I shall make sure those curtains are never drawn again."

Oh, good one, Jo, I thought to myself. *Way to enable the stalker.*

"But if Emily and I are to stay," Jo went on, "one of us should really go back home to get Marmee's permission."

I remained standing where I was. Well, it was her idea.

"Emily?" she prompted after a long moment of silence.

"What?" I returned. I didn't want to leave her alone with Laurie. What I really wanted was to have him all to myself. Even if he was a stalker.

To heck with the pact. If there was only one guy in the story, why should I be the one to go without?

"Well, you are younger than me by one—"

"Oh, fine," I said through gritted teeth.

When I finally returned fifteen minutes later, not only had I gotten Marmee's permission, but my arms were full.

The others had all insisted I bring something for the invalid.

Beth had insisted I bring three kittens to cheer him up, which seemed a weird thing to send to a sick person, plus they kept scratching me. Meg had insisted I bring a blancmange she'd made. I remembered reading about blancmange in the original book and not knowing what it was but thinking it sounded revolting. Now I knew. It was a sweetened dessert made from gelatinous or starchy ingredients and milk. And yes, it was *so* gross. The only thing that saved the disgusting white mess were the flowers and leaves from Amy's pet geranium that she'd insisted I use to decorate the border. Leave it to one of the March sisters to have a geranium for a pet—a March Chia Pet! At least it didn't scratch.

As for me, what did I bring? Myself. Wasn't that enough?

"I'm back!" I called as I reentered the house.

"We're up here!" Jo called from somewhere up above me. "In Laurie's room!"

You fast mover, Jo March, I thought as I took the stairs with determination, juggling cats and blancmange and geranium decorations. *Well, two of us could play at this!*

"Laurie tells me they haven't lived here long either," Jo informed me as I entered the room, breathless, depositing the kittens and blancmange on the first available surface: the astonished invalid's lap.

Wait a second. Did she just say "either"? But I thought we always lived here. At least I thought the Marches did.

"So I've been advising Laurie on how to make friends," Jo said.

HA! For one who never took advice, Jo was awfully good at dishing it out.

"I told him how I've already gotten to know all the neighbors except for him," Jo said. Hands on hips, she looked around the room. "Look at this messy room! I told Laurie it should be set to rights before I read to him."

It really was amazing how much they'd managed to discuss in the time I'd been gone, although somehow I sensed Jo had done most of the talking.

"Emily?" Jo cocked an eyebrow at me.

"What?" I finally spoke. Sometimes it was tough to get a word in edgewise with Jo.

"*The room.*" She glanced at our surroundings with a meaningful look: the messy sheets, the scattered clothes, the disorderly bookshelves.

"You don't mean—" I started to say. "But that's wack!"

"'Wack'?" Laurie asked, looking extremely interested in me all of a sudden. "I love words, and that's one I've never heard before, or at least not quite in that way."

"*Wack* means crazy," I informed Laurie, thinking: *Yay! We have something in common! We both love words!*

"Then why didn't you just say 'crazy'?" Jo pressed. "Or even 'wacky'? Although there is no such word as *wacky*, it would make more sense than *wack* if you were looking for a synonym for *crazy*."

Wait. No *wacky*? What kind of world was this? Oh, right. It was a world in which, not only was there no *wack* yet, there wasn't even a *wacky*. I was going to have to get my hands on a good dictionary, I realized, and memorize the whole thing.

"So what you really meant to say was 'wacky,'" Jo persisted.

"No," I finally said, annoyed. Suddenly I didn't care how wack it made me look in their eyes, I refused to let her win another argument. "I *meant* to say 'wack,'" I informed her defiantly. Then I looked at Laurie, shrugged. "What can I say? I love words and I like inventing new ones."

Laurie's eyes lit up. "Miss Emily! How charming!"

"You can just call me Emily," I said, "now that we're friends."

"Emily," Jo said.

"Hmm?" Gosh, Laurie was cute.

"The room?" Jo said.

"Oh, don't be ridiculous, you silly goose," I said, still gazing into Laurie's beautiful dark eyes. "You know I spend all day every Thursday cleaning our home with Beth. If you think Laurie's room should be cleaned so badly, clean it yourself."

While Jo grumbled around the room, "setting things to rights," it was my turn to learn a few things.

I learned both his parents died when he was little—sad.

I learned Brooke was Mr. John Brooke, his tutor—useful.

I learned his grandfather didn't like him to play the piano—perplexing.

"Are you two just going to sit there and talk all day?" Jo huffed, plumping the last pillow and placing it on Laurie's bed.

"I know!" Laurie clapped his hands on his thighs. Since we'd arrived, he already looked less sick than when we first saw him from the window. At least he was more cheerful. "I'll show you Grandfather's library!"

The library he led us to was even bigger than Aunt March's, with a large portrait of Mr. Laurence dominating the room.

"What an amazing room," Jo said. In moments like these, I didn't resent her at all, because I was feeling the exact same thing—all those books to fall into.

"Grandfather lives among his books," Laurie informed us.

HA! Don't we all! I thought half bitterly, suddenly tired of being a fly on the wall in someone else's life. If this had followed the original book, Jo was meant to be alone here with him. I was just an extra in their play.

Well, at least by being here I could enforce the pact.

"Don't you think Grandfather looks frightening in that picture?" Laurie asked Jo.

"No," Jo said. "I'm not afraid of anything."

And in that instant I realized she *wasn't* afraid of anything and that that was part of her magic. Me? I was afraid of all sorts of things, always had been. I was afraid of remaining in this world, but now I was also afraid of going back to my old life. It's not like I'd ever fit in so great there to begin with, and what with the changes in me since being here, that would probably only get worse. What if I started spouting "shall" at everybody? Kendra would think I'd gone nuts. Plus, if I left here too soon, how would I ever save Beth?

A servant came to inform Laurie that the doctor had come to check up on him.

How quaint—house calls!

A moment later, I was left in the library, studying the old man's portrait with Jo.

"You know," Jo said, "the old man knew our grandfather."

No, I hadn't known that, and it didn't make much sense to me. Didn't Jo say earlier that we and the Laurences were both relative newcomers to our houses? And yet now she was saying that our grandparents had been friends?

I heard a door open and click shut, a sound Jo appeared oblivious to.

"Of course, he's not as handsome as our grandfather," Jo said, comparing the portrait in front of us to some vision in her mind of a grandfather I'd never seen, never known.

I heard the sound of footsteps approaching, glanced over my shoulder.

"Jo?" I warned her.

"And that mouth," Jo went on, "so grim!"

The footsteps drew nearer.

"Jo?" I tried again.

"I'll bet he has a tremendous will," Jo went on.

Oh, to heck with it, I thought. *This could be fun.*

Jo tilted her head to one side. "Although from this angle, he does look like he might be a little wack. But no. I'm not scared of him at all."

I watched as the gnarled hand gripped Jo's shoulder, watched the look of horror on her face as she spun around and saw the person I'd known had been in the room with us for some time: Mr. Laurence.

"Not scared of me, huh?" he demanded.

She may have blushed like crazy, but still Jo stood her ground. "No, sir."

And she continued to stand her ground as he asked her about what she'd said about his mouth and his will. She may never have intended to offend him, but she'd meant what she said and, even having been overheard, wouldn't back down now.

"And you think I look . . . *wack?*" the old man said, puzzling over that last word.

"I only said a little wack, sir," Jo corrected, blushing even more as she shot me a hard look. Clearly this was all to be my fault for having taught her that word in the first place. "Only a little, but yes, sir, in that picture I'm afraid you do."

Good, I thought. *Now he will kick her out, for her rudeness and her impertinence and for calling him a little wack. He will kick her out for good and then I will have Laurie to myself for—*

That's when the old man roared. Only it wasn't in anger, I realized after a moment. He was roaring in laughter. And what was worse, he wasn't laughing at Jo, he was laughing with her.

"How delightfully honest you are!" he said, struggling to control his laughter. "I wish there were more girls in the world like you!"

I glared at Jo.

I couldn't help it, I was jealous. Jo had said all those things, and *still* the old man found her charming? Jo could get away with anything!

One thing Jo couldn't get away with. Spotting the grand piano in the drawing room, she begged Laurie to play so that she could tell Beth about it, and Laurie played beautifully. The part she couldn't get away with was that the old man, hearing him play and realizing she had urged him to, hustled us toward the front door.

"I think that in Theodore's condition," the old man said, "he has had quite enough entertainment for one day. But it would be wonderful if you March girls spent more time in the future with him. I think Theodore could benefit greatly from your society, so long as there isn't any more piano playing."

"I could come every Friday!" I offered. "I'm free every Friday!"

Jo glared at me.

"What?" I said as we trudged off toward home. "It's the truth. I have every Friday free, and—"

"Oh, do be quiet, Emily. Sometimes I think you must be wack."

That night over supper, Jo and I told the tale of our joint adventure that day.

"Did he like my blancmange?" Meg wanted to know.

"I believe, er, he wanted to save it all to enjoy himself later," I said, not wanting to hurt her feelings by telling her he hadn't touched the gross-looking thing.

"I hope he doesn't think the geranium flowers and leaves are edible," Amy said, "for I believe they might be poisonous."

"I am sure," Jo said huffily, "that he is intelligent enough not to eat the flowers."

"That piano sounds heavenly," Beth said, chin in hand. "But it is perplexing: Why does his grandfather not want him to play it?"

That's when Marmee had some insider information to share with us.

"Mr. Laurence doesn't like the boy to play the piano," she said, "because his daughter-in-law, the boy's mother, was an Italian musician whom he blames for taking his son away from him. He worries that the boy will also want to be a musician and that he will lose him as a result too."

"Italians are always nice," Meg said.

"Perhaps," Marmee said, considering. "The boy was born in Italy, and I fancy he is not very strong. Still, I agree with Mr. Laurence. You girls would do that boy a world of good, and I have the feeling he would do the same for you. You have my permission to spend more time with him."

"I have Fridays off!" I piped up.

Jo narrowed her eyes at me. I could almost see the wheels turning in that brain of hers: *Remember the pact, Emily.* But I didn't care. I didn't care anymore about trying to avoid conflict with my new sisters by *not* competing over some guy. I'd once thought I wanted to switch things in *Little Women* so that Laurie would wind up with Jo rather than Amy. But now that *I* was here, why shouldn't he wind up with me?

Laurie was good-looking, he was nice, and he was impressed with my ability to come up with new words. I couldn't remember the last time any guy had been impressed by me. Plus, he was the coolest guy in town. Okay, so maybe he was the *only* guy I knew in town, but still . . .

Meeting Laurie for the first time that day—talk about getting lost in a good book!

I no longer wanted to leave it.

Six

I'd already decided that my purpose here was to keep Beth from dying, but so far, I'd had no opportunity to take much action. After all, other than feeling her forehead after our one visit to the Hummel family, watching her the entire week afterward to see if she got sick, what was there for me to do? Simply wait until the story carried me to a point where I *could* change something, anything, to keep the worst from happening.

Until that time came, all I could do was go about my days.

I'd announced to the others that I could visit Laurie on my Fridays off, but it would be a week before I could go back over.

Sunday. You'd think a family like the Marches would be regular churchgoers, but Sunday came and went with no mention of church at all. *Could we possibly be Jewish?* I wondered as the day wore on. *Muslim?* But no. Of course it was neither of those things. What then?

Then it struck me. The only things that had happened since I'd been here were those things that had actually happened in the original book: visiting the Hummel family; Jo and Meg going off to the party at the Gardiners'; Jo making fast friends with Laurie. The only changes to those scenes? My presence. The story itself didn't change on its own. But perhaps I could change it. I wondered what would happen if I suddenly suggested, "Hey, aren't we going to church today?" Would the others quickly lay aside their reading and sewing and sketching, hastily throwing on cloaks and bonnets? Maybe Jo, looking slightly puzzled by the turn of events, would hurl a "We were all just waiting for you to say something, lazybones" in my general direction?

Sunday passed quietly until Marmee reminded us that Mr. Laurence had said Laurie might—what was the word? Oh, right—*benefit* from our society.

That's when the great pilgrimage began.

Meg took a walk through the gardens, enjoying the winter flowers.

Jo took up position in the grand library, grabbing every book I showed any interest in so that there was little fun for me and tons of frustration.

Amy studied the artwork on the walls, making sketches.

I, the jack-of-all-trades, apparently had no hobbies to call my own, not like the others did, and so I was left at loose ends. It would've been a good chance to flirt with Laurie, but somehow that would've felt weird with so many other sisters in the house. Jo would probably call me on it if I tried anyway, accusing me of breaking the pact. So I had to be satisfied with smiling at him as we came and went, and introducing *dude* to him as a form of address.

Only Beth stayed away, in spite of Jo's description of the piano. She was too shy of the old man, too shy of life.

Monday, it was off to the wretched Kings again with Meg.

Tuesday, it was off to wretched Aunt March's with Jo.

It was Wednesday when things began to change.

On Tuesday night, alerted by Jo to Beth's specific fears about his heavy eyebrows and fears of him in general, Mr. Laurence paid us a visit. As Beth listened, clinging fearfully to her limbless and headless doll—whose name I'd since learned was peculiarly Joanna—he told Marmee that he could really use someone to play the piano and help keep it in tune since Laurie so rarely played. *And whose fault was* that? I wondered. Mr. Laurence assured Marmee that anyone who was kind enough to keep the piano in tune need not worry about being bothered by the rest of the household. In fact, that person could simply come and go as she pleased.

What an awesome invitation. For the first time in my life, I wished *I* played the piano. Too bad the only musical talents I'd ever possessed had been the sort to elicit "You suck" pronouncements from my real sisters.

But it was a perfect opportunity for Beth. And for once, it seemed she wanted something enough to let go of her fears. Slipping her tiny hand into the old man's large one, she offered up her services as pianist.

It was quite a thing to see, the way this gruff and stiff old man melted into a puddle around Beth.

But then it was Wednesday and there was Beth steeling her courage to walk across to the Laurence estate. I went with her and we entered quietly by the side door, and discovered the simple sheet music that I was sure the old man had deliberately left out for her.

Beth took a seat at the piano, touched the keys in awe, breathed a happy sigh.

"You needn't stay any longer, Emily," she said. "It was so kind of you to accompany me this far, but I can manage from here."

"Are you sure?"

She was. And then it occurred to me: she *wanted* to be alone, wanted her first time at this piano to be exactly as Mr. Laurence had promised her it would be—without fear of bothering anyone and no one bothering her.

I went out the music room door, thinking I might find Laurie. Perhaps we could have a little chat, maybe get to finally know each other better without nosy Jo around.

But as I moved to close the door, and Beth began to play, I saw Mr. Laurence open his study door to listen, and then I looked up the winding staircase, and saw Laurie standing guard there, warning the servants away. How *sweet* was that? It was *so* sweet.

Still, I realized then that this wasn't the place for me, or at least not at that moment. It was Beth's moment, Beth's day.

It was time for me to find something else to do with myself, outside of intruding on other people's stories.

What I should do, I thought, *lame as it might be, is go home and do Beth's share of the housework as well as my own. That would be the nice, sisterly thing to do.* But I didn't want to do that.

I decided to walk into town.

So far, I'd only been to the Hummels', the Kings', the Laurences', and Aunt March's, and it was high time I saw something else. The other sisters had all bought Christmas presents for Marmee *somewhere*, so there must be at least one store around here, some sort of town center perhaps.

But, I wondered, arriving at the street, which way was town?

Hmm . . . the traffic on the street, such as it was, the few carriages in sight, all seemed to be heading . . . that way.

Figuring that must be where the action was, and hoping there really was action and that it wasn't too far away—it was seriously cold out!—I followed in the carriage tracks.

Soon there were more carriages in the street, more people walking in the same direction. At last we all turned a corner and there was . . .

A strip mall. Well, not a strip mall like back home—there was no Starbucks, no CVS—but there was an obvious string of businesses: a tearoom, a barbershop, a store selling items for women, a general store, the last being the place where my sisters probably did their holiday shopping. Since I wasn't a man in need of a haircut and since I had no cash to spend, I decided to check out the general store.

There were food items, housewares, there were men's army boots similar to the ones Jo had bought for Marmee. I picked up one of the boots, studied it from all angles. I'd always thought the boots we wore here were ugly, but you never knew when something was going to become fashionable again in a retro way. Maybe when I got back to the real world, I could win *Project Runway* with these?

At the sound of voices, I looked up to see a group of older men standing around the counter talking.

"The war has accelerated since the New Year," one said.

"Since before that," said another, "since back in July when Major General McClellan took command of the Union Army of the Potomac."

"How long," asked a third, "before Lincoln orders an attack on Virginia?"

Attack on Virginia?

That's when it hit me, really hit me: it was 1862 and I was living in a country that was in the midst of a war. Before now, I suppose I had been aware of the war on some peripheral level—the absence of Papa, Jo's incessant talk of wishing she could be where the fighting was—but it had never hit me like this. While we were all safe here up north, leading relatively comfortable lives, terrible things were going on down south. So what if this was a fictitious world. The American Civil War was real. The dying was real.

I felt a sudden sense of urgency, spoke without thinking.

"Can't the Red Cross do anything?" I asked. "People are dying!"

The men looked at me like I was an alien, which, I guess, I was. Maybe the Red Cross hadn't been invented yet?

"*Do?*" the first man who had spoken scoffed.

"You're a girl," said the second, stating the obvious before snorting.

"You can sew socks," said the third with a sneer. "That's all *you* can do."

Socks??? I was outraged.

The very idea—that I could do nothing, simply because I was a *girl*, that it was all above my pretty little head! Didn't these idiots know that girls could do anything guys could? No, of course they didn't. In my time, my *real* time, women were soldiers, fighting right alongside men. But here? I was pretty sure girls weren't even allowed to vote yet!

Well, what were *they* doing that was so important and helpful? Standing around a general store and talking?

And yet what could we really do, outside of talking and sewing socks?

I left the store feeling disturbed at my own powerlessness to influence the larger events around me, the men's mocking laughter following me out the door.

Not ready to go home yet—a new home that felt too safe just now—I walked farther down the street. Soon the shops disappeared, then came a long expanse with nothing, and then . . .

A church.

But it looked so familiar.

As I stepped closer, I saw a tiny metal plaque nailed to the wall beside the front door. It had a year on it, dating the founding of the church to the days of the American Revolution.

I'd seen that plaque before . . .

Suddenly, I remembered a much larger church, with a wing for a bigger congregation and administrative offices, a Sunday school, but with this original tiny building still preserved as part of the entrance.

I *knew* this church!

It stood, or at least in its more modern version, in the town where I lived in my real life, the town I'd grown up in.

Just what the heck was going on here?

Why was I essentially back where I started?

Then the answer came to me: *change*. Somehow, it all came down to change.

I'd already been altered by my time here, even I could see

that. The way I saw the world around me, even the word choices I made—it wasn't the same as before. But if I was really being changed by this world, what changes was I acting upon it? Surely there must be something beyond introducing *wack* into the vocabulary. Surely there must be some reason for all this, some higher purpose.

Was it really all about saving Beth?

Beth must have made quite an impression on the old man and he on her. So grateful was she about him letting her play the piano, she sewed him a pair of slippers as a thank-you in record time, calling on us sisters to help. The slippers had pansies on a deeper purple background, leaving the old man so touched, he sent her a little cabinet piano of her very own with brackets to hold candles, green silk with a gold rose in the middle covering the flat top, a perfect little rack and stool. It came with a note from Mr. James Laurence to Miss Elizabeth March, saying the piano had belonged to his granddaughter, whom he'd lost.

He'd lost a son and a granddaughter? How sad!

But I stopped being sad when Beth began to play. It was just wonderful to see how happy she was now.

Wednesday night turned into Thursday turned into breakfast on Friday.

Jo (trying to appear casual): "So, Emily, how do you plan to spend your day of leisure?"

Me (trying to appear equally casual, but failing): "I thought I might go over to the Laurence place for a bit this morning."

Jo (with ill grace): "Harrumph."

No sooner did my sisters head out the door to their various destinations than I was out the door myself and across the grounds to the Laurence estate like a light. I was *so* excited to be on my first solo visit to him, but not so excited that I forgot to remind myself that the hedge separating our properties was taller than it looked.

Laurie looked only mildly surprised to see me on my own.

"Ah, yes," he said, finally opening the door wider so that I might enter, "I remember now your saying you could come on Fridays."

Then, remembering his manners, he bowed at the waist and greeted me with, "Dude."

"Dude," I returned with a slight curtsy.

He had fully recovered from his cold and asked me to walk in the conservatory with him.

"I like your family very much," he said, strolling with his hands clasped behind his back. "Your mother is a capital woman."

"Capital," I echoed, feeling dumb.

"And your sister Meg, such patience she has with everybody."

"Patience."

"And then there's Jo." He laughed. "Jo can be quite overwhelming."

"Overwhelming."

"Amy is so funny about her nose. I don't imagine anyone but her sees anything wrong with it."

"Nose."

"And dear Beth. Was there ever a kinder, gentler girl in the world?"

"George H. W. Bush." In a speech, he'd once referred to "a kinder and gentler nation." What can I say? We'd studied sayings of the presidents in American history class.

"Pardon me?" That brought him up short.

"Sorry," I said. "I guess I was just free-associating for a moment there."

"Free-associating?" He looked puzzled. "Is that another word you invented, like *wack* and *dude*?"

I ignored the question. "I'm glad you find so much to admire in each of my sisters," I said, "but isn't there someone you've left out?"

"Left out?" He continued being puzzled. "No." He shook his head. "I don't believe there is anyone else."

This wouldn't do.

"Me?" I finally said, coming straight out with it. "Don't you have any admiring things to say about me?"

He laughed then. "Why, of course! You're the middle March, and may I say, you do a capital job of it!"

Harrumph!

No, this *really* would not do.

Didn't he feel the same attraction for me that I felt toward him? He had to!

I decided to test my hypothesis. I placed my hands on the sides of his face and pulled his head toward mine, closing the space between us.

"Miss March!" he cried, just prior to my lips touching his.

I can't say it was the most satisfying kiss in the history of the universe. There were no sparks of electricity, no stomach butterflies, and when I tried to slip him some tongue, all I was met with was a firmly closed mouth.

"Miss March!" he cried again, extricating himself from my grasp and taking a full leap backward.

"Emily," I corrected.

"Very well. Emily. I do not know what came over you, but I am no longer certain your Friday visits are such a good idea."

I just looked at him, curious. He may not have returned my kiss, but I was somehow sure he hadn't totally hated it.

"I'm sorry," he said, gaining control over his innate good manners when I remained silent. Perhaps he thought I felt offended? "I am sure I know what just happened. You have somehow caught the cold that I had last week and now you are delirious. Colds can do that to one—cause delirium, I mean; not, er, kissing other people, although I suspect it could cause that too, since it so obviously just did."

"You must be right," I said, feeling the need to accept his explanation as a kindness to him more than myself. He was so obviously confused and I couldn't blame him: there were no kisses like *that* in the original *Little Women*. I put my hand to my own forehead in that same gesture I found so annoying when Jo or Meg did it. "Oh, look," I said. "I'm warm. I believe I do have a fever!"

I reached for his hand so that I might place it on my forehead, prove to him how feverish I felt to the touch, but he was having none of that.

"I will take your word for it," he said, untangling his hand from mine. "Now, you really must go home and take care of yourself until you are better. I am sorry I spoke so harshly earlier when I said you should not come on Fridays anymore. Of course you may come—when you are feeling all better, that is—and we shall never speak of this dreadful incident again."

Dreadful in——?

Well, that went well, I said to myself as he brusquely ushered me out of the house.

But then I decided he was probably just acting so flustered because on some level he thought I was hot, even if he couldn't allow himself to think that.

At least it wasn't a total loss.

Seven

Oh, what I wouldn't give for some LOL cats right around now.

In the wake of the me-kissing-Laurie disaster, I realized that I had finally found my place among the March sisters. If Meg was the wise older sister, Jo the rebel tomboy, Beth the gentle spirit, and Amy the vain and pretty one, I was ... I was ... I was ...

The family *skank*?

Great, I thought. *That's just great.*

It was Thursday again, my day to attend to Amy: dressing her hair in the morning, walking her to school, picking her up afterward, helping out with homework.

"I should like you to gather some strands in a bow at the back," she instructed self-importantly, "but brush the rest so that it looks lush and free-flowing. Oh, and please don't forget to leave some tendrils framing my face. Tendrils are *so* important in making my nose look more normal. My life was simply appalling before I discovered the finer uses of tendrils."

There were *so* many things a person could've said to that insane "tendrils" speech of Amy's, but it was just too easy. Besides, I was sure I could create something more interesting than what she was describing. But then I puzzled over the incredible array of pins and bows and curling tongs. I'd never been much good with my own hair—back home, Charlotte and Anne could put their own hair into French braids or use a scrunchie and have it wind up looking perfect—and none of this made any sense to me. Perhaps simple would be best.

Finally, I picked up the brush—grudgingly, I must add.

"How's this?" I said not much more than a moment later.

She studied her reflection.

"What have you done?" she shrieked.

"I've put it all up in a ponytail," I said.

"A *ponytail?* I've never heard of such a thing!"

When she put it like that, I had to admit, it didn't sound like the most attractive idea. But I thought it looked fine, plus it was easy to do one.

"Haven't you ever seen a ponytail?" I was somewhat shocked at her extreme reaction.

"Yes," she admitted before adding, "*On a horse!*" She patted her hair in a fussy way. "Meg never does my hair like this."

"Well, I'm not exactly Meg, am I?" I countered. Then I seized on an idea, one I was sure would appeal to Amy. "I saw it in a newspaper when I was in town last Friday. They say it's the latest, er, rage abroad. All the fashionable girls are wearing them."

"Abroad, you say?"

"Oh, yes. It originated in France. They call it, um, *le ponytail.*"

"*Le ponytail?*" She carefully formed the unfamiliar words and for once they came out just right, which was interesting, since Amy was known in the family for botching all kinds of words and phrases, which I supposed was still better than being the family skank.

"But if you really don't like it . . . ," I started to say, reaching for the hair ribbon.

"Oh no!" Her hand flew to protect the bow holding up her ponytail. "I do like it, very much so. It only took me a few minutes to realize it." She studied her reflection some more. "And you say it's French?"

"*Oui,*" I said, speaking the only French I knew outside of *le ponytail.*

But before Amy and I could leave for school, we still had a little bit of Amy drama to get through. Something about limes.

Apparently, pickled limes were as much the rage in Amy's school as ponytails were in France.

"The girls take turns bringing them," Amy said breathlessly, as though she were talking about the most important thing in the world, ever. "You give the limes to girls you like, you eat them in front of those you don't—never offering even so much as a suck— and you hide them in your desk so Mr. Davis won't see."

Back home, my sister Anne was only a year older than Amy. It was tough to picture Anne, usually glued to whatever was on MTV, obsessing about the distribution of limes.

"Is Mr. Davis still so stern?" Meg asked. "I remember when he banished gum."

"Worse," Jo said, "I remember when he confiscated all our novels and newspapers."

"When I still went to school," Beth said, "he forbade what he referred to as 'distortions of the face.' I swear, I didn't even know I *was* distorting my face!"

"Yes," Amy said, "he really is still so stern. But who cares about that? *I* will never be caught, since I cannot afford any limes and now the other girls will all hate me and call me cheap and I will become a social outcast since I have eaten all their limes, except for those of Jenny Snow, who refused to share with me, but never once brought any of my own to share and—"

"Here," Meg said. "Will a quarter do?"

Amy's face lit up like Christmas. Better than that, she stopped talking.

"I'm sure that all the girls will be simply entranced by my pony-tail!" Amy babbled as we continued our walk to school, having first made a detour to town, where she bought a quarter's worth of limes, twenty-four of which she now clutched in a brown paper bag. Seriously, had anyone ever *heard* of anything more absurd than pickled limes?

Leave it to 1862.

Leave it to *Amy*.

I'd give Jo credit for one thing at least: I doubted *she'd* ever allow herself to get caught up in something so silly as chasing the latest fad, particularly if it involved something as ridiculous as pickled limes. Me, I'd succumbed to peer pressure plenty in my time and had to admit that if I still was expected to go to school here, I'd probably be competing over pickled limes with everyone else.

"Of course, the other girls will want a ponytail just like mine," Amy babbled on, "but they will no doubt be excited about it, while Jenny Snow will probably be green with envy."

I had no idea who Jenny Snow was, but with a name like that, she seemed like she might be a frosty person and someone to look out for.

"Probably," I agreed, "Jenny Snow will be green as a pickled lime." We were nearing the schoolhouse and I saw some of the girls entering. None of them wore their hair up, let alone in a ponytail. "Hey," I said, "how many girls are in your school?"

"Silly Emily!" Amy laughed an oddly sly laugh like she knew something about me that I didn't. "How do you not remember? You went here yourself until not long ago!"

I did? I wondered what I'd learned there. Was I considered a smart student? Slow? "Humor me," I said.

"Half a hundred," she replied.

"Half a hundred? Why can't you ever say anything simply? Why can't you just say 'fifty'?"

"I don't know." Amy shrugged, seemingly as perplexed as I was. "It's just how people talk. Somehow it's more complicated to say 'fifty.'"

We were at the door now, she was ready to go in, and I felt it was time for me to say something inspirational.

I placed a hand on her shoulder.

"So, um, study hard," I said, "and one day you may grow up to be president."

"Of what?" she said.

"Duh—of the United States, of course."

Her eyes widened and then she threw back her head and laughed, right in my face.

"Oh, Emily!" she cried, struggling to recover herself. "You really are the strangest creature, aren't you?"

"Good luck with those pickled limes," I said, turning away and leaving her to it.

Once Amy was in school, she was supposed to stay there until I went to get her. And yet for some reason, she arrived home late morning. Did they not like her ponytail?

"What happened?" I asked, seeing how upset she looked. "How did the ponytail go over?"

"It doesn't matter right now about the stupid ponytail—Mr. Davis struck me!" she burst out, shoving her hands up under my nose for inspection. I could see the red welts on her palms where some object had done the damage.

"But that's awful!" I said, outraged on her behalf.

What kind of world was this? At Wycroft we had a zero-tolerance policy about kids hitting other kids, but we also had a zero-tolerance policy about teachers hitting kids. This was child abuse!

"I know!" Amy said, still plenty outraged herself. "No one has struck me in all of my twelve years! I have only ever been loved!"

"Why did he hit you?" I asked.

"Because of the limes! Because of Jenny Snow and the limes!"

I *knew* that Jenny Snow was trouble.

"Jenny got mad because I wouldn't share mine with her, so she told Mr. Davis I had them in my desk and then he made me . . . he made me throw them out the window two by two! And then he made me stand on the platform for fifteen minutes until he called time for recess! But do you know what the worst part was?"

I didn't have a clue, but this all sounded awful to me, at least in a twelve-year-old-girl sort of way.

"As I threw the limes out the window, I could hear . . . *laughter* from down below!"

"Laughter?" I echoed dully.

"Of course laughter! Children were catching my limes as they fell and extruding over their good fortune."

Extruding? That didn't make any sense. But then I realized it was probably just another instance of Amy garbling her vocabulary. She probably meant *exulting.*

"I shall never go back to that school," Amy declared. "When Mr. Davis called recess, I left, vowing never to return." All of a sudden her face took on a worried expression. "Do you think Marmee will be upset with me?"

But no one was upset with Amy.

Meg, whose special pet Amy was, exclaimed over our youngest sister as though she'd been waterboarded at Guantanamo.

Jo strode up and down the room manfully, demanding that Mr. Davis be arrested at once.

Beth, who'd been at home all along but had been too busy playing with her cats and weird dolls to notice Amy's early arrival, was horrified. "I knew no good could ever come from going to school!" she said.

Marmee's response, arriving home later, was slightly more tempered. First she sent Jo with a note for Mr. Davis, informing him that Amy would no longer be attending his school and that Jo was to clean out Amy's desk.

I almost felt sorry for Mr. Davis, in spite of what he'd

done, since I knew what a termagant—another PSAT word!—
Jo could be.

Marmee explained that until she had the chance to discuss
the matter through letters with Papa, Amy would study at home
with Beth.

Oh great, I thought, *more of Amy.* She was almost as bad as Jo,
but for entirely different reasons.

Amy was suddenly looking extremely pleased with herself.
Well, who could blame her? Twelve years old and she didn't
have to go to school anymore, at least not for the time being—
I'd had to wait until the ripe old age of fourteen before quitting
school!

But Marmee shut that down pretty quickly.

She pointed out that the only reason she was taking Amy
out of Mr. Davis's school was that she didn't believe in corporal
punishment but that Amy had broken the rules and deserved to
be punished for her disobedience. In fact, Marmee was glad
she'd lost the limes.

Then came what I'd begun to think of as An Edifying Marmee Lecture—yawn—in which she lectured Amy on the perils
of conceit: how Amy had lots of talents and virtues but was too
inclined to show them off; how much better she would be were
she more like Laurie, who had many accomplishments but no
conceit.

Well, I thought, *he may not have been conceited before he met me, the
March family skank, but now that he had and now that he knew he was thought
by at least one March girl to be exceedingly kissable—*

All of a sudden I had a premonition. There was going to be
some kind of fallout from this silly lime incident, something
more serious than Amy being homeschooled and me having to

put up with her around the house. And yet, try as I might, I couldn't remember anything from the original book that might tell me what that serious something might be. It made me crazy sometimes, this occasional story amnesia.

Still, I told myself, when the moment came, I'd do my best to prevent disaster.

Eight

It didn't take long for that fallout I'd anticipated, that "something more serious," to materialize.

Meg and Jo were preparing to go to the theater with Laurie to see something called *The Seven Castles of the Diamond Lake* that Jo boasted had fairies, elves, red imps, and gorgeous princes and princesses. Amy, who'd had a cold, was angling to go too, but Jo dismissed her request because: one, the show would hurt her eyes; two, she could go with Hannah and Beth the following week; three, she hadn't been invited.

I wondered why no one mentioned the possibility of *me* going to the show, either with Meg, Jo, and Laurie then, or with Hannah, Beth, and Amy the following week. Was I not known to like the theater? I debated whether I wanted to go or not. On the one hand, it would be a new form of entertainment here, plus, if the play was good, I could tease Jo about how much better it was than the one she and Meg had performed soon after my arrival; it was always fun to tease Jo. But on the other hand, I didn't really like fairies, elves, red imps, and gorgeous princes and princesses—it all sounded so Disney.

But I didn't get to debate the pros and cons of staying versus tagging along because suddenly Amy was screaming, "You'll be sorry about this, Jo March!"

Did I miss something?

Maybe I should have been clued in about what was to come based on what I knew about my sisters: that both Amy and Jo were hot-heads, but that Jo had the least self-control and was always sorry afterward. Well, maybe it wasn't accurate to say that she had the *least* self-control, since I was fairly certain Jo had never tried to slip Laurie the tongue.

But I should have been clued in when Amy disappeared, and I could have sworn I heard her rooting around in the room I shared with Meg and Jo.

And I *really* should have been clued in when I saw Amy emerge from our bedrooms, back her way over to the fireplace, and toss something in before we could see what it was, whatever she tossed in causing the flames to leap higher and flare brighter.

But I wasn't clued in because I'd started to write a story, one about a girl at a bad time in her life who finds herself mysteriously sucked into a favorite book. Back home, being a reader and writer were two of the things I'd always loved so why not do it here?

So it wasn't until the next morning that we all became aware of Amy's unpardonable crime.

When Meg and Jo had returned from the play the day before, they told us stories of fairies, elves, red imps, and gorgeous princes and princesses—enough so that I wasn't sorry I missed it, particularly when Meg declared Jo to be a superior playwright to the one who created that awful-sounding theatrical mess. Meanwhile, Amy adopted an air of nonchalance as though she'd never been interested in the play in the first place.

Now Jo discovered that while she was at the play, Amy had burned Jo's story—a half-dozen fairy tales she'd been working on with the intent of finishing it as a book before Papa got home. That copy, Jo said, had been the *only* copy.

How could I have forgotten! In the original book, Amy burned Jo's writing after the lime incident. It was such a mean-girls thing to do to someone else—I'd thought that even at eight years old when I'd read it for the first time. It was worse than little boys pulling the wings off flies. Was Amy some sort of sociopath?

And oh, the awful look on Jo's face when she said it was her only copy.

"I'm sorry," I said to Jo, feeling as though I alone in that room could understand what she was going through. It would be terrible to lose the only copy of something I'd written.

"I'll hate you forever, Amy March!" Jo cried, giving Amy one last box on the ears—she'd already shaken Amy so much, her teeth had nearly chattered out of her head—before huffing off in the direction of the garret.

Overdramatic? Sure. But for once I couldn't blame her.

Even Meg, Amy's usual champion, couldn't blame Jo for her anger.

Nor could Marmee, although as she tucked us in that night, I heard her lecture Jo softly about the inadvisability of letting the sun go down upon her anger. But Jo wasn't ready to forgive.

The next morning Jo announced that she was going skating with Laurie.

Somehow overnight Amy had convinced herself that *she* was the injured party. Hey, she'd already apologized, hadn't she? So no matter what she'd done to make Jo mad in the first place, if Jo wasn't willing to forgive her instantly, then Jo was now in the wrong.

Amy informed any who would listen that the last time Jo had gone skating, she'd promised to take Amy the next time, and this was the last ice of the season. Spring would soon be here.

The last ice? Spring?

Just how long had I been here already? And what was going on back home? Would I *ever* get back home again? I almost wished things would move along quicker with Beth, so that I could do something heroic to save her, and finally return to my real life. Not that I didn't like it here—I'd grown used to the unpasteurized milk, and then there was Laurie—but it wasn't my real life. Not that my real life was so hot anyway, come to think of it.

Meg, in all her eldest-sister wisdom, advised Amy that she should go skating; that she should follow Jo and Laurie at a discreet distance, waiting for the golden opportunity to make friends with Jo again. Everyone knew Jo's moods changed like the weather.

Amy had already grabbed her skates and was halfway to the door when it struck me what was about to happen.

My story amnesia lifted and I saw the scene so clearly: Laurie oblivious; Jo seeing Amy coming up behind them but pretending she didn't; Laurie skating ahead to see if the ice was safe before racing; Amy never hearing the warning Laurie gave Jo to stay near the shore, that it wasn't safe in the middle; Jo not caring if Amy heard or not; Amy heading for the middle of the river because she thought the ice would be smoother there; and Jo turning just in time to see Amy fall through.

So what if somehow Jo and Laurie pulled her out afterward, this was something dangerous *I* could prevent. Maybe, in addition to saving Beth at some future point, maybe I was supposed to keep Amy from falling through the cracks ... literally!

"I'm coming with you!" I shouted after Amy, thinking to avert disaster with my presence.

Amy froze in the doorway, stunned.

"But you hate the cold!" Beth objected.

"You don't even skate!" Meg further objected.

Well, she was right about that. In my real world, I hated any sport that involved giving up physical control, which included all winter sports, as far as I was concerned: skating, skiing, sledding, the luge—whatever the heck that was. And yes, I did hate being cold. Still ...

"I don't care!" I shouted, suddenly feeling the weight of my purpose in this world. "I'm coming with you!"

"But you don't even *have* skates!" Amy said, walking out.

Meg, perhaps seeing how urgent I felt even if she didn't understand why, shoved a pair of decrepit-looking skates upon me. "Here, take mine."

With hurried thanks, I grabbed them from her and raced off after Amy.

Brrrrr!

As much as I hated the cold when I was on land, it was even worse out here on the ice.

Were they sure spring was right around the corner?

One thing I knew was right around the corner was Laurie, who'd skated out of view around the bend in his fur-trimmed coat and cap, just like I remembered in my vision from the original book. Everything was going according to plot, right down to Jo being aware of Amy but pretending not to be, everything right down to Jo hearing Laurie say that the middle of the ice was too dangerous and her not caring if Amy heard him or not.

Everything was the same, except for the addition of me, of course.

Normally I would have been jealous of Jo and Laurie spending time alone together—this was different from them going off to a play in the company of prim Meg—but I didn't have time for that now. As I teetered and wobbled and stumbled after Amy in the unfamiliar skates, it was all I could do to keep my balance.

Amy turned to call over her shoulder to me impatiently, "If you're going to come, come!" Then she began to head toward the precarious middle of the ice.

"Wait!" I called after her.

"What *is* it, Emily?" she asked in exasperation. "I'm in a hurry here."

I knew I had to stop her, had to keep her close to the shore where I still was, so I did the only thing I could think to do: I forced myself to fall.

I remembered a line from an old television commercial. "I've fallen and I can't get up!" I shouted, sprawling around on the ice as though I really couldn't. Okay, I'll admit it: I really couldn't.

It's hard to stand up on ice when you have nothing to hold on to, no real sense of balance, and you don't know how to skate.

"Oh . . . *fine*." She shook her blond locks and headed in my direction.

She was halfway to me when the crack came.

C-RACK!

It was so loud, like a gunshot, I don't know how it was possible that people in the next town didn't hear it.

I looked across the ice in time to see Amy's arms shoot up into the air, and then her body disappeared into the black water that filled the space where the ice had cracked open, her little blue hood bobbing on the surface.

This is still fine, I said to myself, forcing a note of calm into my internal voice. *So I didn't stop her from falling through the ice. So what? This will be just like the book. Jo will have turned in time to see Amy fall through and Laurie will lie down flat and grab Amy while he sends Jo to go fetch a rail from that fence over there.*

Only it wasn't *still fine.* When I looked up in the direction Jo and Laurie had been just a minute ago, they weren't there, so Jo hadn't seen Amy fall through the ice.

Oh no, I realized with an even greater horror. This meant that the only person left to save Amy was . . . *me???*

Oh shoot.

"Amy! Hang on!" I called to the bobbing blue hood.

Then, still unable to rise in my skates, I dragged myself along the ice.

After much heaving and pulling, I finally edged up on the black hole. I'll admit, I was a little scared to get close. What good would it do the world—any world—if I fell in too and we both drowned?

But then I realized that this was all my fault. In my misguided effort to avert disaster for Amy, I'd managed to make things worse. Now, instead of simply suffering a scary dunk in the water as she'd been meant to do, she could drown.

I had no choice. I had to save her.

Like the Grinch, my sometimes-ten-sizes-too-small heart grew three sizes that day.

I inched up all the way to the edge, not caring about my own safety anymore.

"Grab on to my hand, Amy!" I urged her.

But she didn't seem to hear me, struggling as she was to keep her head above water, to keep it from disappearing beneath the surrounding ice.

If she didn't hear my voice, did she hear the much louder crack that soon followed?

Because there it was—*C-RACK!*—and the ice beneath me was giving way and now I was in the black water beside her.

It was the coldest I'd ever been in my life, but I didn't care. Somehow, I got my arms around her waist and with one enormous heave I threw her out of the water and onto the ice, like landing a really big fish. Then I tried to heave myself out too, using the ice border like I would the side of a swimming pool to leverage my body, but every time I bore down on another section of ice, it gave way beneath me.

And I was getting cold. So cold.

My hands became ice, my breathing shallow, and then suddenly I began to feel warmer even though I was still in the frigid water.

Was this how my life was going to end, I wondered, *far from my real life, stuck in the middle of blasted* Little Women?

And then there was Jo's voice, yelling, "Emily March! What *have* you gotten yourself into? Get out of there this instant!"

And then there was Laurie, lying down on the ice, reaching out a hand until he could grasp on to my wrist tightly, keeping me above water while he yelled to Jo to get a rail from the fence over there.

And then they were handing me the rail, pulling me up and out to safety.

"It took you both long enough," I said accusingly to Jo and Laurie.

"What happened?" Laurie asked, his concern so strong I would have felt hopeful for our future as a couple if I weren't nearly dead.

"*That's* never happened before," Amy said oddly. Then she added with awe in her voice, "Emily saved my life."

"Huh," Jo said. "Well, I highly doubt that. Emily can't even skate."

Back home, Amy and I were wrapped in blankets and put before the fire, our teeth still chattering.

Jo couldn't do enough for Amy. Apparently death was a great reminder of love.

"Well, no harm done," Marmee said soothingly. "A little cold water never hurt anybody."

I nearly choked on my tea.

No harm done? my mind screamed. *A little cold water?* I wanted to strangle Marmee. Amy had almost died out there. *I'd* almost died out there! Hadn't any of these people ever heard of hypothermia before?

Oh, wait a second . . . 1862 . . . perhaps no one had invented hypothermia yet . . . or maybe they just didn't know about it . . .

And then they were hurrying Amy and me off to our beds, and I could hear Jo and Marmee talking over Amy's snoring in the next room.

Jo was feeling guilty over her temper, worrying that one day she'd do something so awful it would destroy her life and make everyone hate her.

Serves you right, I thought. *If we were in* my *world and you pulled a stunt like that—letting someone go out on thin ice when you knew the risks, and then if that person died, we'd call it negligent homicide and lock you away.*

Wait a second. Maybe Amy wasn't the resident sociopath. Or perhaps she and Jo were *both* pathological?

But there was Marmee's voice, soothing Jo with stories about her own temper, how it had taken Marmee most of her life to conquer it.

"How did you?" Jo asked with rare timidity. "Conquer your temper, I mean."

"I didn't conquer it permanently," Marmee said. "It came back to me again when I had four young daughters and we were poor."

"Four? Don't you mean five?" Jo said.

"Oh, that's right," Marmee said sounding puzzled. "I don't know why, but for some reason, I forget at times that there are five of you and think there are just four."

Gee, I wonder why that is? I almost snorted out loud. It was some comfort to realize that I wasn't the only one here who was confused at times by all of this. Maybe the story mostly seemed preadapted to me, but there were these occasional wrinkles, as though the story still had to stretch to accommodate me.

Then Marmee droned on about Papa, how his goodness and perpetual patience had been the beacon that had led to her current temper-less state. He'd encouraged her to be the kind of woman her girls would want to grow up to emulate, a woman who would be proud and happy to have her girls confide in her.

It would have been so easy to snort then. So much of what she was saying was snort-worthy, like the idea of Papa being perpetually patient. Well, of course he was—because he never actually had to be there!

I thought about what Marmee and Jo had discussed about Jo's temper being something she needed to work on and I remembered those books Marmee had given us for Christmas: the four—no, *five* copies of *Pilgrim's Progress*. It occurred to me that Marmee knew that Jo's temper was her weak spot; and further, that Marmee had intended for each of us to work on our character. Meg, I figured, needed to become less superior; we all knew about Jo's temper and Amy's vanity, not to mention Beth's shyness—shyness might not be a huge flaw like a pathological temper, but it did keep Beth from fully enjoying her life. But what then was my character flaw, the big thing I had to work on? Surely, it had to be something more than conquering my tendency to be the family skank.

"I still don't believe that story Amy told about Emily saving her," Jo said. "*Emily?* Perhaps Amy was imagining things?"

"It does seem unlikely," Marmee admitted.

Hey! I was outraged. I would have objected, loudly, but I was the eavesdropper here. And what did they mean by that? What did these people know about me that I didn't? Was there something about me that made it seem unlikely I *would* ever save anyone else's life?

Then Marmee said how much she missed Papa but how she'd told him to go to war because she wanted to give her best to the country she loved, and then Marmee counseled Jo to turn to her Heavenly Father for guidance, Amy woke up with a happy cry to see Jo there, the two hugged and kissed, and everything was forgiven and forgotten.

Well, *I* wouldn't forget.

Amy could have *died* because of Jo . . . and Amy destroyed Jo's *book!*

These Marches were nuts!

Nine

I needed to find out what a fortnight was.

It had been making me crazy for years. Why hadn't I ever looked it up before?

I'd come across the term when reading *Little Women* when I was eight and I'd been puzzled by it, so I'd asked my mother. She'd said, "Look it up in the dictionary!" And I'd automatically assumed her advice really meant "I have no idea!" and I'd of course failed to look it up, coming up with my own definition. I'd figured a fortnight referred to four nights, something like a long weekend. Fortnight. Four nights. It made sense to me.

But now as I watched Meg pack what the others termed the "go abroady" trunk for a fortnight at the Moffats', and I observed all the junk she put in that trunk, it struck me that my definition couldn't possibly be right. A fortnight had to be longer than four nights ...

It would have been nice if there were a dictionary handy, and with Jo being such a great writer, you'd think there would have been, but I'd long since become aware that whenever I wanted a particular thing, it was impossible to find it in the March household. So I did the next best thing: I pulled Beth aside from the others. It's not like Beth was known for her brain power, but at least she could be counted on not to laugh in my face if I asked what the others thought a stupid question.

"A fortnight is fourteen days," Beth whispered, "or some people think of it as two weeks, but it is somewhere in there."

What was wrong with these people? They expanded "fifty" to the lengthier "half a hundred" while compressing the precise "fourteen days" to the confusing "fortnight." Why couldn't they be straightforward for once?

That was when Beth laughed straightforwardly in my face.

"Silly Emily!" she said between giggles.

Silly Emily? *Seriously*, Beth?

I was used to the others laughing at me at various times—or casting aspersions on my character by implying I wasn't the sort of person who'd save my own sister's life when she'd fallen through a crack in the ice—but never Beth. In fact, I was so stunned by her outburst, I couldn't reply at all.

"I'm sorry," Beth said, at last managing to gain control of herself, "but don't you realize that I can see what you're up to?"

"Up to?"

"Why, yes! You are asking me a question that everyone knows the answer to, while pretending you do not."

"And, er, why am I doing that?"

"Why, to make me feel just as intelligent as the others, of course! You know that I am shy about my lack of book learning, and you want to make me feel as smart as anyone else." She gave a happy sigh before turning serious. "That is so like you: always looking to do the kind thing."

I was getting credit for being kind? Coolio!

"Yes, well, *kind*." It made me feel suddenly guilty that Beth thought of me that way, when all I cared about now was figuring out the meanings of terms I had no clue about. "I don't know about that. But while we're on the subject, could you tell me what a tarlatan is?" I'd heard Meg say something about packing hers.

"Silly Emily!" She started to laugh again. "There you go again, being kind!"

"Yes, heh, there I go."

It turned out that a tarlatan was a type of fabric, in this case referring to a slightly shabby-looking gown Meg intended using as her "ball dress." It was obvious Meg wanted something finer— apparently the Moffats were very wealthy compared to us—but there just wasn't enough money.

"Anyway," Jo said cheerfully, "Marmee has given you so many things from the treasure-box, I wouldn't think you'd mind so much wearing an old dress to the big party, since so much else of what you'll have on that night will be new. Well, at least to you."

The treasure-box—I'd been able to figure that out without resorting to pumping Beth—was an old cedar chest where Marmee had a few things to give to each of us when she thought the time was right. I was very curious about that chest. Since Marmee sometimes forgot there were five of us, not four, was there really anything for me in there?

"Marmee says that fresh flowers are the perfect ornament

for any girl anyway," Amy said to Meg, "so isn't it wonderful that Laurie has promised to send you some while you are at the Moffats'? I'll bet the other girls will be green with envy!"

Wait a second here. Laurie stood guard while Beth played the piano, he took Jo to the theater and skating, and now he was sending flowers to Meg? Off the top of my head I couldn't think of any particular favor he'd shown Amy, but just what was going on here? When was Laurie going to romance *me*?

But I didn't have time to wonder about that anymore because Meg was fretting over her material things not being perfect.

For the second time that day, Beth did something surprising. She got a little PO'ed.

"Just the other day all you wanted in the world was to be allowed to go to Annie Moffat's," Beth said, "and now, even though Marmee has given you new gloves and silk stockings, it still isn't enough?"

"Yeah!" I agreed forcefully. I found myself liking Beth's slightly skewed perception of the world with me cast in the role of kindness while Meg was an ingrate.

If Jo had to work on her temper, Beth her shyness, and Amy her vanity, Meg definitely had to work on that dissatisfaction thing of hers.

Perhaps sensing that dissatisfaction, the other three began exclaiming over the pretty things Marmee had given Meg and talking about all the fun and parties and new experiences she would have on her fortnight away.

Fun. Parties. New experiences.

Suddenly I had to get out of that room.

The others were too busy squeeing to notice my quiet exit. As I gently closed the door behind me, I saw Marmee standing across the hallway.

"Talk with me for a while, Emily?" she requested.

How could I refuse? It wasn't like back home, where I could say: "Not now, Mom, maybe later."

She led me to the small living room, took her special seat before the fireplace.

"I am very worried about Meg," she said, "but without Papa here, there is no one else I can confide in but you."

Whoa! Since when was I someone anyone could confide in?

"You know," Marmee went on, "I was reluctant to allow Meg to go to the Moffats' in the first place."

"Well, yes," I said, "with her being gone for a whole . . . *fortnight*, the King children will be neglected for two weeks unless I go to them myself."

"I wasn't thinking of Meg's job," Marmee said. "But yes, you are right: you will have to go."

Rats.

"No," she continued, "it's that I fear this time away, being exposed to the Moffats' grander lifestyle, Meg will return even more discontented with her life here than when she left."

Grander lifestyle? Suddenly, I wanted more than anything in the world to be where there would be fun and parties and new experiences.

"I have a solution!" I offered eagerly.

Marmee waited expectantly.

"I could go with Meg!"

"Of course you can't. You weren't invited. Jo wasn't even invited."

"Well"—I hurried to think of some useful purpose I could serve—"I could act as lady's maid to Meg, helping her dress her hair and things like that. Remember that ponytail I gave Amy that time?"

Funny. She didn't look impressed.

"I'm sure all the Moffats have their own ladies' maids," I rushed on. I was sure of no such thing, but what the heck? "I wouldn't want Meg to do without. Plus, it would be good training for me—you know, to learn the ropes so I know what to do when I'm old enough to attend house parties."

Would I still be here in a few years? I shuddered at the thought. It was already spring.

"'Learn the ropes'?" Marmee echoed. "Sometimes, Emily, you say the strangest things. And while your offer is tempting . . ."

Please say yes! Say yes!

". . . I'm afraid I must say no."

I could feel my face fall.

"It was a kind offer, Emily, but I fear that Meg must learn to conquer her discontent on her own. Besides . . ." She paused. ". . . you'll be too busy taking care of the King children."

I felt outraged. Hey, this woman wasn't my mother. She wasn't the boss of me!

But I couldn't tell her that.

Wretched King children!

Wretched stupid everything!

I had to finally admit it: my chief problem in life, the one I needed to work on in a *Pilgrim's Progress* sort of way, was jealousy. Sometimes it seemed as though I was jealous of everybody and everything: jealous of Meg's opportunity in going to the Moffats', jealous of Amy's pretty blondness, jealous of Jo's writing— specifically the fact that she'd done more of it than I had—plus her friendship with Laurie, even jealous of the tender way everyone treated Beth.

"Doesn't it bother you," I said to Jo a few days after Meg's departure, "Meg getting to go to the Moffats' while you and I have to stay here? After all, we *are* almost as old as she is."

"Bother me?" Jo looked startled. "Of course I'm not bothered. I hate parties and getting dressed up. Why should I mind some-one else getting something, especially when I don't even want that something for myself?"

Apparently, I was the only March sister to be plagued by jealousy.

In fact, the others seemed just as happy to rely on their imagi-nations as they would have been to go to the house party in the first place. Just like when Meg and Jo had gone to the New Year's party at the Gardiners', leaving me behind with Beth and Amy, the other three now spent their evenings discussing what they were sure Meg must be doing *right that second*.

"I've heard," Amy said, "that one of the older Moffat girls, Belle, is engaged. I'll bet Meg finds that extremely interesting and romantic. I know I would."

"I hope Meg isn't feeling too badly," Beth said with a worried frown, "that her dresses are somewhat shabby compared to those of the other girls."

"Well, she won't feel bad for long," Jo said. "Laurie told me he was sending her a box with roses, heath, and ferns in it for the small party tonight."

"Doesn't anyone else find it strange," I said, "how much attention Laurie spends on each of us?"

The others stared at me as though I'd said the oddest thing in the world. Apparently I was the only one who found Laurie's behavior strange.

"You're not going to bring up the pact again, are you?" Jo said witheringly. Then she shook her head as though shaking off my peculiar words. "I'll bet it'll be like Amy said before—the other girls will be green with envy over Laurie's flowers. But if I know our Meg, she'll play a trick on them. She'll pretend they're from the old man, Mr. Laurence."

I wasn't sure what was so funny about a sixteen-year-old girl pretending a man old enough to be her grandfather was sending her flowers, but the others apparently found it a hoot, because they started laughing.

"The ball is going to be a week from Thursday," Amy said with a wistful sigh.

Now *that* I understood. What I wouldn't give to be a fly on that wall.

Every now and then, a person gets what she asks for. In this case, I got to be a fly on the wall at the ball, although not in the way I'd imagined.

The Moffat girls were so impressed with the flowers Laurie sent Meg, Belle Moffat sent Laurie an invitation to the ball. Laurie's initial inclination was to decline politely—he said he didn't like dressy parties any more than Jo did—but Jo convinced him. Jo, who never seemed to care at all what she herself looked like, wanted him to report back on how Meg looked.

And Laurie consented, just like that.

It would be nice, I thought, thinking of Jackson, *to get guys to do what you wanted them to do.*

The day after the ball was a Friday, which worked out well for me, Friday being the day I had free from my jack-of-all-trades work. While Jo grumbled off to Aunt March's, and Amy and Beth stayed behind in the house to work on their lessons and do housework, I practically skipped across the newly green lawn to the Laurence estate and knocked loudly on the door.

I hadn't been over by myself since that . . . *last time,* and at first Laurie looked vaguely shocked to see me standing there. I wondered if he was scared I'd try to kiss him again.

My concern grew when he tried to shut the door in my face.

"I'm not going to try to kiss you again!" *Or at least not today,* I mentally added as I pushed back forcefully against the door.

Laurie stopped trying to shut the door so abruptly, that with no resistance anymore, I immediately fell at his feet. As he reached out a polite hand to help me up, I saw he was blushing.

"Of course I wasn't worried about that," he said. "I know you will never do such a thing again."

A lot you know, I thought.

"It's only," he went on, "that I promised Meg I wouldn't say anything to anyone about last night."

If *that* wasn't catnip . . .

"You have to tell me now!" I said.

"Oh no, I mustn't!" he said.

"But you can't say something like that and not expect me to ask any questions."

"But a promise is a promise. And Meg made me promise I wouldn't tell anyone at home."

I had an inspiration. Grabbing on to his arm, I tugged him outside.

"What are you doing?" he shouted.

But I didn't answer. I just kept tugging.

"There," I said, satisfied with myself now that I'd tugged him so far across the lawn, we stood exactly in the center between our two houses.

"I'm not sure I follow you," Laurie said, "although I just did—follow you, that is, but that was only because you tugged me so hard."

"There's your home," I said with a nod in one direction, "and there's mine." I nodded in the other direction. "Since neither of us is technically *at home* right now, then there's no reason why you can't tell me what Meg didn't want you to tell anybody."

"Well, while I suppose that might be literally true—"

"Besides which, I'm not *anybody*. I'm just Emily. I won't say a word, and it's not like anyone listens to me anyway."

"Yes, well—"

"*Spill*, Laurie."

"*Spill?* Is that another new word you invented?"

I simply waited, hands on my hips.

"Very well." He sighed, then: "It was awful, I tell you!"

"What was?"

"Meg! They had her dressed up like a, like a . . . *doll*. There were high-heeled silk boots to match the blue silk gown Belle insisted she wear. The dress was so tight she could hardly breathe, the train so long she could barely walk. They put makeup all over her, crimped her hair . . . and the neckline on the dress!" He blushed again. "It was so low, they put tea-rose buds in her . . . *bosom* . . . and her shoulders were bare!"

That didn't sound much like prim Meg.

"And as for the young gentlemen!" Laurie said.

"Yes? What about them?"

"They were begging introductions and lining up to dance with her when I showed up!"

After the practically guy-free months I'd spent in the March household, that sounded awesome.

"And the worst was that after I told her I didn't care for the way she looked, that I didn't care for fuss and feathers, and after she made me promise not to tell any of you, saying she'd tell you all herself, after all of *that*, later on I saw her drinking champagne with Ned Moffat and his friend Fisher. And even after I made it clear I disapproved, she kept drinking!"

"There, there." I made vague patting gestures with my hand on his arm, meanwhile thinking of how much I'd learned in the past few minutes:

One, Laurie could talk a blue streak when he wanted to, and he was a little priggish about certain things.

Two, when let off her leash, Meg was something of a tarty lush—so *that's* what the March girls were really like when readers weren't looking!

Three, Laurie really didn't like fuss and feathers, not at all. I figured this knowledge would serve me well in my romantic war against Jo for Laurie's heart. And I still did want to win his heart. In a weird way, it was insanely cute how worked up he was getting on Meg's behalf. Back home, if a girl's neckline was so low you could see her . . . *bosom*, the only thing any guy might say would be "Lower! Lower!"

"Oh!" Laurie added, newly outraged. "I almost forgot: the Moffats nicknamed Meg 'Daisy,' of all things. Can you believe it? Daisy!"

Four, Laurie had something against nicknames, unless it was his own.

Oh, and five, I had the power to get Laurie to spill secrets.

Meg returned the next day, Saturday. She looked ragged and I thought she might be suffering from a hangover. Champagne'll do that to a girl. Or so I'd heard.

Meg said she was happy to be home, even if home was unspectacular.

Marmee let that "unspectacular" pass.

But once Beth and Amy went to bed, Marmee was all ears, which was good, since Meg was suddenly all mouth.

"It was awful!" Meg echoed Laurie's words to me from the day before. Then she confessed about the dress. "But that wasn't the worst part. Oh no. The worst part was that at one point I heard Mrs. Moffat telling her girls how smart you are, Marmee, how you had such plans for us girls, chief among which was that we should all be kind to Laurie because he is rich, and wouldn't it be wonderful if he married one of us!"

Well, when she put it like that, it didn't sound like *such* a very awful idea. I mean, someone had to marry him.

"I would like to confront Annie Moffat!" Jo sprang from her chair.

Geez. What a hothead.

"You'll do nothing of the kind," Marmee said.

"Marmee's right," Meg said, going on to add something about how she'd forget the bad, only remembering the good—*HA!* I thought. *As if that ever worked for anybody!*—and that she wouldn't be dissatisfied with her life any longer.

HA! again. I'd heard that kind of talk before. I'd *talked* that kind of talk before. I'd never been able to follow through, though.

"Of course, I must admit," Meg said, "I did like being praised and admired."

And cue the violins for a Marmee Speech . . .

It turned out that Marmee wanted Meg to be modest as well as pretty but that further, she did indeed have plans for us:

". . . to be loved and chosen by a good man is the best and

sweetest thing which can happen to a woman"—*No wonder,* I thought, *girls get so guy-gaga they'll do almost anything to get one; it's because of stupid books like* Little Women!—"but if it doesn't work out that way ..."

Hey, what if I turned out to be the lesbian March girl? I bet that would screw up their story!

Never mind that, though.

Would it ever work out for me in the way that Marmee described?

Ten

Okay, maybe after getting upset about Marmee saying "... to be loved and chosen by a good man is the best and sweetest thing which can happen to a woman"—barf—it was hypocritical of me to change the way I dressed to suit a boy. If that's the case, sue me. Anyway, there was a world of difference between Marmee's version, in which the guy was the center of the universe, and mine, in which the guy was just a fun and interesting part of it.

Since learning that the wealthy boy next door didn't like "fuss and feathers," I'd started dressing down in order to attract Laurie's attention. So far, that didn't seem to be working, but it looked as though my new shabby dress might benefit me in another way. Now that it was fully spring, with longer afternoons for work and play, I'd discovered that the March girls all loved gardening. Every year, they were each given a plot of their own in the yard.

So one Saturday, having seen the others put on their shabby

attire too, I grabbed a little spade and followed them out to a square section on our small property that someone had staked out with wooden posts and twine.

"Oh, look!" Meg exclaimed. "My little orange tree is doing nicely! Now, about some roses . . ."

"I haven't decided what to plant this year," Jo said, rubbing her chin. "Maybe sunflowers? A whole plantation of them?"

"I like my larkspur best of all the flowers," Beth said, "but I am happiest to grow chickweed for the birds and catnip for my cats."

People *grew* catnip?

"I'm thinking of redoing my bower this year." Amy stood with hands on hips. "What do you think of more morning glories and honeysuckles?"

As I observed them excitedly planning their gardens for the year, I realized something was wrong. Where was my little plot of earth to till?

Quickly I did the math in my head, counting off the subdivisions of the squared-off plot. I was able to do it quickly since it doesn't take long to count to four.

"Hey!" I shouted to the others. "What about me?"

"What about you?" Jo said, not even bothering to look up from her digging.

"Where's my little plot of earth to till?"

"Silly Emily!" Beth laughed.

"You've never liked gardening," Amy said.

"You don't like getting your hands dirty," Meg said.

According to them, I didn't like this, I didn't like that. So who was I supposed to be here, some kind of negative no-personality idiot?

I threw my spade down in disgust and trudged back to the house.

Every Saturday evening at seven p.m., like clockwork, the other four disappeared. Happy to have a rare hour or so alone where I could work on my writing, I'd never asked where they were going and they never said. But the night of the gardening incident, curiosity got the better of me and I followed them at a safe distance, keeping silent so they wouldn't know I was there as they chattered amongst themselves.

Eventually, I followed them up to the garret. I again remained silent, observing as they each picked up badges off the table. The badges had "P.C." printed on them, and they wore those badges around their heads like paper crowns. With great solemnity, Meg took a seat behind the table, while the others sat in chairs across from her.

"P.C."? What could that mean? Not "politically correct," but it was the only thing I could think of at the time.

"I hereby call this meeting of the Pickwick Club to order," Meg announced.

The Pickwick Club?

"Mr. Snodgrass." Meg turned to Jo. "Do you have this week's edition of *The Pickwick Portfolio*?"

"Yes, Mr. Pickwick," Jo said.

"Please present it," Meg directed.

"Well, sir," Jo said, "your own entry about a masked marriage is quite good, and the piece about the squash by Mr. Tupman"— she nodded at Beth—"was also quite good, if a little on the simple side." Jo turned to Amy with a glare. "Unfortunately, this week all Mr. Winkle had to offer was *yet another* apology for laughing during club and for failing *yet again* to deliver a suitable piece for publication."

In spite of Jo's stern look, Amy giggled.

Pickwick? Snodgrass? Tupman? Winkle?

What *were* they doing?

The strange things people did for entertainment before You-Tube was available. And yet, they looked like they were having fun.

"What *are* you all doing?" I burst out.

The four others gave little jumps in their chairs as they turned to look at me. Apparently, I was better at acting invisible than I'd ever thought.

"Why, you know," Meg, the first to recover, said.

"We've been doing it for a year," Jo said.

Well—I mentally gritted my teeth—*I haven't been here a year, thank you very much!*

"Jo got the idea from reading Dickens," Amy said. "She liked *The Pickwick Papers* so much she thought we should put out our own paper."

"So we each assume different characters from the book," Beth said, "even though some of us haven't read it yet and probably never will."

"Well," I said grudgingly, "it looks like fun. Why wasn't I ever invited?"

"What do you mean you weren't invited?" Jo snorted at me. "You said you hated Dickens. You've never wanted to come before."

"Well, I do now." I pulled over a chair from against the wall. "Perhaps I could sit in just this once . . ."

I tried to stay silent, I really did, but soon I realized that in spite of Meg being the symbolic head of the group as Samuel Pickwick, the real force behind *The Pickwick Portfolio* was Jo, who in addition to writing most of the pieces was also the editor.

"Here, let me see that." Sick of being left out of things all the time, I snapped my fingers at the paper, which I began to read for myself.

"Yes," I muttered, "Beth's 'History of a Squash' does have something sweetly simple about it."

"In here," Jo said, sitting up straighter in her chair, "we address Beth as Mr. Tupman."

"Fine, fine." I read some more. "Oh, *come on*, Jo!"

"That's Mr. Snodgrass to you," she said.

"Fine. Mr. Snodgrass. But *come on*. Did you really write an ode to a dead cat?"

"Well, the cat did die." Jo sniffed haughtily. "It's good to have poetry in a paper, and odes do have to be about something."

"And what about these advertisements in the back? 'Hannah is to give a cooking lesson'? By all means, alert TMZ!"

"What?" Amy said, puzzled, but the others ignored her.

"Well, Hannah *is* going to give a cooking lesson." Jo reddened. "Or, at least, she's going to make us dinner."

"And these hints and the weekly report? Meg using less soap on her hands would keep her from being late for breakfast? And while you accurately grade yourself as *bad*, Meg as *good*, and Beth as *very good*, you only give poor Amy *middling*?"

"*Middling*?" Amy echoed. "Not again, Jo! I swear you only do that because you're still mad at me for burning your book that time!"

"The *middling* person is to be called Mr. Winkle," Jo said

heatedly. Then she turned on Amy. "And don't forget to call me Mr. Snodgrass!"

Freak.

"I don't care what any of you call yourselves," I said, tossing *The Pickwick Portfolio* aside, disgusted. "This paper of yours is rubbish."

"I suppose you think *you* can do better?" Jo said.

"Yes," I said coolly. "I believe I can."

"Fine." Jo crossed her arms. "Prove it."

I got up from my chair and went to stand beside Meg. "Do you mind?" I looked down at her, gesturing at her seat.

With reluctance, she relinquished the seat of power, assuming the less important one I'd vacated.

I sat down behind the table and surveyed the four journalists.

"And take those silly badges off your heads!" I directed.

Looking sheepish, they complied.

"Now then, I should like to call to order this meeting of"—and here inspiration struck me—"the Twist Club!"

"The Twist Club?" Jo echoed.

"Yes," I said. "And our new paper will be called *The Twist Times.*"

"But I don't understand," Jo said. "Why would we call our club and our paper that?"

"For *Oliver Twist*, of course. You seem to have this obsession with Dickens, so I just figured—"

"It made sense with *The Pickwick Papers*," Jo said. "But what does *Oliver Twist* have to do with newspapers or any papers at all?"

Huh. She had me there.

"It's the only Dickens I know," I admitted, not adding that

I'd only ever seen the movie musical version. "Now then," I barreled on, ignoring Jo's snort, "what I really think we need to do is liven up this dreadful rag you've been producing. We need punchier headlines, and more timely stories—"

"And we'll also need new names," Beth cut in, although I must point out, she cut in as timidly as possible.

"New names?" I echoed.

"Well, yes," Beth said. "It doesn't make sense for me to be Mr. Tupman if I'm writing for *The Twist Times* now."

"Anyway," Amy said, "I was growing tired of being Mr. Winkle."

Jo glared at her.

"Okay," I said. "What new names would you like to have?"

"You pick, Emily," Beth said. "I don't know anything about *Oliver Twist.*"

"How about the Artful Dodger?" I suggested.

Beth smiled at this. "Oh, I like the sound of that very much: *Mr.* Artful Dodger."

"What about me?" Amy asked eagerly.

I studied her. "Fagin, I think. You know—the nose."

She didn't look quite as pleased as Beth.

"And me?" Meg asked.

"Nancy would suit you," I said. "She dies horribly; but before that, she's terribly and tragically romantic."

"Mr. Nancy," Meg said, pleased.

"And what about me?" Jo asked.

"How about Bull's-eye?" I suggested.

"The *dog*?" Jo was aghast. "I have read the book, you know."

"Fine then," I said, "you can be Bill Sikes."

"But he—"

"And I'll be Oliver Twist, of course. I guess now that we all have our names, the next thing to do would be to start writing."

"But what should we write?" Beth asked. "I always do better if there's a specific assignment."

"Er, write what you know!" I said, remembering a phrase Mr. Ochocinco used to use. "But punchier! More timely! More lively!" I shooed them with my hands. "Get to it now!"

Jo regarded me. "And what will you be doing while we're doing all the work?"

"Why, I'll be editing your work as you hand it in," I said, "just like you used to do."

"This ought to be good," Jo said.

The following Saturday night, the first edition of *The Twist Times* was presented, which I read aloud to the others.

THE TWIST TIMES

A HAPPY DEATH
by Nancy
It is a tragedy that Nancy died
But a triumph that she loved Bill,
Even while he was killing her.

OF CATS AND DOLLS
by the Artful Dodger
Cats and dolls have more in
common than people think. For

you can love them all even when
they have no limbs, or even a head,
and they make messes on the furniture.
Oh, and pianos are very nice too.
And squash.

THE TRAGEDY OF HER NOSE
by Fagin
She would have had such a good life,
but her nose got in the way of everything.
Whenever she tried to drink something,
her nose banged against the lip of the cup.
When she slept at night, her nose was so
large that the snores from it kept waking
her. People her own age shunned her.
Small children ran screaming from her
path. So she died.

ON WRITING
by Bill Sikes
When one first makes the decision
to be a writer, she must.

ADVERTISEMENTS
Hannah will once again be
offering a cooking lesson—

"Wait a second!" Jo interrupted me. "What's going on here?"

"Oh, sorry," I said. "It's just that with all the confusion—you know, the friendly takeover at the newspaper and all—there simply wasn't any time to seek out new advertisers, but I promise that next week—"

"I'm not talking about *Hannah!*" Jo was clearly exasperated.

"What else could be wrong?" I asked.

"I'm talking about my piece!" Jo said. "All you read was, 'When one first makes the decision to be a writer, she must,' and then you stopped reading without finishing the rest."

"But I did finish," I said, holding up the newspaper so she could see her piece with its two lines.

"What happened to the rest?" she demanded. "The piece I gave you was ten pages long!"

"Well, see, that was the problem," I said. "Your piece was simply too long, so I had to cut it."

"You cut it from ten pages to two lines?"

"Why, yes," I said. "Space considerations, you know." I held up the newspaper, pointed to the item about Hannah. "I had to leave room for our advertisers, didn't I?"

Two things happened then.

Jo lunged for my throat and Laurie came out of the closet.

"What are you doing here?" I could only gasp out the words because I was still busy trying to pry Jo's fingers off my throat.

Seeing him there, Jo instantly let go of me.

"I invited him," Jo said.

The others gasped.

"I just thought he might like to write for the newspaper," Jo said.

"But he's a . . . *boy!*" Beth said.

"No, he's not," said Jo. "He's Teddy." Teddy was Jo's *special* name for him. Figured.

"But we've never had a boy write for the newspaper before," Amy said.

"Yes, but wouldn't it be nice to get a fresh perspective?" Jo said. "And as I say, it is only Laurie . . ." She picked up the paper, handed it to him. "What do you think?"

Why, you little rat! That's what *I* thought. She wanted him to write for the paper? *HA!* I'd bet anything she'd hidden him away in that closet hoping that when he saw my first issue of the paper, he'd think it lame. I'd bet anything that was it because it was certainly the kind of thing I'd do to her.

And it was lame, I saw that now as I looked over his shoulder: "A Happy Death," "Of Cats and Dolls," "The Tragedy of Her Nose"—it was as lousy as Jo's paper had been.

"*The Twist Times.*" He chuckled over the title. "Very clever."

Well, maybe it wasn't *so* bad . . .

"I do think there could maybe be more local news," he continued, "you know, since it is a newspaper. And that piece on writing does seem to be a bit, er, truncated . . . hmm . . . Do you think Hannah might be willing to teach me to cook?" He folded the paper, not waiting for an answer, and turned to me with an admiring smile. "Nice work." Then he added, surveying my dowdy dress, "I'd think, though, as editor you'd get to dress better."

Was there no pleasing him fashionwise?

"I hope you'll let me write for your paper," he addressed me as though we were the only two there.

Why had his attitude toward me changed? I wondered. Oh, well. He was probably only being overly nice to me so he could get published. Everyone wants to see their names in print—fifteen minutes of fame and all that.

Still, might as well take advantage of the situation . . .

"Of course you can," I said.

"But it's not up to just you," Jo said testily. "There has to be a vote."

What was this? Now that it turned out that Laurie admired my paper, she no longer wanted him involved?

"Well," I said sweetly to her, "it was *your idea* to invite him." I turned to the group at large. "All those in favor?"

"Aye!" Amy said.

"Aye!" Meg said.

"Aye!" Beth said, adding, "even if he is a boy."

"Aye!" I thrust my hand up in the air in Jo's direction. "*Aye!*" I waved that hand insistently.

"Fine," she said sourly, raising a limp hand. "Aye."

"But he's going to need a male name to write under," Beth said. "I mean, I realize he's already got one. But you know, like the rest of us use from the book?"

But I'd exhausted all the names I could remember from *Oliver Twist*.

"Bull's-eye okay with you?" I asked Laurie with a doubtful smile.

"It's perfect." Laurie's eyes sparkled as he smiled back at me. "I don't mind being the dog."

Then Laurie informed us about how, in anticipation of being invited to join our merry journalistic group, he'd set up a make-shift post office in the hedge between our properties. The box had a roof that opened so that messages and books and things might circulate more freely among us.

The others thought this was a capital idea—that was Jo's word for it: "capital"—but I could see trouble down the road.

What if one sister intercepted a letter from another sister to Laurie? What if one sister stole a letter from Laurie to another sister?

A post office between our two houses?

How reckless!

Eleven

Poor Pip was dead!

Who the heck was Pip?

Turn back the clock five days, to June 1 . . .

The Kings had gone to the seashore, leaving Meg with three weeks free. Aunt March was off to Plumfield, and while Jo had feared right up to the last minute that the old woman would either decide not to go after all or would insist on Jo coming with her, the carriage that took her away only contained one Aunt March, one driver, and about twenty-two trunks. Then, since Meg and Jo both had a vacation of sorts at home, Beth and Amy begged Marmee to let them take a break from their studies too.

And Marmee agreed to all of it, saying that while three weeks might be too long, she would allow her girls to experiment with one week of leisure, a life with all play and no work.

Funny, no one asked what I thought of all this, what I wanted to do.

The truth was, much as I might have grumbled about my duties, I'd grown used to my round of regular responsibilities. But now, with no King children or Aunt March to go to, no Beth and Amy to help with their lessons, I was out of a job. Or jobs.

The jack-of-all-trades had nothing to do.

They say that idle time is the devil's hands.

Isn't that what they say?

Well, something like that.

The others settled into their first day of leisure. Meg said she would just laze around the whole time. Jo intended to read in the old apple tree and go on "larks" with Laurie—well, we'd see about *that*! Who was violating the pact now? Amy was going to spend her time drawing, while Beth had her dolls to attend to.

That left me.

The *Pickwick Portfolio/Twist Times* having renewed my energy for writing, I spent my time working on the story I'd started about a girl who time travels to an earlier era. With no other distractions, I figured I could make real headway on it in a week.

Of course, I was finding there were problems with writing in this world. For one thing, there were no computers. Everything had to be done in daylight or by candlelight and by hand. It was all write, write, write with my right, right, right—I swear, my right wrist was getting muscular, at least two times larger than my left! If this kept up, my right wrist would be the equivalent of Amy's nose: something to be self-conscious about and laughed over.

Okay, maybe I was getting carried away.

But it was awful not having a computer. I couldn't move text around easily and the sheets of paper I worked on got muddled-looking with all the strikeouts and arrows indicating something should be moved here or there; never mind that there was no Internet for me to procrastinate with.

Then there was the added problem of finding a safe place to hide my increasingly large stack of pages. I didn't want the others to see what I was writing. I mean, it wasn't like I was giving away the secret recipe for Snapple, but some people around here might be . . . *offended* if they, oh, I don't know . . . *recognized* themselves in any of my characters.

I snuck up to the garret, used a stick to pry loose a floorboard, and shoved the day's pages inside, on top of pages I'd hastily stuffed in there on previous occasions.

There!

It was a good story, I thought. I wondered if, if and when I returned to my real life, I'd be able to take it with me.

Everyone was bored.

Of course, no one would admit it. But when Marmee asked at day's end, "How was your first day of leisure, girls?" after a moment of silence Meg responded, "Wonderful! Although for some rea-son, the day did seem extraordinarily long."

"Interesting," was all Marmee said, but her smile struck me as smug.

I studied her. *What a shrewd . . . Marmee she is!* I thought. When she'd said we could try this "experiment" for a week, I hadn't seen right away that she was the one conducting the experiment . . . and that it was on us! It was like she was some sort of mad scientist.

"If I do *X* and allow the girls to do *Y*, I predict that I will wind up with *Z* result . . . and then *I* can have the pleasure of pontificating on it all!"

That would be a fun speech to endure!

I hadn't realized, all those times I'd read *Little Women* when I was younger, how pompous Marmee could be.

Of course, unlike the others, I hadn't been bored at all that day. I'd liked having so many hours to work on my short story that was really turning into more of a book. But it wasn't the sort of thing I'd want to do all day long every day.

If I did, my right wrist would fall off!

It really was boring, I thought to myself the next day with a yawn, *having no specific duties to fill my day with.* When I was back home, I'd loved free time because there was so much that I could do for fun. But here? In the 1800s? There was no TV, no computers, no phones to talk or text on all day long if I wanted to. There was definitely no Twitter. There was just sitting around the house. For short periods of time, it wasn't bad. But like this? It was too *much* quiet.

Marmee and her wretched experiments!

That's probably why I felt so much excitement and relief when on the second day of the experiment, Jo walked in with a letter that Laurie had left in our post office.

"He says it's going to be a perfect day for rowing on the river!" she announced, looking as relieved and excited as I felt.

I quickly hurried to get a bonnet, finally settling on Hannah's because it was the largest by far.

The sun—I hated it as much as I hated winter, I thought as I tied a bow beneath my chin. With my auburn hair and fair skin, I burned easily, and I'd left my SPF90 back in the real world some-where.

"Emily, what *are* you doing?" Jo demanded irritably. "Where do you think you're going and why on earth are you wearing Hannah's bonnet? You look ridiculous."

I ignored the last part. "I'm getting ready to go rowing with Laurie," I said brightly, sailing out the door before she had the chance to say anything else.

I knew what she'd say if I let her: that the invitation had been for *her* and I wasn't invited.

But I wouldn't give her the chance. I didn't care what she said or thought about my going because: 1) as far as I was concerned, she and Laurie had already spent way too much time alone together— I'd lost one guy to an older sister and then a younger sister, back in my real life, and I wasn't about to let that happen to me again, pact or no pact; 2) there was no way I'd spend a whole day in that house, unable to write because my wrist was sore, watching Meg laze on the sofa, Amy draw, and Beth play with her dolls.

You'd almost think that this rowing thing was yet another of Marmee's little experiments . . .

So many things in life have a way of widening the gap between ideals and reality.

My hands were getting sunburned already—I hadn't thought to wear gloves—plus there were so many flies out on the water! Not only was there no sunscreen in this world, but there wasn't any bug spray either.

And was there a good reason, I thought as I watched my redden-ing hands pulling backward on the oars in a great heave, *that I was the only one doing any rowing?*

Oh, that's right. I'd offered.

In my mind, I did a snotty imitation of my own voice: *"I can do all the rowing!"* I'd said, figuring Jo couldn't turn me away if I made myself invaluable to the expedition. *"But I've never known you to row a boat in your life!"* she'd said, sounding just as snotty, only for different reasons.

This rowing was hard work! There was no time to do anything else.

Like flirting with Laurie, which was exactly what Jo was doing right now.

"That post office you installed between our houses," she said from underneath her wide-brimmed straw hat, which, I must say, looked cooler in every way than Hannah's bonnet. "That post office is really such a marvelous thing!"

Okay, so maybe it wouldn't seem like flirting to most people, but coming from Jo it was.

"I never knew a boy could be so inventive," Jo said.

Honestly. She was practically throwing herself at him! *Why not just jump in his lap and lick his face like a puppy?* I thought grumpily.

Oh, that's right. I'd already done that. Well, not the lap and licking parts.

And what was Laurie doing while I rowed us around the lake where Amy had nearly drowned and Jo now flirted? You'd think, being a boy, he'd want to do his share of the labor. But no. I was on one end of the boat, rowing, while he lazed indolently—PSAT word! Woo-hoo!—on the seat at the other end, with Jo on the middle seat, her back to me.

Maybe he was so lazy because he was used to having servants do things for him? *Well,* I thought, *at least he isn't insolent.*

"Why?" Laurie said to Jo, a long blade of marsh grass dangling from the corner of his mouth. "You don't think boys can be as inventive as girls?"

"I don't think boys can do anything as good as girls." Jo laughed, still in the Jo mode of flirting. I swore, I liked her better when she walked around with her hands shoved in her skirt pockets like she was a boy, saying "Christopher Columbus!"

"But that's ridiculous," Laurie said, not argumentative at all, but as though he were simply making a statement of fact. "Everyone knows that boys are superior to girls, in every way imaginable."

Jo had her long chestnut hair tucked up under her straw hat and I saw her naked neck redden instantly.

And it wasn't with sunburn.

"You take that back, Theodore Laurence!" she threatened, half rising from her seat.

I was surprised by her reaction. Was she really that upset about what he'd said? Or was she so bored after yesterday that she was mad at the world and picking a fight?

Whatever the reason, I decided I liked the mad Jo better than the flirting Jo.

"Don't be ridiculous," Laurie said with a lazy smile, tilting his head back to catch the sun. He closed his eyes, happy. "I am bigger than you, stronger, I have greater speed, and I am smarter on every measure that matters."

Yeah. I could have told you he thought that. Guys always do. That's why they had to be humored, for example . . .

"I like that about you," I called across the boat to Laurie, having to crane my neck around Jo. "Bigger-than-girls is a good feature in a boy."

Laurie opened one eye and, I swear, winked it at me.

But Jo, apparently, didn't know anything about guys or how to talk to them.

"Emily may be silly enough to agree with what you say," Jo began.

Hey! I resented that.

"But not me," Jo said hotly. "I *know* that I am superior to boys." She paused. "At least most boys," she added, showing that she had some sense if she was reluctant to insult Laurie completely. What guy would really want to be with a girl who kept saying "I am better than you, I am better than you, I am sooooo much better than you."

That's the guy's job.

"So you take back what you said," Jo instructed Laurie.

"And if I don't?" he challenged, looking for once as though he might be getting a little angry. Maybe the heat was beginning to get to him too.

"If you don't," Jo countered, "I'll throttle you . . . and then I'll never speak to you again!"

I couldn't have that, I thought as Jo rose from her seat, prepared to deliver on her threat. Oh, I didn't care if she never spoke to Laurie again. That would be fine with me—welcome, even! Although she was such a chatterbox, I figured she'd never be able to stick to it.

It was the throttling part I couldn't allow. Laurie was bigger than Jo, but she was still pretty big for a girl. Plus she had anger and scrappiness on her side. I was sure she could take him.

No, I couldn't allow that: my poor, sweet Laurie, throttled black and blue by my crazed sister.

That's when I saw my opportunity.

Not far from where I'd been rowing, a rock jutted out of the water. I swung the boat around, rowing toward it as fast as I could, keeping my eye on my goal all the time.

When we struck the rock with a surprising degree of force, we only teetered on it for a moment before all—Jo, Laurie, and Emily—were dunked in the water.

There! I thought. *That would cool Jo off! It was certainly cooling me off,* I thought, rolling onto my back for a moment and just floating.

"You did that on purpose!" Jo sputtered at me angrily, little drops of water spraying from her mouth.

I ignored her, turned on my stomach, and dog-paddled over to where Laurie was sopping wet, laughing.

"Did I mention," I said, treading as water dripped from my lashes, "how much I like it that you're bigger than I am?"

Four days later, the whole household was still bored, Marmee had decided she and Hannah would take the day off since the rest of us had already had most of the week off, Jo and Laurie had had their fight and were not speaking as far as I could tell, and my hands were only beginning to lose the lobster-red color they'd acquired that day on the lake.

Rotten rowboats.

And rotten Hannah for accepting Marmee's offer of a day off.

Wasn't *anybody* going to do any work around here anymore?

With Hannah off, there was no fire in the kitchen, no break-fast in the dining room. No breakfast?!

With that bracing thought in mind, I offered to help Meg, who'd wanted to surprise Marmee with breakfast in bed.

But even preparing a simple meal like breakfast proved a

challenge in the 1800s. Meg had obviously never done so before, and while I had, there were no Pop-Tarts nor was there a microwave to be found.

Suffice it to say we burned everything, which Marmee didn't seem to mind at all.

Then Jo informed us *she'd* make our dinner. Apparently, while we were busy upstairs delivering the burned breakfast to Marmee, Jo was busy putting a letter in the post office for Laurie. She'd invited him to dinner, I guessed to make up for the argument she'd instigated.

I didn't offer to help Jo like I had with Meg.

But that was okay, Jo said, she had everything under control.

"I may not know how to make a salad," Jo said, wrapping an apron around her waist, "but I've a book here that will tell me."

"You don't need a *book* to make salad," I said. "Just rip up some lettuce and toss it in a bowl!"

"How would you know?" Jo looked down her nose at me. "And anyway, I'm fairly certain there's a lot more to it than that!"

"Not much." I grabbed an apple from the bowl on the table. "But suit yourself."

As I exited the room, I heard Jo muttering something about lobsters and strawberries.

It was going to be a fun dinner.

And it would have been a fun dinner, if Pip hadn't died.

"Poor Pip is dead!" I heard Beth scream, her voice trailing off into a heartbreaking sob.

With no clue what she was talking about, I raced through the house after the sound of her.

When I found her, she was using the hem of her skirt to wipe at her eyes as sobs shook her shoulders. In the room with her was a birdcage, inside of which lay a dead canary.

Huh. I hadn't even noticed we *had* a canary!

"There, there," I soothed.

Awkwardly, I fitted my arms around Beth. I'd never been very good at the whole hugging thing, but I was sad to see her so upset, even if it was only over a bird.

Then, before I knew it, the others were in the room with us. When Beth tried to blame herself for Pip's death, because perhaps she had forgotten to feed him during her week of leisure, the others pooh-poohed this. One of my brain-surgeon sisters even offered to put Pip in the oven in the hopes of reviving him.

"We can have a funeral right after my dinner party," Jo offered, a bit self-absorbedly I thought—after all, we'd had a death here!—but it seemed to calm Beth.

Sooooo . . .

Jo went to market, Marmee went out to dinner, a gossipy spinster named Miss Crocker—who was apparently a friend of the family even though I'd never met her before—showed up expecting to eat with us, Laurie came, Jo rang the dinner bell an hour late, and the food she made was gross.

Salt instead of sugar with strawberries?

I think not.

And then we had the funeral.

As we stood in the backyard, Laurie—being the only man and therefore the strongest, as he would no doubt want people to know—used a small spade and dug a hole in the earth where Beth could lay Pip before the cats got to him. In fact, she'd been carrying his dead body in her pocket all day to avoid the problem of the cats, in spite of my warnings that it might not be the healthiest thing to do. Unfortunately, I couldn't tell her that any self-respecting health inspector would shut this place down in a minute for all the violations—Beth had gone from cradling a dead canary to the table without a hand-washing in sight!

But none of that mattered now as poor Pip was finally laid to rest.

It was as Beth bravely tossed the first clod of earth over his body that the first involuntary sob broke from me. I don't know why. Maybe it was just that the idea of death itself—even if in this case it was only a canary—reminded me that there were more serious things in the world than the silly things I mostly thought about? Maybe it was just the reminder that anyone could die at any time?

What was going on back home, in my real life? Suddenly I missed my own world so much, and not the things, for once, but the people. I even missed Charlotte. And then a thought occurred to me, a scary thought: if I was so oblivious to things going on around me here that I'd failed to notice a canary in the house until that canary up and died, how in the world was I ever going to save Beth?

I began to cry harder.

"Huh." Jo eyed me strangely as she offered me a handkerchief that looked none too clean. "I didn't even know you liked Pip. As far as I could tell, you never even noticed he was there."

It was a big job, doing the cleanup after dinner. Beth was still too upset over Pip to help, Meg felt she'd done enough that day in making breakfast, and Jo thought she'd done enough in making dinner, and so I had to do all the work, since Laurie had offered to take Amy for a drive in his carriage.

Hel-lo! I thought as I scraped dishes. *What was up with* that?

Then Marmee came home, Amy came back, we were all together again, Marmee asked how our day was, we confessed that it had been fast and awful.

And then Marmee gave a speech about the need for a balance between work and play, concluding with:

"Work is wholesome."

That Marmee! I thought. *What a sly boots!*

Twelve

Beth had been appointed our postmistress, meaning it was her job to unlock the little door in the box Laurie installed and then distribute our mail. She'd been appointed because she was the one who spent the most time at home. Also, because we felt sorry for her, having so little in her life that most people would find exciting and feeling that such an important job would mean a lot to her. Also, because some of us were hoping to wean her away from that wretched Joanna doll.

Okay, that last was me.

On that day in July, when Beth entered the house with the mail, her arms were filled to overflowing. My, we were a popular group!

"Here's the nosegay for Marmee that Laurie always sends," Beth announced as she began distributing the mail.

HA! What a kiss-up Laurie could be at times.

"Here's one letter and one glove for Meg." Beth handed the items over.

The letter was from Mr. Brooke, Laurie's tutor, translating a song from German that Meg had requested. As for that single glove, it was a puzzle, since Meg claimed to have left two at the Laurence house.

HA! I thought about the single glove. I didn't really know what the single glove meant, but it was odd and did seem as though it could be *HA!*-worthy.

"Two letters for Jo, a book, plus a funny old hat from Laurie so she won't burn her face." Beth looked relieved to be rid of so much of the mail burden in one shot.

HA! But then I realized there was nothing to *HA!* about. Instead, I was resentful: Jo always got the most mail, plus I needed that hat more than she did. *I* was the one with the fair skin that always burned.

One of Jo's letters was from Marmee, congratulating Jo on the good progress she'd been making in controlling her temper.

HA! Her efforts to control her temper—Marmee hadn't been there that day in the rowboat when Jo had tried to throttle Laurie.

Jo's other letter was from the boy she'd tried to throttle. Laurie wrote that he had some English boys and girls visiting the next day—friends he'd made abroad—and he wanted the March girls to join them all at Longmeadow, where a tent would be pitched, a fire lit, lunch eaten, and croquet played. He also said that Mr. Brooke would be going along to keep the boys in line, while Kate Vaughn, the oldest of the English girls, would be in charge of the rest of us.

Jo insisted Marmee must let us go, claiming that she, Jo,

could be such a help to Laurie with the rowing—*HA!* She hadn't rowed a single row that day on the lake—and Marmee agreed.

"Amy's got chocolate drops here," Beth said, continuing with the mail distribution, "and a picture she wanted to copy, while I've got an invitation from Mr. Laurence to come play the piano for him tonight before the lights are lit." Beth gave a happy little sigh, although I couldn't see what was so happy-making about the idea of playing piano in the dark.

HA! Who wanted to eat chocolate drops?

HA! Who cared about playing some stupid piano anyway?

The others continued cheerfully studying the items that had come to them through the post office, while I stood there.

"Ahem," I said.

The others finally looked at me.

"Isn't there anything else?" I said. "From the post office, I mean."

Spreading her arms wide, Beth revealed their emptiness. "What else could there be?" she said with a puzzled frown.

"Ohhhh, never mind," I grumbled.

But I wasn't grumbling when I got up in the morning. Instead, I was actually excited about the day ahead.

Something new and different to do—coolio!

Then I saw what my sisters had been up to overnight.

OMG.

Meg had put curling papers all over her head, like the heat and humidity wouldn't drag any curls straight down. Jo was slathered in cold cream—she looked ridiculous, like a not-too-scary movie monster. Amy had a clothespin on her nose—nineteenth-century cosmetic surgery!

Well, I thought, *I may not have had any mail the day before, but at least I didn't have any of their peculiar grooming habits.*

As for Beth, she never cared what she looked like. But she did have her own fetish. She'd spent the night cuddling the headless and limbless Joanna.

"I wanted to atone in advance for our day's separation," she told me as the others pranced and preened.

Oh brother. Apparently, she was still feeling guilty about Pip's death and was worried that the day's separation would result in a similar fate for her doll as that which had befallen her bird.

I was tempted to explain to her that it wasn't the same thing at all. But there was no point in telling that to Beth, I realized as I watched her croon over the doll. It would only hurt her.

"You're a good girl, Bethie," I said. "Joanna's lucky to have you and I'm sure she'll still be . . . *alive and well* when we return."

Beth and I may not have had anything in common in terms of our feelings about dolls, but we did share one thing. Neither of us liked to fuss over our appearance, so we were ready long before the others.

As we stood outside waiting, I wondered: If Beth and I shared an indifference to fashion, what qualities did I share with my other sisters?

Meg was prim, to the point of being boring. I was nothing like that. Would a prim girl be the March family skank? Amy was vain to the point of absurdity. Nope. Nothing like that either. Look at the shabby clothes I'd been willing to wear to impress Laurie with my lack of vanity. As for Jo: HA! We had even less in common than I had with any of the others.

Just then Meg, Amy, and Jo came spilling out of the house.

"Emily, do you think you could at least make an effort to be presentable?" Jo snapped at me.

"Don't you think that hat Laurie gave you makes you look ridiculous?" I snapped back at her. "You look like you're wearing an umbrella attached to your head."

Honestly. Jo and I were nothing alike.

Kate Vaughn was so prim, she out-primmed Meg, I thought once we were all gathered on Laurie's lawn. Was that a lorgnette she occasionally placed over her eye? The only other person I'd ever seen use one was Aunt March. Kate had three siblings with her: Frank and Fred, Jo's age—Fred was wild, while Frank was lame, causing Beth to be extra-kind to him—and Grace, around nine or ten, who immediately latched on to Amy. It was obvious that Laurie liked the boys but didn't have much use for Kate. Well, who could blame him?

Making up the rest of our party were Ned and Sallie Moffat. Meg looked happy to see Sallie there, but less so about Ned. Maybe she was still embarrassed over her flowers-in-her-bosom drunk-on-champagne display?

As for Laurie, he was dressed up in a sailor costume. A *sailor* costume? I tried to convince myself it was cool in a retro sort of way, but it was too much of a stretch.

Then we were all being herded into boats and we were off to Longmeadow.

Laurie rechristened Longmeadow "Camp Laurence" and when we arrived there, I saw that someone had set up the tent, arranged wickets for croquet, and deposited hampers of food.

Before anything else, it was decided that a game of croquet must be played.

Well, *I* didn't decide that. It was Laurie, egged on by Jo. Didn't any of the others notice how hot it was out here? Maybe if I'd been wearing shorts and a T-shirt it might not have been so bad. But in a long-sleeved, neck-high, grass-length dress and boots? It was awful!

I elected to sit croquet out, taking up a spot under a nice shady tree with the lame and the young.

They chose up teams. On one side were Laurie, Jo, Ned, and Sallie, all Americans, while the other team was a mixture of Mr. Brooke, Meg, Kate, and Fred. In spite of the fact that the opposing team was half American, Jo decided to refight the Revolutionary War.

True, Fred cheated at one point, rather obviously, but it seemed to me little reason for Jo's nasty remarks, all about American superiority: Americans not cheating, Americans being generous to their enemies even while beating them. *HA!* was all I could think. Just wait, Jo, until we start screaming "We're number one!" in the world's face every few years at the Olympics.

When the war was finally over and it was time to eat, Mr. Brooke asked who could make good coffee.

Jo immediately volunteered.

Double HA! was all I could think. Just because she had a used cookbook, it didn't mean she'd learned anything from it. And the coffee she made was proof of that.

As the meal drew to a close, I heard Laurie tease Jo, offering her salt to go with her strawberries, and she replied that she preferred spiders, immediately—astonishingly!—locating two and squishing them to death between her fingers.

Gross!

I was all out of *HA!*s. All I could think was, at least she didn't eat them.

After lunch, it seemed like a perfect time to me to play croquet. I wouldn't mind walking around a bit, exercise off some of
the food I'd eaten. But none of the others were interested. Wasn't
that just like me? Out of step with everybody else?

Something else was out of step. Laurie had quietly informed
me that the real reason he'd brought Mr. Brooke along was as
company for Kate, but as far as I could see, the tutor was spending all his time around Meg: choosing her for his croquet team
earlier, sitting next to her during lunch, yakking to her about all
things German.

Hmm . . . could there be something going on there? And why
didn't anyone else seem to notice? Looked like maybe my role was
that of the observant March sister. Well, when I wasn't being the
completely oblivious March sister like I'd been with Pip.

"Let's play a game," Laurie suggested.

"I brought Authors," Jo offered.

I had no idea what Authors was, but it sounded like it was
probably a game involving specialized knowledge. It was probably
all about Dickens—or at least Jo would make it so—leaving me
to look like an idiot when the only questions I could answer were
those about *Oliver Twist*.

So I was relieved when Kate vetoed the idea with a scathing
look at Jo as though playing Authors was just soooo *yesterday*.

"Well, what do you suggest we play?" Jo demanded of Kate,
returning scathing for scathing.

"Rigmarole," Kate answered simply.

"Yes," I piped up, agreeing with her, "I know how you feel. Jo
is always engaged in confusing and meaningless talk." I laughed.
"I'm often tempted to say 'rigmarole' to her too."

Kate placed her lorgnette over one eye, regarding me closely
for the first time. "Rigmarole," she finally uttered, "is a *game*."

Oh, *snap.*

"Rigmarole," Kate explained, "is a game where one person begins a story. Then that person talks for as long as he or she likes, halting right before the exciting part, at which point the next person takes over."

"Huh," Jo admitted. "That does sound as though it might be fun."

A lot more fun than Authors! I thought.

"I'll start," Mr. Brooke offered before anyone else had the chance.

"There once was a man," Mr. Brooke began, "who had a . . . *job.* Yes, he did have to work for a living, unlike some of the other people in the town. Also living in this town was a girl he liked—"

"But one of the other people in the town," Laurie cut into the story enthusiastically, "one of those who didn't have to work, also liked the girl." Laurie paused, puzzled. "Or maybe he liked a different girl?" He paused again. "Or maybe even a different girl than that? Or—"

"She got drunk one night at a house party!" Ned cut in exultantly.

"I'd like to meet a girl like that," Fred said with what could only be described as a leering smile.

"Stop! Stop!" Kate cried, waving her lorgnette at everybody.

I looked around at the others. Meg in particular looked uncomfortable, her cheeks reddening.

"You're not playing it right!" Kate said. "People are just talking whenever they like, not really building the story at all, not stopping it just shy of truly exciting parts. Besides, so far only the boys have gone but none of the girls."

"Well, I can remedy that," Jo said. "There once was a girl who lived in a town, and she liked a boy who—"

"May have been a boy who didn't work," Meg cut in, "or may have been a man who did, only—"

"He loved her no matter what her nose looked like," Amy said, excited. "Which was good because—"

"Noses are meant to be loved," I said, "only there was just one problem."

I paused and was surprised that no one else cut in. Instead, they all just stared at me, waiting to hear what the problem was.

"This girl," I finally went on, "could never be sure if the boy, and I do think he was the boy and not the man, really liked her best, or if it was that other girl instead, or that one, or—"

"Stop!" Kate shouted again. Then she threw her lorgnette down on the grass in disgust. "You Americans are hopeless."

Looked like Jo wasn't alone in still fighting the war.

"A game of Truth, anyone?" Sallie suggested cheerfully. "That's always fun."

Except when it isn't, I thought, my hand growing sticky, trapped in the middle of the stack of other hands.

Truth, it turned out, was even worse than Rigmarole.

The way it was played, we stacked up our hands one on top of the other, then a number was selected at random and whoever's number got called had to answer every question the other players thought to ask.

Lucky me. My number came up first.

"What's your favorite color?" Amy asked.

That was simple. "Red," I answered quickly. Then I shook my head, annoyed with myself. "No, it's green."

"It wasn't exactly a trick question," Jo pointed out.

"Well, it can be." I shrugged. "I change my mind on these things."

"Did you even notice Pip existed before his death?" Jo asked.

"No, I'm afraid not," I admitted, not daring to look over at Beth when she let out a little outraged gasp. "But I'm still sorry he's dead."

"No one asked you if you're sorry," Jo said. "What do you think of Teddy's sailor costume?"

"You already asked a question."

"Sallie never set a limit."

"Fine," Meg said. "Then it'll be my question: What do you think of Laurie's sailor costume?"

Seriously, Meg?

I didn't want to answer, but I had to, and I had to do it truthfully. Oh, why couldn't this be Truth or Dare instead of just Truth? I was much better at dares.

Stupid game.

"It's awful," I said. "It's the most ridiculous outfit I've ever seen, unless the person wearing it is actually in the navy, and I'm only glad he's not wearing knee pants. Seriously, he looks about twelve."

Laurie's cheeks colored as he gave me a look that said he felt I'd betrayed him. But it wasn't my fault—the stupid game *was* called Truth!

"What's wrong with being twelve?" Amy demanded. "I'll wager a person can spend the majority of her life being twelve and not mind it."

What? What a weird thing to say!

"I think that's enough questions for Emily," Sallie said diplomatically. "Jo? I believe your number's next."

"What do you want most?" Laurie asked her before anyone else could get a question in.

Everyone shut up then. It was as though people sensed there was more behind the question than just the words on the surface. It was as if even Jo—maybe even me—knew what answer Laurie was hoping to get.

"Genius." Jo finally ended the uncomfortable silence.

"HA!" This time the *HA!* actually left my body.

"What?" Jo whirled on me.

"Sorry," I said, still laughing. "I mean, you're smart enough and everything, but I think you're a little late for genius."

"How about Laurie?" Sallie suggested, possibly hoping to nip a sibling skirmish in the bud.

"I don't have any more questions for Jo at this time," he said, subdued.

"I didn't mean that," Sallie said. "I meant for others to ask you."

"I've got one," Fred offered mischievously. "Who, Laurie, do you like best?"

I saw Laurie color slightly as he opened his mouth to answer.

Would he say Emily? I dared to hope.

He did look at me first, briefly, considering, but then his eyes veered off and . . .

And suddenly I realized I had to stop the words from coming out of his mouth. He was going to say "Jo, of course." He was going to say it because I'd made fun of his sailor costume and because, in spite of Jo saying that "genius" was what she wanted most when he'd probably been secretly hoping she'd say "Laurie," *she* was the one who always played hard to get.

I had to stop it from happening. I had to keep those words from exiting his mouth.

"Bee! It's a bee!" I began shouting, extricating my hand from the tower of hands and running maniacally in circles.

"Bee?" Jo said. "I don't see any *bee!*"

"Borrow Kate's lorgnette then!" I shouted, still running in circles. "Can't you see? There's a whole swarm of them!"

Before long, I triggered mass hysteria, everyone running maniacally in circles, including practical Mr. Brooke and lame Frank.

At last, I collapsed on the lawn.

"The danger's over," I gasped, waving my hands to indicate the others could stop running too.

"How about a nice game of Authors?" I suggested when all the others had also collapsed. After all my exertion in the heat, I felt practically delirious. "And I'll even go first. I'll take Dickens for eight hundred dollars, Alex."

"What *are* you taking about, Emily?" Jo demanded.

"I don't know," I said. "I only know that if the answer is Bull's-eye, I'll stand a chance."

"You're making no sense," Jo said.

"I know," I admitted.

But one thing did make sense.

I'd prevented Laurie from saying that he liked Jo more than he liked me, that he liked her best. If I could only keep him from ever saying that, I still might stand a chance.

Then Kate was rude to Meg about being a governess; Mr. Brooke stood up for Meg and taught her to read German; Mr. Brooke said Laurie would be off to college next year, making me wonder what a convent-like existence ours would be without him; Mr. Brooke said he'd be off to become a soldier at that time but that he didn't have a mother or sister to miss him; Amy told Grace we had an old sidesaddle at home that we put over a low-lying apple tree branch to pretend we were riding a horse, proving yet again how odd the March girls were; Amy said she longed to go abroad; Beth was nice to Frank; the party ended and we all went home.

The Vaughns would be off to Canada the next day.

As I lay in bed that night, I felt pleasantly exhausted.

But then I shot up as a disturbing thought struck me.

At some point—a ways off, but still—the story of *Little Women* as I knew it would reach the end.

Where would I be when that happened? What would become of me once I ran out of story?

Thirteen

It was a warm September afternoon, the summer holiday was drawing to a close, and the other four had just tramped off to do that thing they'd been doing every day now and that I wanted no part of: self-improvement.

Marmee liked for us to be out-of-doors as much as possible. So each day the others would put on what I considered to be ridiculous costumes: floppy hats and brown linen pouches slung over one shoulder, long walking staffs in one hand, various items in the other. Then they'd traipse up the hill between the house and the river, ultimate destination unspecified, and do whatever it was they did. They said they brought their work with them and played at being pilgrims, but for all I knew they could have been casting spells over the town and playing at being witches. As I say, I wanted no part of these self-improvements.

But there was something boring, not to mention a little lonely,

in being left behind, so once they were safely out of view I went
to visit Laurie.

"I'm bored, dude," he said when he came to the door.

"There's a bit of that going around, dude," I said. "Maybe
we need to do something out of the ordinary?"

"I already tried that," he said. "I frustrated Brooke by deliberately making mistakes in all my studies, then I scared the
maids by implying that one of the dogs was going mad."

"That last sounds like it has possibilities," I said.

"It did, but how long can terrified maids be fun?"

"I don't know." I shrugged. "It sounds like the kind of thing
you could make a whole day out of."

"No." He looked depressed. "It was only fun for about five
minutes. Then all the screaming just became boring."

"Yeah, I could see where that might happen. Maybe we
could—"

"What are your sisters up to?" he cut me off.

"Nothing interesting." I snorted. "I can tell you that much!"

"Yes, but what are they doing today?" he persisted.

"Oh," I answered vaguely, "I think they were headed up the
hill to do some . . . *thing* . . ."

His eyes brightened immediately. "I'll bet they are going
boating. But they'll need the key, of course, which of course
they won't have, so I suppose I should get it and then bring
it to—"

"No, I don't think anyone said anything about *boating*," I
said, feeling exasperated as I had to race after him to get the key
and then hurried to keep up as he traipsed up the hill. "I'm sure
I would have noticed if they'd said they were going *boating*, so I
don't think anyone—"

"Oh," he said, looking dejected, when we'd at last climbed the hill, reached the river, and found the boat bobbing on the water, unused. "I guess not."

Honestly. Why couldn't he be content to just spend some time alone with me?

"We're here now," I suggested, "and you have the key right there. Maybe we could go boating? It'll rock."

"Rock?" he echoed. "Is that another new word when used in that fashion?"

I shrugged.

Suddenly he looked appalled. "Boating? Just the two of us?"

"Hey, I wasn't planning on trying to k——"

He cut me off before I could even say the whole word, never mind finish my sentence. "No." He blushed. "I wasn't worried about that."

"Anyway, I thought we agreed I was suffering from a fever that day," I said, still certain he *was* worried about *that*.

"No, really," he said. "It's just that . . ."

"It's just that *what*?" I demanded, hands on hips.

"Do you know you look just like Jo when you stand there like that? Well, except for the hair and the height and just about everything else being all wrong."

All wrong? I was *all wrong*?

"But other than that?" he went on. "You look just like her." He shook his head abruptly, as though trying to rid his mind of an image. "No, all I meant was, you're not exactly the best person to go boating with, are you? I mean, you do have a tendency to overturn the boat."

"Oh, thanks a lot. I make just one little mistake, just one time and——"

"But if they're not here," Laurie spoke as if I wasn't even there anymore, "where could they be?"

We found them in a pine grove.

If they didn't annoy me so much, I'd think they looked cool there in their floppy hats, their skirts spread all around them on the ground so it was like an ocean of colorful fabric connecting each girl to all the others. They looked like, oh, I don't know, something out of a painting of the 1800s or something.

Before we'd been able to see them, we'd heard their voices chattering, which was when Laurie had put a finger to my lips, cautioning me to keep silent. I was tempted to bite that finger, or kiss it, but then it occurred to me that it might be fun to sneak up on them and scare them—almost as much fun as scaring maids by implying one of the dogs was going mad.

Laurie and I had crept up behind a tree and were silently watching, Laurie enchanted, me less so, until I revealed our presence with a sneeze.

What? I shot him a defensive look. Was it my fault I suffered from seasonal allergies no matter what century I found myself in?

"Who goes there?" Jo said in a voice full of challenge.

What sort of person says "Who goes there?"

"It's just us," Laurie said with a nervous laugh, leading me out from behind the tree.

I didn't know why his laugh should be nervous, but then I noticed that, in order to lead me into view, he'd grabbed my hand. I liked that. And I really liked it when I saw that Jo had noticed too.

"Oh," Jo said, going red in the face. "Well, you can't be here."

"I'm afraid it's true," Beth said sorrowfully. "Only those who are working are allowed to be here."

"There's a rule against being idle here," Amy said.

"That's why we call it the Busy Bee Society," Meg said primly.

The Busy *what*? Seriously. Where did they come up with these things?

I looked around at the evidence of what they'd been doing before we interrupted. Meg had been sewing, Jo knitting while reading—multitasking showoff!—Amy sketching ferns, and Beth sorting pinecones.

My, they did look busy.

"Well, *we* didn't know to bring any work with us," I said, tugging on Laurie's hand, "so since there's a rule against being idle, I guess we'll just be on our—"

"If I find some work to do," Laurie addressed the others, yanking his hand from mine, "may I stay?"

"What sort of work?" Jo narrowed her eyes.

"Well, I don't know," Laurie said, casting his eyes about. "Oh! I know! I could help Beth sort these pinecones." Before anyone could say anything else, he dropped down to the ground beside Beth and began sorting like mad.

"And what sort of work do *you* plan on doing, *Emily*?" Jo hit my name so hard, she might as well have shot a gun through it.

I looked around and thought how ridiculous all the imagination games they played were. Seriously? These were supposed to be *teenagers*? What would I be doing back home right now? Back at my *real* home?

Playing Wii. Texting friends. Going to the mall to buy clothes.

"You're right, Jo, as always." I sighed. "There's no work for me to do, no place for me here, so I guess I'll just—"

"There are plenty of pinecones here!" Beth piped up desperately, the minute I started to turn away. "Really, Emily, there are so many pinecones here, even with Laurie to help, I could never get them all sorted, not if I lived forever!"

Reluctantly, and feeling Jo's glare, I sat down beside Laurie and Beth.

I had no idea what guidelines were being used to sort the pinecones, but pinecones I would sort!

Beth wasn't usually much of a talker, but it turns out there were certain hot-button subjects that could get her mouth motoring.

"When we are up here," she said, sorting away happily, "we pretend that we are on the Delectable Mountain from *Pilgrim's Progress* and that from here we can see the country where we hope to live sometime."

As the others selected places, mostly in Europe, except for Beth, who wanted to stay home, I wondered where that country would be for me. What would I want my life to be like if I felt as though I had any choice?

Gack! It was so easy to fall into the . . . *March Sisters Trap.* Spend enough time with them, and before long a person found herself sucked into their imagination games.

"Of course," Meg interrupted my thoughts with one of her Marmee-like pronouncements, "there's a lovelier country than any we can see, and we shall all get there eventually if only we are good enough."

The others all nodded solemnly, but I had no idea what she was talking about.

Good enough? I wondered. Good enough for what?

"I wonder if I'll ever get in," Jo said.

Oh. Right. They were talking about heaven—that's what this was all about.

Then Beth said she wished she could go right now, Laurie said he hoped Beth would put in a good word for him if he showed up late, and I felt a cold shiver in spite of the heat.

Beth was going to die.

If I didn't find a way to stop it, Beth—who longed for heaven and who only ever wanted to remain at home—would die.

But when?

And, most important of all, what could *I* possibly do to prevent it?

"What about you, Emily?" Jo's voice invaded my thoughts.

What about me, what? Then I realized that while I'd been deep in thought, my hands had gone idle. *Shoot. Jo was probably admonishing me for not being a busy enough bee*, I thought as I forced my hands to sort pinecones at a rapid pace.

"What about me, what?" I said aloud, my hands flying so fast, I could have gotten a job on the assembly line at a candy company. "See? I'm working. Busy bee, busy bee, that's what I am, no idle hands here."

"I wasn't talking about that." It was amazing. Even without looking at Jo, I could tell she rolled her eyes when she said that.

"What then?" I said.

"We were all making up our castles in the air." Another dramatic eye roll, even if still I wasn't looking at her. "You know, our personal definitions of heaven on earth?"

Heaven on earth—there was no such thing, I'd have liked to tell her. I wasn't even so sure there was a heaven in heaven.

"The others all said theirs already," Jo went on, "so it's your turn."

"Well, what did the others say?" I wanted to know, figuring

there'd be no point in me saying "all the gold in the world" if everyone else had picked "peace on earth and goodwill to all mankind."

"Honestly, Emily." Jo again.

Honestly. What sort of annoying person said "honestly" all the time?

"Don't you ever pay attention to the world around you?" she demanded, exasperated.

"Frankly . . ." I paused to peer closely at a pinecone before deciding, *sort it into this pile or that pile*. ". . . no."

"Fine." Jo sighed heavily. "To remind you what's been said, I'll go first . . . *again*. I want, of course, to be a rich and famous writer."

Oh. *Of course*. HA! She wouldn't get very far with that dream if she kept writing idiotic stories like that play when I first got here.

"I want to be rich and live in a nice house," Meg said.

"I want to be rich," Amy said, "and I want to make my fortune in clay and I have lots of other wishes, but mostly I just want to live in Rome, even though I don't know where that is."

"I want to be a musician," Laurie said.

I noticed he didn't say he wanted to be rich, but then, he already was.

"What about you, Bethie?" I asked.

"I just want everyone else to be happy and I want to stay home with Marmee and Daddy and my piano."

"Are you finally ready to say what you want most, Emily," Jo said, "now that we've all repeated our castles in the air?"

"I honestly don't know," I said honestly. Perhaps that had been one of my problems in my real life: that I'd never really known what I wanted, only going after things because those things seemed like the cool things to have. Had I ever even *really* liked Jackson? Or had I just wanted him because he wanted Charlotte?

"Well, you have to pick something." Jo was thoroughly disgusted. "Everyone else has."

"Fine." I straightened my spine. "For my castle in the air, I wish for peace on earth and goodwill to all mankind."

Jo's jaw dropped so low, she was going to need help getting it off the ground.

As I looked at the faces of the others, I saw real admiration there.

"That's quite a thing," Laurie spoke at last. "You have the opportunity to spin a castle in the air, to wish for anything for yourself that you would like, and yet you use that wish for something to benefit the rest of the world."

"I hope I am as wise as you when I am your age," Beth said, grabbing on to my hand impulsively.

"I could never be as generous as you are," Amy said, taking my other hand. "I keep forgetting how you saved my life that day on the ice."

I blushed at their words, but really, I hadn't done anything so great. How hard was it to be generous when you didn't know what you wanted for yourself in the first place? One of these days, I was really going to have to figure out what was worth going after or fighting for.

"Sometimes, Emily," Meg said, "you reveal depths in you none of us have ever seen before."

The only one not tossing adulation in my direction was Jo, who let us all know what she thought by snorting.

"Why don't we meet in ten years' time," Jo suggested, "and compare where we are with our wishes?"

The others all thought that was such a *capital* idea—their word, not mine—and left me no choice but to agree.

What could I say? That in ten years, poor Beth would probably be dead, unless I found a way to stop it? Or that if I did manage to stop it I'd be back living where I belonged, in the twenty-first century?

Besides, because I'd studied history in school, I already knew one castle in the air that wouldn't come true:

There would be no peace on earth.

There would no be goodwill toward mankind.

The American Civil War would end, but eventually, other wars would come to replace it. Some things couldn't be stopped or changed.

The others tried to convince Laurie that he should be a musician if that was what he wanted most. What was there to stop him? Of all of us—as a male, as a *rich* male—the world should be his oyster.

That's when Laurie explained that his grandfather wanted him to be an India merchant, as he was, but that he hated the idea and hoped that going to college for four years would appease him. Why, if the old man had anyone else in the world other than him, Laurie would leave tomorrow for Europe to pursue his music.

Meg continued on with her advice, accidentally making it clear that she knew an awful lot about Mr. Brooke, and telling Laurie that we only teased him because we regarded him as our brother.

Huh.

Did Jo regard him as a brother?

How did he regard each of us individually?

And what did I really think of him?

Fourteen

I'd become a stalker.

Just like that, October had arrived and with it, a strong chill in the air. The other thing that had arrived was a new industriousness in Jo. She spent more and more time alone in the garret, writing. When Meg asked her if she got lonely up there—didn't she miss "our society"?—Jo replied that her pet rat, Scrabble, provided excellent company and that his eldest son was quite amusing too, although she failed to name him.

I wanted to know what she was working on, but when I asked, she wouldn't say. As for my own story, I was still working on it in stolen moments.

I did try sneaking into the garret one night after the others were all asleep, my intent being to ransack the old tin receptacle where I knew Jo kept her pages, but she'd booby-trapped the thing. By candlelight I saw that she'd taken so many of her long chestnut hairs, draping them across the crease in the drawer in an intricate pattern, I knew that if I tried to move them, I'd never get them back again the way she had them.

And then she'd know someone had broken in. And she'd probably guess it was me.

One chilly day, I secretly observed her doing a suspicious thing: putting on her silly hat and coat and then, when she thought no one was looking, taking a package wrapped in red ribbon and lowering herself out the back window! Naturally, I had to follow her.

I tailed my suspect to what the others called an omnibus, a public vehicle drawn by horses. Hoping to avoid being seen, I hopped on the back at the last minute, situating myself behind an old man. When we got into town and everyone else got off, I again waited until the last minute before hopping off and following her at a safe distance.

At last she arrived at a small office building. Hiding behind a fat oak tree, I peeked around the corner, observed her as she circled around to the front entrance no less than three times.

Why was she so nervous?

I squinted up at the signs as she finally entered.

The dentist? Was that why she was so nervous? Did she have a cavity? I could see why she'd be nervous. I had no idea how they filled cavities in the 1800s, but I had a feeling it involved more pain than it did where I came from.

Poor Jo. I may not have always liked her very much, but the idea of dental work without Novocain was scary to think about.

But wait a second. A bad tooth didn't explain that mysterious package she was carrying.

I squinted up at the signs again, and that's when I saw it.

The Eagle.

Huh. That was our local newspaper. Most people liked to wrap their fish in it.

But why would she . . . ?

Why, that little . . . !

She'd brought her stupid stories here to beat me to the publication punch.

Well, we'd see about *that!* I huffed as I raced down the hill.

For a long time, I'd felt in competition with Jo as a writer. First, there was the fact that we did both love to write, which sometimes could be enough in itself. Then there was the fact that she thought she was *all that.* Not to mention that competition over the *Pickwick Portfolio/Twist Times.* And now she was going to try to sell a story to a newspaper before me?

I hurried faster. I had to get home as quickly as possible.

I had a short story to finish.

Who does she think she is? That was the furious thought that filled my mind, alternating with every sentence I wrote in my story. That and, *I'll show her!*

That's what I was doing, writing furiously and furiously writing, when the object of my fury found me in the garret two hours later.

"Emily, can I have a word with you?" Jo asked, with a rare shy tone.

Before answering, I quickly covered my pages with my arms.

"I'm not trying to steal a look at your silly *writing!*" she snapped, returning to her typical exasperated mode of addressing me.

"Oh, sorry," I said, blushing as I loosened my arms.

Then I thought: *Hey! What did I have to be sorry for?* After all, she'd been so paranoid of her own writing being seen, she'd placed that basket weave of hair over it. Well, two could play at paranoia!

I returned my arms to their protective posture over my work.

She rolled her eyes at me. But when I asked, "So, what did you want to talk to me about?" a sad look came over her face.

"I need to talk with someone," she said, "and there is no one else with whom I can discuss this particular thing."

That was weird. Jo and Meg always confided their secrets in each other. Or else they spoke to Marmee. Nobody ever came to me.

In a way, I felt flattered. Even if it was Jo doing the asking.

"How can I help?" I offered magnanimously, feeling just a little bit like the head of a Mafia family.

"I was just in town—"

"And what were you doing there?"

"Does it matter? I was in town and, when I finished my business, I ran into Teddy . . ."

It took me a minute to remember that Teddy was what she called Laurie.

"What was he doing there?" I asked.

"I don't know! I thought I saw him coming out of a billiards saloon, he claimed he was taking fencing lessons, but I'm still not sure. The point is, we got to talking and—"

"Talking about what?"

"I'm trying to tell you! So we decided to trade secrets—"

"What sort of secrets?"

"*I'm trying to tell you!* And Teddy's secret was . . . Teddy's secret was . . . Teddy's—"

"Yes?" I was on the edge of my seat here.

Her next sentence came out in a breathless rush. "Teddy's secret was that he knows where Meg's other glove is."

"Is that all?" I collapsed back into my chair. "And what glove?"

"The missing glove." Horse that she was, Jo rolled her eyes at me and then snorted. "Remember the time Beth was delivering the mail and we all got a lot of things—well, except for you—and Meg got a few things as well, one of which was a single glove from the set of two she said she accidentally left over at the Laurences'? *That* glove."

"Sounds vaguely familiar," I said. "But what of it?"

"Teddy told me that Mr. Brooke has kept it as a treasured memento of our sister. He carries it in his pocket at all times. Apparently, Mr. Brooke . . . *likes* our Meg."

"Oh!" I had to admit, that did strike me as a bit icky, the notion of someone carrying around someone else's sweaty glove at all times. But then, that was the Victorians for you. You never knew what crazy things they'd do when under the spell of love. So probably, there was nothing too terribly psychotic about Mr. Brooke's behavior. He'd carry her glove, she'd probably press his dead flowers in some book, and eventually they'd call it love.

"So he likes her." I shrugged. "I fail to see the harm that—"

"*Fail to see the harm?*"

"Well, there's no need to get—"

"*Fail to see the harm?* But this is the most awful thing ever! She's too young for love!"

"Well, she is seventeen now. How old was Marmee when she married your—I mean *our* father?"

"Then *I'm* too young to have her be in love," Jo said, ignoring my question. "Oh, why do things have to change? Why do we have to grow up?" She paused. "There is one hope."

"Yes?"

"When Teddy and I were in town, we ran into Meg. She was just coming from the Gardiners', where Sallie had been telling her all about Belle Moffat's wedding. Belle's in Paris for the winter now, you know. Anyway, I could tell that Meg was envious of Belle's grand wedding. So maybe she can be persuaded to leave off her fancy of Mr. Brooke, since he is a poor man, and wait for a rich one? With a little luck, it could be years before one comes her way."

Well, there was Laurie . . .

But I knew Laurie wasn't destined for Meg. Having recovered from some of my story amnesia, I also knew where Meg and Mr. Brooke's storyline was heading. Of course, I couldn't tell Jo any of that.

I was still thinking about Meg and Mr. Brooke's future when Jo's annoyingly annoyed voice cut in.

"Aren't you paying any attention to me, Emily?"

"Sorry?"

"I was trying to tell you about the other problem."

"Which is?"

"Teddy."

"Oh. Is he holding some girl's glove hostage too?"

She ignored that. "That thing about me seeing him come out of the billiards saloon. I know he told me he was just taking a fencing lesson, and he even offered to teach me when I asked him, so that our fight scenes might be realistic when the time comes for us to do *Hamlet*, but I'm not sure if I believe him. What if he's lying?"

"So?"

"*So*? You know how Marmee feels about such things. Why, she won't even let Ned Moffat come to call—who, I might add, would make a much better secret suitor for Meg than Mr. Brooke, being rich and all—because he spends far too much of his leisure time in billiards saloons. So I told Teddy that he must be simple and honest and respectable so that he will always be welcome here."

"And what did he say?" I asked, curious. I couldn't imagine a guy appreciating being lectured to by Jo.

"He said that he didn't go to the billiards saloons all that often anyway, but that he did like to go sometimes. Said he had a billiards table in some room in that huge house of theirs, but that it was no fun for him to play alone at home."

A billiards table? Hey, wait a second here. *I* shot pool.

I decided the news of the billiards table and Laurie's interest in the game was useful information to be filed away for later.

Two weeks later, I was writing in the garret when I heard a racket outside. Going to the tiny window and peering out, I saw Jo and Laurie in the garden. He held something in his hands and Jo kept racing after him, trying to steal it away.

Soon, they came inside, breathless, and we all gathered around to see what the commotion was.

Jo held a copy of *The Eagle* and, flipping to an inside page, she began reading a story called "The Rival Painters."

When she finished, I had to admit, the story did show *some* promise, but nowhere near the praise all the others were heaping on after seeing the byline "by Miss Josephine March." Laurie even declared Jo "the Shakespeare of our town," which actually wasn't *that* soaringly over the top, given the crummy fish-smelling paper it appeared in.

"Of course, Teddy's known all along that I'd submitted some stories, because I ran into him the day I brought them to town," Jo told everyone smoothly, neglecting to mention the glove, I noticed. "At first, he thought I was there to get a tooth pulled or something. Can you believe the silliness of such a thought?"

Well, I could.

"I hope to one day earn enough money to support myself and help out with the girls," Jo went on self-importantly. "Of course, I wasn't paid anything for this story and the other one I gave the newspaperman."

"Not paid anything?" I may not have been published, *yet*, but even I knew you weren't supposed to just give it away. Even if you were only paid a dollar—or, in the 1800s, a few cents—you were still supposed to get paid.

Jo shrugged as if it didn't matter to her.

"The newspaperman said I should be happy enough if he liked my story sufficiently to print it," she said happily. "Then, once I saw my name in print, and he saw what sort of a reaction the public had to my writing, we'd see about him paying me for subsequent stories."

I got paid more than Jo.

Just barely.

The newspaperman gave me "two bits" for a short story after my inspired speech about money always flowing toward the writer.

When the next issue of *The Eagle* arrived, I waited impatiently as Jo's latest story was read aloud by its authoress and then breathlessly as she slowly paged through the rest of the paper to see what other short fiction she was competing with.

" 'The Woman from the Future,' " Jo announced the title before starting to read.

The others all looked at one another, puzzled expressions on their faces.

"But that makes no sense." Amy wrinkled her nose when Jo was finished. "Why would someone from one hundred years plus in the future travel back in time to live in a town that sounds awfully similar to ours?" Amy turned to me then, as if I might be able to answer her question.

But I just shrugged, not wanting to give myself away.

"If there is such a thing as time travel," Beth said, "which I don't believe there is, I hope people get to take their cats and dolls with them."

"Of course there's no such thing as time travel." Jo snorted. "Who does this Evelina Massachusetts think she is?" she asked, referring to the pseudonym I'd used. "What a preposterous name! Whoever wrote this tripe was undoubtedly embarrassed to attach her real name to it."

"I'll tell you one thing," Meg said. "Whoever she is, she's no Jo March."

Ohhh, go lose another glove, I was tempted to tell her.

"If you're done reading that," Hannah said, "can I have that last story?"

Oh! I brightened considerably. My first fan!

Then Hannah added, "I have some fish I'd like to wrap in it."

Fifteen

So what if no one in my entire family, in this entire stupid town, liked my story of a time traveler.

I'd still keep writing it. After all, I was living it.

November was the dreariest month ever.

At least that's what all the others said, and they went on and on about it so much, eventually I decided to just put on a coat and go out, if only to get away from their complaining.

"But you don't like the cold," Amy said, when she saw me all bundled up.

"Yes, yes," I agreed waspishly, "but I'm still going out in it."

I went.

Knock, knock, knock.

I gave my request to the maid who answered the door and a moment later my request appeared before me.

"Emily!" Laurie sounded surprised, I hoped not unpleasantly. "What brings you out on such a miserable day?"

"A while back," I said, "Jo told me that you have a pool"—I had to correct myself—"I mean, a billiards table here but that you don't often play at home because it's boring to play alone." I took a brave breath. "So I thought I could remedy that for you."

"*You?* I don't mean to laugh," he said, laughing anyway, "but what could you possibly know about billiards?"

I knew this question would come up, so I'd given the matter some advance thought and devised an answer.

"Oh, I read all about it in some book. There are pretty colored balls, you hit them with a stick called a cue, you try to get them in pockets. Don't you know that you can learn a lot from reading books?"

Since no one had asked me to stay awhile, I took off my own coat, looked around.

"So," I said. "Where do you keep your billiards table?"

C-RACK!

Laurie broke the balls on our second game.

Nothing went in and it was my turn.

As I bent over the table to shoot, trying to remind myself what ball I was supposed to be shooting at, Laurie interrupted.

Interrupting a player who's about to shoot—back home, in the real world, a person could get beaten up for doing that.

But that didn't stop Laurie.

"It is the most peculiar thing," he said. "You are very good at putting the balls in the pockets when you shoot—and, I confess, you have even sunk some combinations that would never occur to me to even attempt—and yet you do not appear to have a clue as to how the game is played at all in terms of the rules."

Of course I didn't. That's because the game he played bore no resemblance at all to my eight ball. When he'd said he had a billiards table, he meant a billiards table, as in English billiards, not a pool table. And instead of the rainbow of solid and stripe balls I was used to, all he had were white, yellow, and red balls.

And I couldn't ask for help since I'd already boasted that—

"Didn't you say you read a book about billiards?" he said.

"Maybe it was in German," I said, "in one of those books Mr. Brooke is always giving Meg."

"But it really is just so odd. I watch you play and you appear to be playing very well at some game, just not this one."

I took another shot.

"Nice shot!" he cried. Then: "Too bad it was the wrong ball."

Before either of us could take another shot, we were interrupted by a maid announcing Miss Josephine March.

Why'd she have to interfere with everything? I thought. Well, at least billiards was a game I could beat her at. So what if I didn't know the rules? Even Laurie admitted I had a great shot.

"What's wrong?" Laurie asked immediately upon seeing Jo enter, breathless.

"A telegram has come," she said, looking at me with concern.

"For me?" I said dumbly. Who would be sending me a telegram? And weren't telegrams almost always bad things?

"No, not for *you*." Typical exasperated Jo. "For Marmee. It was from some man in Washington saying that Papa is in the hospital and that she must come at once."

Laurie was standing close to me and he grabbed on to my elbow then as though to steady me.

"Are you all right?" he asked, concern in his voice.

I swallowed, nodded.

The truth was, I felt numb. I'd registered that something potentially awful had happened to this man everyone in the household referred to as Papa, but he wasn't anyone I knew.

"I'm fine," I said at last.

"Oh, why did the others, why did we *all* complain so much of being bored?" Jo, a girl I could never have pictured wringing her hands, did so now. "We said if only something exciting happened—but this! There was a ring at the door, Hannah answered, then she came back with that wretched telegram. Why could we not have been content as we were?"

"What can I do to help?" Laurie asked. "Anything!"

"Oh yes," Jo said, getting a grip on herself. She produced a letter. "This is for Aunt March. Marmee is to leave for Washington on the first train in the morning to go nurse him. She is already gathering supplies, says the hospital stores are not always good, but she will need money from Aunt March for the trip. Could you please deliver the letter?"

"At once," Laurie said. "I'll go get my horse now."

"And I have an errand of my own to run," Jo said, "so hurry on home, Emily. They need you there."

It felt good, the idea of being needed.

I started to follow Laurie out but then I heard Jo's annoyed voice.

"Emily, what *were* you doing playing billiards with Laurie? You don't know how to play *billiards*."

Apparently not.

When I walked in the door, it was as though they were already holding a funeral.

It was so weird for me being there then, the weirdest moment since I'd arrived there back around Christmas. Once again I was an alien. The others were all crying into handkerchiefs, holding on to one another, absolutely devastated. Although I could feel upset for them, I didn't know this man they called Papa, had never met him.

I wished I could do something to help them all, to make it better for them.

"Oh, Emily!" Beth cried, throwing her arms around my neck.

I hugged her back, patted her when Meg came to me with a piece of paper in her hand.

"Here is the awful telegram," she said.

It was just a greeting, plus two short sentences, signed by an S. Hale. But then I noticed the address at the bottom:

Blank Hospital, Washington.

Blank Hospital? What the heck sort of name was that?

"I feel so guilty," Meg said. "There I was complaining how hard times are, how men have to work and women have to marry for money, and then Hannah came in with that telegram." She began to sob again.

I pulled her into the embrace so now there were three of us in that hug.

"It is my fault," Amy said miserably. "When Meg said that,

I said that Jo and I would make our own fortunes—her through her writing and me through my work with clay." She glanced over at the little clay figures of birds and fruit and faces she'd made, the objects Hannah referred to as mud pies. "It was vain of me to think of personal fortune as if it mattered." She began to sob again too.

"There, there," I said.

And now we were four in this group hug.

It would have been comical if it weren't so tragical.

"I wish I could be as strong about this as you are, Emily," Meg said, wiping at her eyes. "I never pegged you for the stoical type before."

Easy to be strong and stoical, I thought, *when you don't have a personal stake in anything.*

Then Marmee bustled in and looked at us for a long moment as though counting heads.

"Where is Jo?" she asked.

None of us knew.

"No matter," she said. "I am all packed and ready."

Then Mr. Laurence came and told Marmee that Mr. Brooke would be going with her to Washington as her personal escort, which made Meg straighten up, suddenly looking very grateful and surprisingly pretty.

And then Laurie came in with a letter from Aunt March, saying she was enclosing the requested funds but first needed to deliver a lecture on how she'd always said March shouldn't have gone into the army, which made Marmee mad enough to crumple up the letter and toss it on the fire, after pocketing the money, of course.

And then—the last then!—Jo came in.

She had a bonnet on her head, one that I didn't remember see-ing on her when I'd seen her back at Laurie's. It looked ridiculous.

With one swift move, she tore the bonnet from her head.

We all gasped.

Her hair, all that beautiful long chestnut hair, gorgeous as a healthy horse's mane, had been cut off, leaving her with a short, choppy crop.

"What have you done?" Marmee asked.

I didn't even have to listen as Jo explained to the others.

She'd sold her own hair, the one thing she could think of for which she could get any cash, so she could give it to Marmee to help out Papa.

I watched as she pressed crumpled bills, totaling twenty-five dollars, into Marmee's hand.

Jo wasn't a pretty girl, but her hair had been, and now it was gone. Now she looked like a naked bird.

But she looked like something else too as she stood there, defiant.

She looked glorious, magnificent.

Where others would wring their hands over something but then be content to leave it at that, Jo had taken action.

Tomorrow, I'd no doubt go back to resenting her, thoroughly, but for today she had all the admiration I'd ever felt for anybody.

Sixteen

That night, I lay in bed listening to Jo finally cry over her lost hair and then Meg speaking softly in the most glowing terms yet about Mr. John Brooke. Once the room fell completely silent and the house was fast asleep except for me and one other person, I heard Marmee making her nightly rounds, going from bed to bed to lay a kiss on each of our foreheads. She began in the other room with Beth and Amy before coming to our room, where she kissed Meg and Jo before coming to me last.

I don't know why she saved me for last, since by rights I should have been third, or middle, but as I heard her approach I made sure to shut my eyes tightly. I didn't know what words of comfort I could possibly offer this strong woman who was so worried for her husband, the man who was supposed to be my father. So I just lay there feigning sleep when she kissed me, but in my heart I wished her well.

The next morning the household rose at an insanely early hour so that Marmee could catch the first train to Washington. After waving her and Mr. Brooke off with promises on our parts to be good and strong and instructions on her part that we were to rely on Hannah's faithfulness, Mr. Laurence's protection, and Laurie's devotion, saying further that she wanted us to work and hope and remember that we could never be fatherless—oh, right, she was talking about God again; well, I supposed we couldn't possibly escape a Marmee lecture on such an occasion—we were left on our own.

After Hannah made us a rare pot of coffee and Meg remarked that with Marmee gone the house felt a full half empty—"a full half empty"? Was it full or was it empty? I wished she'd make up her mind!—it was time for Meg to go to the Kings', Jo to Aunt March's, Beth and Amy to do housework and schoolwork, and me to go wherever the day of the week told me to go.

Mr. Brooke wrote every day and the news was good: Papa's pneumonia was getting a little bit better all the time.

Naturally, we were expected to write letters too, first to Marmee, but then as it appeared that Papa was finally strong enough to receive letters, to him too.

This presented me with a huge problem. I saw the others eagerly bend their heads to the task, some thoughtfully (Meg), some energetically (Jo), some gently (Beth), and some with excruciatingly poor spelling and grammar (Amy). They all seemed to have a lot to say, perhaps giving him news or reminding him of shared remembrances to brighten his day. The thing was, I had no past with this man. What could I possibly write that wouldn't sound totally asinine? What comfort could I possibly offer?

"Haven't you started yet, Emily?" Jo asked crossly. "We want to get these off with the early post."

"Simply composing my thoughts here," I said brightly, while inwardly I groaned.

What do you say to someone you don't know?

Get well soon was usually a crowd pleaser, but not with this crowd, since Jo would yell at me for not putting enough time and thought into it.

Then I remembered something *he* had written to me in a packet of letters the household had received shortly after my arrival, and then I too bent my head to the task, trying my best to pick words a March would use.

Dearest Papa,

> *I know, as you told me once, that even when I feel there is no clear place for me, there is always one in your heart. And so I write to give you a full report on the state of the March household.*
>
> *Meg is now the head of the table at meals. The role seems right for her and I think when the time comes for her to have a bunch of kids, she will do a good job. She hardly ever yells at any of us.*
>
> *Jo is, well, Jo. She and Laurie got in a fight, but even though she still claims to be right, she was willing to apologize the moment he was.*
>
> *Sweet Beth! You should see her. So kind, and even with these letters, it's like she's determined to take up as little space as*

possible. Honestly, I wish she would take up more. Do you ever
stop and think how much better the world would be if it were
filled with Beth? Or how empty it would be without her?

Amy's handwriting and grammar are terrible. But I suppose
you can see that? It's hard to believe she'll one day m——

Whoops! If I predicted who Amy would end up marrying
(so crazy!) and one day it came true (still crazy!), Papa might
think I was a witch. No one, to look at Amy now, chewing her
pen and then writing "contradick" and "punchtuation," would
ever believe who she was destined for.

Sorry, one of Beth's kittens just jumped on the paper and I
lost my train of thought.
Where was I . . .
Okay, so perhaps this was not a full report, but please
know that everyone here—including me—wishes you a speedy
recovery. So GET WELL SOON!
Anyway, Jo is now glaring at me, so I had better wrap this
up. I hope it will give you comfort to know that while Marmee is
down there in Washington with you, I am keeping an eye on things
up here and seeing that the others remain the little women you love
so well. I even read Pilgrim's Progress *every day for strength.*

A lie. The others read it religiously but I'd barely cracked
the spine on mine. Still, it wouldn't be good for him to think
one of his little women had gone heathen.

So continue mending and, as I say, GET WELL SOON!
There are many here who miss you.

A truth. Many did miss him, even if one of them technically wasn't me.

> *Signed,*

"Aren't you going to sign this?" Jo asked when she was about to put all our letters in the packet.

"Oh," I said vaguely. "I thought I did."

"Well, you didn't," she said, thrusting the sheet back at me.

I stole glances at how the others had signed theirs.

> *Ever your own Meg.*
> *Hugs and kisses from your Topsy-Turvy Jo.*
> *Come home soon to your loving Little Beth.*
> *Your affectionate daughter, Amy Curtis March.*

Well, at least Amy was capable of spelling her own name right.

Even Hannah had signed hers: *Yours respectful, Hannah Mullet.* As though he might not know which Hannah she was if she didn't write out her whole name. And what kind of last name was Mullet anyway?

What to write, what to write . . . how to sign, how to sign . . .

And then it hit me: the one thing that if I included it in a letter to him was sure to put a smile on his face.

I smiled myself as I took up my pen again and scrawled across the bottom of the page:

> *Your Middle March.*

Seventeen

We spent the next week being so virtuous it would have made my teeth hurt if it weren't for the fact that I felt just as caught up in the purpose as the others did: the purpose being to keep the household running as smoothly as possible in Marmee's absence so that she should have nothing to worry about while she continued to nurse Papa.

But then Jo got sick and everything got crazy.

At least for me.

"You must go to Aunt March in Jo's place," Meg in her role as Marmee in absentia directed me.

"But I've never gone there on my own before," I objected.

"What can be so hard about that?" Meg wanted to know. "Jo goes there every day of the week on her own save the one day you go with her."

"The old lady terrifies me," I admitted.

"Don't be absurd," Meg said, proving herself to be no real Marmee at heart. Marmee would never mock one of our fears. "What can one little old lady do to you?"

"She can pound her cane at me," I said with a shudder. "She can cry for 'E-mi-LY!' until I think I'm going crazy."

"That doesn't sound so bad," Meg said.

"Try it sometime," I challenged. "If she addresses you as Margaret, you'll be surprised at how many syllables she can turn your name into, and the longest will sound like there's a shriek buried inside it."

Meg tilted her head to one side for a moment as if considering what her name might sound like: "Mar-ga-REET!" But then she shook her head as though annoyed at me for forcing her to consider it at all.

"Never mind that," she said. "Jo's sick and Aunt March doesn't like to be read to by people who sound sick. She says it spoils her pleasure. And since Aunt March has been kind enough to finance Marmee's journey down to Washington to be by Papa's side—"

"Kind enough?" I cut her off. "It's not kindness when a person gives an 'I told you so' lecture before forking over the cash!"

"'Forking over the—' What?" Meg shook her head again. "Whatever the case, we cannot afford to anger Aunt March at this time. After all, what if Papa takes a turn for the worse and Marmee needs to stay longer and needs more money to do so?"

I was finally impressed. I could see Marmee's pragmatism in Meg.

"Fine," I said, pulling my bonnet down off its hook. "I'll go in Jo's place today. I'll go and read to the old bat no matter how crazy she makes me with all her pounding and screeching my name and—"

"A mere *day?*" Meg laughed. "You can't be serious!"

"Excuse me?" I'd been tying the bonnet under my chin, but my hands froze now mid-tie.

"A day won't be enough—you have to go every day this week!"

A week of Aunt March pounding her cane at me.

A week of Aunt March screeching, "E-mi-LY!"

They say you can get used to almost anything given enough time and no other option: like bad prison food or no air-conditioning or hairy armpits if you accidentally stumble into the wrong century.

But "they" never met Aunt March's parrot, Polly.

"E-mi-LY!" the parrot would croak at me. "Is that hair color real?

"E-mi-LY!" the parrot would croak at me. "Are you sure you belong with the March family?"

The answers were respectively "yes" and "no," but I refused to talk back to a parrot.

"Why does Polly say those things to you?" Aunt March demanded. "She's rude to everyone, of course, but the things she says to you never make any sense to me."

"I don't know, Auntie," I said. I liked to call her Auntie because I knew it bothered her. "I don't speak Parrot."

She started to sputter and I knew from experience that if I gave her enough time, that sputtering would turn into some kind of pronouncement concerning my rudeness.

So I didn't give her enough time.

I picked up *King Lear* and found a place that was different from where I'd left off.

"Shall I continue?" I sighed. "I'm pretty sure we're almost at the part where one of his daughters kicks him out for the last time."

Take a week off from your regular duties in order to go read to some old bat and things really do get crazy, and not just for me. Life: it's what happens when you're looking in the wrong direction.

Beth was finally sick.

Every morning that week I'd gotten up early to avoid Aunt March screeching at me for being even a second late.

And every morning after I left, apparently Beth had reminded the others of their responsibility to look in on the Hummels in Marmee's absence.

But no one else wanted to go.

Jo was sick, Meg was too busy running the household, and Amy was just, well, *Amy*.

Not to mention, it was dreary going to the Hummels.

So Beth went dutifully, bravely on her own.

And the others let her.

If I'd known, if she'd said anything about her visits when I returned from Aunt March's each evening, I would've found a way to prevent her. Or I would've forced one of the others to go, or even gone myself in the evenings. After all, this was my whole reason for being here: to change that one thing, to keep Beth from dying. With only that one job to do, how had I failed at it so miserably?

But she never said a word, so I hadn't known.

I knew something was up, though, when I returned one evening to find Beth in bed, her fever raging, her tongue red as a strawberry.

"I'm sorry," Beth apologized as Meg and Jo nursed her. "But there was no one else to go. Mrs. Hummel goes to work and the baby is—the baby *was*—so sick, although Lottchen did her best to take care of it."

Normally, I would have been puzzled over the name of Lottchen—Lottchen? Seriously?—but a word in her last sentence stopped me cold.

"*Was?*" I echoed. "You mean the baby is better now, right?" I asked hopefully.

But a look around the room told me that Beth had already shared this tale and that the outcome wasn't a good one.

"No." Her eyes filled with tears. "The baby died . . . in my arms."

Oh no!

"The doctor came," Beth went on bravely. "He said it was scarlet fever."

"And now Beth has it too," Meg said.

Scarlet fever. The disease that would kill Beth—*had* killed Beth every single time I'd read the story. My mind raced—could I still avert that final outcome? There must be *something* I could do. But what? If only I hadn't been at Aunt March's, if only Amy wasn't so . . . *Amy*. There must be *something!*

"The doctor told her to come home and take belladonna," Jo added.

"It's contagious, isn't it?" I asked.

"Very," Meg said.

"But both Meg and I had it when we were younger," Jo said.

Had I been vaccinated against it? Was there even a vaccine? And if I had been vaccinated against it, would a vaccine in the other world still apply in this world?

Without thinking, I took a step back from the bed and felt immediately guilty when I saw the look in Beth's eyes. But the look wasn't disappointed; it was forgiving.

I stepped forward again.

"Well." I laughed as though it didn't matter. "I probably had it too then." Pause. "Didn't I?"

"How can you not remember if you had scarlet fever or not?" Jo scoffed. "It's hardly the sort of thing a person forgets!"

"I agree," Meg said, but she looked puzzled. "But it is funny, because suddenly *I* can't remember if Emily ever had it or not! It is odd about Emily, how sometimes a person mysteriously forgets things about her as though great gaps of her life are just one blank slate."

"Well, *I* remember!" Jo snorted. "Meg and I were the only two to get it."

Now that I knew I'd never had scarlet fever in this world, I was tempted to step away again. Would this be how I'd die? Of scarlet fever, in a world that was only fictional until a year ago? And if I did die here, would my own body mysteriously show up dead in the real world?

Still, I forced myself to step closer to Beth, taking her hot little hand in both of mine.

"Is it very bad?" I asked quietly. "Do you feel awful right now?"

"Not awful," she said, far more calmly than I could have been in her position. "There is the headache and now the sore throat and I do feel queer, like somehow I am not even here, not even completely me, but it is not awful."

"I'll stay with you until you're better," I said, forcing a bright smile, knowing somehow that she'd never be all better.

"I'll stay," I went on more brightly still, "and read to you from your favorite books." I forced a laugh. "I'd much rather read to you than to Aunt March! And I'll even take care of all your dolls for you while you're sick, even headless and limbless Joanna, so you don't have to worry about them being neglected. I'll—"

"Don't be ridiculous." Jo cut me off. "Dr. Bangs has already been here. He asked Beth which one of us she would most like to have nurse her and she said *me*."

"I'm sorry, Emily," Beth said apologetically. "It was very hard for me to choose, but you see I did remember you hadn't had it before and I don't want to endanger you."

"That's right," Jo said. "Come to think of it, what are you still doing here, Emily?" She began to shoo me like she would one of Beth's kittens. "Get out! Get out! What do you want to do, get yourself sick so that I have to take care of you too?"

I didn't want to go, didn't want to leave Beth's side, but . . .

"Please go, Emily," Beth urged. "If I were ever responsible for getting you sick, it would kill me."

I hated to hear her speak those words, but how could I refuse?

Okay, I may have been willing to leave Beth's bedroom, but leave the house completely? And to go stay at Aunt March's?

"I'm sorry, Emily," Meg insisted, "but there simply is no

other way to keep you and Amy safe from catching scarlet fever."

Amy kicked up even more of a fuss than I did.

"I won't go! I won't go!" she shouted when informed of Meg's plans. "I can't stand that old bat!"

It was no comfort to think that one other family member thought of Aunt March in the exact same terms I did.

But then Laurie came by to see how we were doing.

"Couldn't we stay at Laurie's house until the danger's passed?" I suggested.

Meg looked shocked. "I can't let you go stay unchaperoned at a *boy's* house!"

Laurie looked shocked at my suggestion as well, a little fearful of it too.

Why was he so scared of being sort-of alone with me?

"Please, Meg," Amy pleaded. "It is, after all, only Laurie, so it's not as though it were a real boy."

Before Meg could respond to this odd claim, Laurie stepped in.

"It won't be so bad," he reassured Amy. "Every day you're at your aunt's, I'll come by to take you on walks and for drives. I'll even take you out trotting in the wagon with Puck and to the theater."

Amy was immediately satisfied. She may have claimed Laurie wasn't a real boy—who did she think he was, Pinocchio?—and yet she certainly managed to simper and flirt with him now as though he was one.

As for me, why wasn't I reassuringly offered walks and rides in the wagon with Puck? Whoever Puck was.

"It's wonderful how strong you are about these things," Laurie said to me in a low voice when Amy had skipped off to pack a trunk and Meg had followed to help her not pack anything fool-ish. "The others are lucky to have you. You're such a brick."

No one had ever called me a brick before. It was a bizarre compliment, but one that made me feel good.

Then everyone was back in the room.

"Should we write to Marmee and tell her about Beth?" Jo wondered aloud.

"No," I said, determined to remain a brick now that some-one had decided I was one. "It'll only worry her when she can't do anything about it anyway. What kind of choice would that be: Stay with her sick husband, who has no other family in Washing-ton, or leave him to come tend to her sick daughter? No, I say leave her in ignorance unless a time comes when she absolutely needs to be told."

I'd done my best to deliver a persuasively Marmee-ish speech and the others took it well enough. Even Jo nodded a grudg-ing approval.

Then:

"Emily," Jo said exasperated, "why aren't you packed yet? Always holding everybody up!"

As I rushed around the bedroom, throwing items into a trunk like a crazy person—mustn't forget my spare corset!—sadness and worry returned: worry because, having failed to prevent Beth from getting sick, now I might get stuck here forever; and, more importantly, sadness because I'd grown to love Beth and I really hated to leave her behind.

Not to mention that in my mind's ear I could already hear that wretched parrot taunting me.

"E-mi-LY want a cracker?" it would croak.

Then I brightened.

Once installed at Aunt March's, there was nothing to prevent me from sneaking back to the house in order to spy on Beth's progress, was there? And maybe when I did sneak back, I could find something to do to save her.

It was a long walk, but I was strong—a brick, even!

I could do it.

Eighteen

It was a lot easier to make the long walk from Aunt March's house to the March home than it was to find a good time to sneak in. As I stood freezing under Beth's window in the gray of a dying day, occasionally going on tiptoe to risk peeks over the ledge, only to see Jo sitting at Beth's bedside, I kicked myself: I should have waited until the middle of the night, when even Jo would have to fall asleep for a bit. As it was, my feet felt like blocks of ice, my legs too stiff, the road between that house and Aunt March's too long to go back only to make the trek again later.

And so I waited, waited through the long hours of dying day turning to deeper dusk and finally full night.

For some reason, I'd never noticed how many stars there were. The sky was blanketed with them. Finally, when it must have been long after midnight, I peeked over the ledge to see Jo nodding in her chair.

Now if only Meg and Hannah are asleep, I thought as I stole into the house, careful not to let the door *snick* shut behind me. I even removed my boots so that the wooden floorboards wouldn't clack. Then I tiptoed through the house to Beth's room and stepped softly to the side of her bed.

It'd be nice to be able to say that she looked peaceful in her sleep, but she didn't. She made no sound, but she tossed and turned violently as though fighting with something I couldn't see. Without thinking, I removed my chilled hand from inside my muff and placed it on Beth's feverish cheek. Almost immediately, she stilled her jerky movements. For a horrible second I thought I'd killed her, but then I saw a peaceful smile on her lips.

Poor Bethie.

I would've stood there longer, happy to be Beth's personal refrigeration unit for however long she needed me, forever even, but then I heard Jo make restless noises.

Oh honestly. Was she already waking again? What was the girl, a vampire?

Not wanting to risk getting caught, I dove into the half-opened closet, pulling the door nearly shut behind me.

Oh great, I'm stuck here now, I thought.

It turned out to be a good thing I was stuck, because I got to hear how good Jo was with Beth when Beth wakened suddenly from some fever dream.

But then it turned into a bad thing when morning came and with it Dr. Bangs, who had Jo leave the room while Hannah stayed with him and he examined Beth.

That was when I learned that Beth was far sicker than anyone but Dr. Bangs and Hannah realized.

❧

It was even more of a nuisance sneaking out of the house than it had been sneaking in. First I had to wait for the doctor and Hannah to leave, then I had to wait for Jo to go to the bathroom, which seemed to take a very long time before she did—the girl was like a camel!

But I wasn't. I hadn't gone in hours and hours.

So it was with great relief that when Jo left the room, I crossed to the window, stopping briefly to kiss Beth's forehead before pushing the window open and crawling out.

Only then did I put on my boots.

And pee behind a tree in the woods.

And begin the long journey back to Aunt March's, where hopefully pretty Amy was occupying her attention enough with her accomplishments that Aunt March wouldn't notice I'd been absent from breakfast.

Hopefully, I'd get a nap in at some point today, since I'd be coming back to Beth's room later on, only this time I'd plan my visit better.

I did plan my next visit better, and all the ones the entire week after that.

I would set out at about ten p.m. Then, whenever I saw Jo dozing, I would make sure to stop at the kitchen first to grab some small food item that I could eat when hunger grew to starvation point.

Sometimes Jo would sleep for longer periods, allowing me more time with Beth. Then I'd watch as she twisted and turned in her sleep. But no matter how violently she moved, she never relinquished her hold on headless and limbless Joanna.

And sometimes in the mornings, before I had a chance to

sneak back out, I would hear Beth trying to sing as she used to love to do, her voice through her sore throat coming out a heartbreakingly agonized croak. Those were *almost* the hardest moments. The hardest was when it became obvious she no longer recognized anyone, when I would hear her calling Hannah "Amy" or calling Jo "Emily." In normal times, Jo would no doubt resent the mix-up, while I'd enjoy it, but these weren't normal times. I wanted nothing more than to hear Beth recognize Jo as Jo, and I was sure Jo felt the same.

That was the first time I heard Jo and Meg seriously consider writing to Marmee to tell her what was going on. But then Hannah brought in a telegram from Washington saying Papa had taken a turn for the worse and that we shouldn't expect Marmee for some time. Hannah didn't think we should worry Marmee when she could do nothing about it.

There was another morning when I heard the voice of the Hummel woman coming from the living room, apologizing for Beth being sick and asking for a shroud in which to bury her baby, Minna.

I felt sorry that the baby had died, but a part of me couldn't help but be angry with her over Beth getting sick.

Others came to visit too—so many others! Neighbors, the milkman, even the butcher! People I'd never heard of before came to the house, all worried about Beth, taking the risk to come because they loved her so much.

It would be so easy for kids I knew back home to make fun of Beth for being such a homebody and all her other simple ways—and don't get me started on her love for the doll Joanna. But she was so *good*, and yet not in an annoying way. No wonder people couldn't help but love her. Me, on the other hand? No matter what century I was in, I wondered who would be there if I got sick . . . or worse . . . But Beth?

I pushed the thought away. I didn't want to think of that anymore.

But then I had to think about it.

Because then came the horrible night when, after Jo had fallen asleep, I heard Beth moaning for Marmee. Beth had never called for her since getting sick, at least not when I'd been there. I'm sure she must have wanted to—Beth was the type of girl who would want her mother when sick; they all were—but I'm also sure that of all the people in the world, Beth never wanted to be a burden on anybody.

Why wasn't Jo waking and going to her? Beth's cries sounded so loud to me. Then it occurred to me that Jo must be exhausted from staying awake twenty-three hours a day.

I couldn't let Beth go on crying for Marmee that way. I had to do something.

Pushing the door gently open I crept to Beth's bedside, took one of her hot hands in one of mine.

Her eyes fluttered open and then locked on my face.

"Marmee?" she croaked wonderingly.

"No—" I started to say, then cut myself off when I saw she really didn't know the difference.

"Yes," I corrected myself, soothing her brow with my free hand. "It's Marmee. Now I need you to rest and concentrate as hard as you can on getting well. We all love you so much."

She breathed a happy sigh. "Could you sing me back to sleep?" she asked.

Sing? I wished she'd asked for anything but that. Not only would I wake the others, I was an awful singer.

But it was Beth. How could I refuse her?

"What would you like me to sing?" I asked.

"'Onward Christian Soldiers'? You always like that one."

No, I didn't. I didn't even know that one!

So in the quietest voice possible, I sang "The Climb" by Miley Cyrus.

It was the only song I could think of just then that might be something Beth might like.

"I don't know that one," she said.

"That's because you missed church on Sunday," I said, thinking fast. "It's a new hymn. The whole town can't stop singing it."

"I like it." She rolled over with a yawn. "Could you sing it again, Marmee?"

"Yes," I said, settling down beside her, wrapping my arms around her and rocking her body. "But you must promise to try and rest now."

"I promise."

So what could I do? I sang again.

"I've never heard that song either," came Jo's voice, surprising me that she was now awake, "and anyway, we don't even go to church. You know that."

"Does it matter?" I eased my hold on Beth's sleeping body.

"What are you doing here?"

"Does it matter?" I adjusted the pillows under Beth's head.

"You could catch the fever."

I bent to kiss Beth's brow. "Does it matter?"

Apparently it did matter to Jo and Meg.

They understood why I'd snuck in—who didn't love Beth?—but still they sent me back to Aunt March's.

And still I snuck back that night.

It was the first of December, almost a year since I'd arrived. I'd been fourteen when I got here. I was fifteen now. Back home, Anne would be in the Upper School at Wycroft and the fall term would be nearly done. She and Jackson were probably a couple by now, not that it mattered to me anymore. So much had changed, including me.

I was in the closet to hear Beth become increasingly incoherent, tossing out words in her troubled sleep that made no sense. And I was there to hear it when Dr. Bangs came to examine Beth, finally saying with a sad sigh that it was time to send for Marmee.

No!

Not yet! I was almost sure Beth wasn't supposed to die yet! Didn't a whole lot of stuff from the original book still have to happen first? But maybe I was having story amnesia again. Maybe this *was* when she would die.

Dr. Bangs said he expected there would be a great change, for better or worse, around midnight. To me it sounded no better than the sort of mumbo jumbo found in horoscopes, but what did I know?

I heard the others leave the room, Jo going to get a telegram they'd already prepared for such an event, which she'd take into town herself, even though a storm had whipped up outside.

When the room was at last empty, I emerged and kissed Beth, thinking I'd sneak out myself for a bit. It did get cramped on the floor of the closet. I stretched my aching muscles and then, realizing how hungry I was, went in search of some food. Sure, I might run into Meg or Hannah, but they wouldn't be nearly as tough about kicking me out of the house as Jo would be if she were still here.

I was in the kitchen making a snack when Hannah entered.

"What are you doing here?" she demanded.

"What does it look like?" I said. "I'm making a snack."

"That's not what I meant and you know it." Hannah put her hands on her hips and looked at me sternly, but when I coolly gazed back at her, she dropped those hands in defeat. "Ach, you always were the most stubborn."

This surprised me. "Not Jo?"

"You must be joking." She waved a hand. "It was always you."

News to me!

I wasn't buying it.

I was still eating my snack—I didn't care what it was or what it tasted like with Beth sick, I just needed to put something in my stomach—when Jo returned, breathless.

She looked at me in disgust.

"You back again?" she said.

I shrugged. "I never really left."

I prepared to be kicked out again, but before that could happen Laurie showed up.

He looked just as breathless as Jo as he grabbed her by the elbow and steered her into the living room.

"I have some news and also something to confess," he said.

Figuring I might as well hear this too and figuring that since he hadn't even greeted me he probably wouldn't notice my presence, I trailed after them.

"First the news," Laurie said. He brought out a telegram.

Jo scanned it quickly. "It says here that Papa is improving." She looked up at him, tears of hope in her eyes. "But this is wonderful news!"

Then she began really crying, telling him how with both parents gone she felt as though God was far away too.

Laurie comforted her, saying Beth was too good to die,

that God would never take someone like her. This bothered me. If God wouldn't take a good person, then what about all the other good people he'd taken over the last few millennia? Laurie's argument may have comforted him, but it sounded like a bunch of nonsense to me.

Apparently Jo thought so too. "But the good and dear always die," she said.

Laurie couldn't find a thing to say to counter this, so he made his confession instead.

"I took it upon myself to telegraph your mother yesterday to inform her Beth is ill and that she is needed at home. Brooke says she'll be here later tonight."

The look Jo gave him then—I thought I was seeing thunder—and when she flew at him I was sure she intended to beat him up for doing such a thing without permission.

But then I realized she was hugging him. She was *grateful*.

Laurie must have realized it too, because he tried to kiss her, at which point Jo pulled herself away.

Idiot. I wouldn't have pulled away!

Laurie didn't seem to mind her reaction, though. Maybe it dawned on him that this wasn't the best time to put the make on a girl?

"The last train comes in at two a.m.," he informed Jo. "I shall be happy to go to the station now and wait for your mother however long it takes."

It was when he turned to leave that he saw me standing there.

"Oh!" He blushed. "What are you doing here? Aren't you supposed to be staying with Amy at your aunt's? I could have sworn I saw you there earlier in the day."

"Oh, you know Emily." Jo waved her hand here, but for once it wasn't in disgust. I figured maybe she was so relieved Marmee was coming, she didn't care about what I did just then. "Emily just comes and goes as she pleases. I only wish there were some way to help Beth. If only there were some medicine for what she has . . ."

A way to help Beth . . . Some medicine . . .

Suddenly I remembered something from science class and an idea occurred to me. I stared at the remainder of the piece of bread in my hand.

"Do we have any old bread in the house?" I asked Jo urgently. "Something with a bit of mold on it?"

The sudden thought I'd had was about something I vaguely remembered learning in science once. Hadn't penicillin been discovered from mold on bread? Maybe that could save Beth!

"How should I know?" Jo asked, irritable once more. "Ask Hannah."

I asked Hannah and she *did* have some moldy old bread.

"Here," I said, returning to Jo with the bread. "When you sit with Beth, please, *please* get her to eat this."

"Moldy bread?" Jo wrinkled her nose. "But why? I should think, if she has any appetite at all, she'd want something other than moldy bread."

"*Please*, Jo," I pleaded, desperate now. "For once just trust me. I think this might help Beth."

The shadow of death hung over the house.

Even though it was night already and Laurie had left for the train station, it seemed a long wait until midnight, the witching hour that Dr. Bangs had declared should represent a turning point for Beth.

I was back in the closet, urged there by Jo.

"Meg's been through enough this past week," she'd said, shooing me along, "what with worrying about Beth *and* running the household. She shouldn't have to worry about you too right this minute."

So back into the closet I'd gone.

"I am so worried about Beth," Jo said in a loud whisper, almost like she wanted me to be able to hear them, as she and Meg hovered over Beth's bed.

"We need to trust in God," Meg said, sounding more confident than I suspected she felt, "and Marmee."

"You're right," Jo agreed.

Hey! What happened to the girl who agreed with me that God would take a good person as easily as a bad person?

I sighed. Looked as though I was the only person questioning authority left in the foxhole.

Then Meg vowed to never complain about anything again if God would only spare Beth.

Me, I was making no vows to God or anyone else, because I knew I'd never keep them.

Or maybe I'd make one, just to myself, that if Beth lived through the night I'd never again mock poor headless and limbless Joanna, not even in my own mind. But no, that wasn't a big enough trade. If Beth lived through the night, I'd do my best to find a way to be a better person.

"Did you see that?" Meg said in a hushed voice just after the hall clock struck midnight.

I poked my head out and saw a long shadow fall across Beth's bed. It was as though something had come to claim her.

If I hadn't been there to see it with my own two eyes I'd never have believed it.

And then . . .

Nothing happened.

Nothing appeared to change: her face still flushed, her breathing still labored, her body still fighting in its fevered sleep.

We all settled back into our respective positions to wait, some of us more comfortably than others.

One o'clock.

Two o'clock.

Suddenly Jo leaped from her chair. "Oh, Meg!" she cried. "I think she's dead!"

She began to say good-bye then, but Hannah, having no doubt heard her cry, rushed in.

In the instant before she spoke, I saw the shadow was gone. Somehow, it had receded without any of us noticing.

"She's not *dead*," Hannah said. "She's only sleeping. Peacefully. Her fever's turned."

Her fever had *turned*? Did this mean, then, Beth wasn't going to *die*? That I had somehow saved her? But . . . but . . . *how* had I done it? Was it the Miley Cyrus song? The moldy bread?

Had *I* invented penicillin?

Dr. Bangs was sent for.

"She will pull through, I think," he said, adding, "this time."

I didn't like his cautious note, but I told myself he was just being careful—malpractice suits and all that. Beth had survived the witching hour, had survived scarlet fever. She'd be fine in time. Thank you, Miley Cyrus! Thank you, moldy bread!

I could almost feel Jo's eyes boring through the closed door, almost hear the words in her head as she wondered: *Did Emily somehow do* this?

The others began rejoicing then even though Dr. Bangs was giving instructions on what to do once Beth awoke.

Good thing *I* was listening!

There was the sound of bells and then Hannah and Laurie shouting Marmee's arrival.

Oh, *now* she comes home! Talk about anticlimactic.

But wait a second. If my purpose here had been to save Beth, Beth had been saved.

So what was I doing still in Alcott-land?

Nineteen

Meanwhile, over at Aunt March's . . .

There were two things to come out of the time Amy and I spent living there while Beth had scarlet fever: 1) I realized for the first time just what a ginormous suck-up Amy March really was; and 2) Aunt March was buying into the whole thing, resulting in statements like:

"Emily," Aunt March confided, "I find that I like having Amy here so much more than having Jo."

"Emily," Aunt March observed, "Amy is so well-behaved. She has such pretty manners."

"Emily," Aunt March complained, "why can't *you* be more like Amy? My word, you're just as bad as Jo. As a matter of fact, I think you're even *worse* than Jo!"

"Worse than Jo!" Polly the parrot taunted. "Worse than Jo!"

Obviously, the parrot was buying into Amy's suck-up act too.

Oh, and there was one other thing that came out of our time at Aunt March's, an odd thing. There came a day when I admit I was complaining even more than usual about having to do whatever insane thing it was that Aunt March wanted us to do.

That's when Amy turned to me and said, "Honestly, Emily, your time here would go much faster and be more smooth and pleasant if only you'd get into the spirit of the thing."

"Maybe I could make things more smooth here at Aunt March's," I said, "but I don't see how I could ever make it pleasant."

"I didn't mean *here* specifically," Amy said.

"Then what did you mean?"

She opened her mouth to speak, but then she tilted her head to one side, considering me. "Never mind," she said at last. "Forget I said anything."

Twenty

Having returned at Laurie's urging, Marmee refused to leave Beth's side, even though Beth was clearly on the mend. But just because Marmee wouldn't leave Beth, it didn't stop her from insisting that others do so.

"Laurie," she instructed, "please go to Aunt March's to inform her and Amy that I have returned, and that the worst regarding Beth appears to have passed.

"Emily," she instructed, "please go with Laurie and do your best to stay put at Aunt March's as instructed until I say that it is safe for you to come home."

As I left the room, wondering what I was even still doing there since somehow I'd managed to save Beth's life, I heard her address Meg and Jo. "Honestly, girls. How *could* you have allowed Emily to visit here when you know she has never had scarlet fever? You should have sent her back to Aunt March's the minute you saw her face."

"*Allowed?*" Jo used a rare scoffing voice with Marmee. "*Sent?* Have you ever tried to tell Emily to do anything when she has already determined to do the exact opposite?"

There was a brief pause before Marmee finally admitted, "Indeed."

The first snow was on the ground when I rode with Laurie to deliver the good news to Amy.

"It is too bad," he said as the carriage bounced along, "that you have not been able to accompany Amy and me on our afternoon outings. I have seen a different side to your youngest sister in the time we have spent alone. Perhaps if you had been there more, you might have seen it too."

"A different side to Amy? What different side could there possibly be? With Amy, what you see on the surface is definitely what you get."

"You mean that she is vain and foolish?"

I certainly wasn't going to disagree.

"Of course she is that," Laurie continued when I said nothing, "more vain and foolish than any girl I know. But when one spends time alone with her, one realizes that she is also strong and even shrewd."

Shrewd? Amy???

But then I remembered something else she'd said about a week or so ago when she'd advised me: "Your time here would go much faster and be more smooth and pleasant if only you'd get into the spirit of the thing."

At the time, I'd interpreted "here" as our stay at Aunt March's.

But what if Amy had in fact meant something deeper? What if this strong and shrewd Amy, according to Laurie, was instead referring to my time here in Marchville? Had Amy somehow figured out that I didn't come from *here* at all?

No, of course that wasn't the case, I reassured myself as Laurie delivered Marmee's message and Amy flew at Laurie's head in gratitude just like Jo had done. Amy wasn't shrewd enough to figure out something like that. How could she?

But she was smart enough for one thing, I saw now. Laurie had said his impression of Amy had changed. And I saw for the first time clearly just how shrewd she was: Amy was an opportunist and, having the opportunity of Laurie all to herself, had seized upon it. Now the most eligible boy any of us knew had started to look at Amy in a new and more favorable light.

Hmm . . .

Oh, well. If Laurie was feeling a new passion for Amy, he certainly wasn't showing it now. No sooner did Amy let him go than he collapsed on a sofa, like some frail lady in a Victorian novel, claiming to have slept not at all since the day before.

Soon he was snoring softly.

"I guess I'll write to Marmee now," Amy said, with a disappointed glance at the snoring boy.

It wasn't easy for me to stay away from home and Beth, but I did my best the first few days, knowing that Marmee would be firmer in kicking me out than Meg or Jo had been.

I was helping Amy straighten up the parlor, yet again, when Marmee came to call.

"Beth is doing well enough now," she said, "although I prefer you both remain here for the time being, but I did so want to see the one daughter I have not seen yet."

Marmee opened her arms wide and Amy flew into them.

Then, as if I wasn't even there, Amy sat in Marmee's lap and told her all about how hard things had been for her, being away from home.

"Oh. You're here," Aunt March said to Marmee, rousing from where she'd been napping in a chair. "I hope you don't plan to take Amy away from me just yet. In fact, I wish I could have her with me forever."

"No, I'm not taking them yet," Marmee informed her.

"Oh." Aunt March looked disappointed as she cast a glance in my direction. "I was hoping you'd take away just the one. Really, anytime now would be fine."

"Marmee!" Amy cried, holding out her hand. "Look at the ring Aunt March gave me! She originally planned to leave it to me in her will, but decided I should have it early, because I am so good."

Marmee agreed that the turquoise was a very pretty ring, even if it needed a double guard to fit Amy's finger. But she also thought Amy too young for such "adornment."

That's when Amy proved her shrewdness once again.

She spun some convoluted reasoning about how the ring would serve as a constant reminder that she must strive to be unselfish, like Beth.

The very idea of Amy taking an unselfish approach to life for any length of time—HA!

But Marmee swallowed it whole.

I couldn't keep myself away from home and Beth forever.

And so, a few days later, I made the long trek through the snow to see how my favorite sister was doing.

But as I peeked over the ledge to Beth's room, I saw that Marmee and Jo were there, and neither looked like she'd be leaving anytime soon.

The window was slightly open—Dr. Bangs had probably prescribed that a little pneumonia was just the thing for an invalid—so I was at least able to eavesdrop on them.

Marmee and Jo were discussing John Brooke—the stalker with Meg's glove.

First Marmee said what a help he'd been to her in Washington and how glad it made her knowing he was still there, tending to Papa.

Then Jo surprised me by spilling the secret about how Mr. Brooke had kept Meg's glove so that he could have a piece of her.

Then Marmee surprised Jo *and* me by saying she knew all about John's love for Meg—if not the glove—and that he'd confessed it to her and Papa.

"He wants to earn enough money and position himself better," Marmee went on, "before marrying her, but your father and I told him that we will not allow Meg to wed until she is at least twenty."

Then Jo went on and on, her usual predictable blather about wanting to keep Meg with them forever, blahblahblah. I was about to fall asleep out there when she said something I couldn't have predicted, not in a million years.

"I had always intended," Jo said, "that Meg should marry Laurie."

What the—

It was mind-boggling to think that Jo was so dense she thought Laurie should marry Meg, the March girl least suited for him. The rest of us, even Beth, had more fun in our little fingers than Meg had in her whole body. Even more mind-boggling was the idea that Jo had so little self-awareness, she didn't see that *she* was the one best suited for—

What was the girl—nuts? Anyone who'd ever read the story—anyone with half a brain—could see that Jo and Laurie were meant to be together. Yes, even *me*. The way they talked so easily, the way they clicked over everything, the way she affectionately called him "Teddy" and "my boy"—it was so obvious how much Jo liked him. And yet, no matter what anyone who'd ever read the story thought, no matter what anyone with half a brain could see, there remained just one tiny problem:

I still wanted Laurie for myself.

Twenty-One

A few weeks had passed and I was still living between worlds: spending part of the time at Aunt March's with Amy, and the rest of the time back home.

There was constant chatter about the possibility of Papa returning now that his health was improving, and I wondered what it would be like to come face-to-face with the one remaining family member I'd supposedly known my whole life and yet never met, but no specific date was on the calendar.

Now that Marmee had returned and Beth had turned her dark corner—Three cheers for Beth! as Jo might say—the household had rearranged itself once more. Beth could actually lie on the sofa in the study now, playing with her cats and sewing clothes for her dolls. I'd kept my silent vow to never think another bad thought about the headless and limbless Joanna and even gave an outward showing of this newly turned leaf by praising the garment Beth had sewn for her: a gown with a high-necked collar that somehow served to emphasize the lack of head.

"Joanna looks extremely happy in that," I told Beth.

"How can you tell?" Beth asked.

"By her smile, of course," I said. "Joanna always smiles like that when she's particularly happy about something. It's like the sun coming out."

Beth seemed particularly happy herself at my words, my willingness to finally play along.

Now that we were into the shortest days of the year, Jo'd taken to lifting Beth up in her arms, blanket and all. Then she would carry Beth around from window to window so she could see cheerful nature and the changes in the out-of-doors.

I had to grudgingly give Jo credit, for being generous and for being strong enough to carry her. One time when Jo was out of the room, I tried, and nearly dropped Beth.

Beth had lost so much weight it occurred to me that if my friends in the twenty-first century knew how effortlessly scarlet fever peeled away the pounds, they'd probably do anything to catch the disease. Hmm ... maybe I could somehow take a vial of scarlet fever–infected blood with me when I time traveled back home? I'd probably be rich and famous!

Not that I seemed likely to time travel back home anytime soon. I was beginning to wonder if I was doomed to remain here forever.

I pushed that thought away.

And in the meantime, while I was here, I focused my attentions on Laurie.

My mom used to say that when a guy teased a girl it meant that he secretly liked her. I'd never believed that warped little theory, since whenever any boy teased me it seemed to only mean that he hated my guts. But maybe I was wrong. Maybe Jo had been right and there was some sort of weird chemistry between Laurie and Meg?

I was thinking this because Laurie had played a prank on Meg.

Laurie, being Laurie, took what little he did know about John Brooke and Meg and made a big mess out of everything. He forged two love letters to Meg, and she'd actually replied to one. When it all got out, there was much hand-wringing on her part. First Meg was upset that Mr. Brooke had written to her in such an "indiscreet" fashion. Then she was upset with herself for writing back in an even more indiscreet way. Personally, I'd have *loved* to see those letters. What could a man who'd stolen a girl's glove as a romantic memento put in an indiscreet letter—"I find your ankles, when glimpsed beneath the bottom of your voluminous skirts, irresistible"? And what could my prissy older sister possibly have replied that made her blush—"I do love the idea of you looking at my ankles, but do wait until I am a bit older before gazing at them so forthrightly"? The mind reeled. Finally, Meg freaked when she discovered Laurie had written those letters after all, and that Laurie had read her reply.

And now Marmee was upset by all of the above.

Basically, she reamed Laurie out. How could he do such a thing? What sort of friend was he to either Meg or his tutor to think that such behavior was acceptable?

And then everyone else piled on.

Laurie seemed appropriately ashamed of himself. In fact, when he headed for the door, I could have sworn I saw a tail sticking between his legs.

"Do you think, perhaps," Jo said once the door had closed, "we were a little too hard on him?"

"*Too hard?*" Marmee looked like she didn't know what to do with such a comment. Unlike in my real life, where my sisters and I constantly pushed back when our mother yelled at us about something, I'd never seen any of the March girls push back against Marmee. Her and her pontifications: they were judge and executioner around here.

"It's just that," Jo went on, "it *is* only Teddy. He never means any harm, even if he does sometimes cause it. Plus, it was sort of my fault for acting as though I had a secret, forcing him to angle for it."

"I suppose . . . possibly . . ."

It was the closest I'd ever heard Marmee admit to being even remotely mistaken about anything.

"I know!" Jo said brightening. "I have a book I need to return to his grandfather. I'll bring it now and while I'm there, I'll just stay around long enough until I run into him, and then I'll fix everything. If I know anything, it's how to handle Teddy."

HA!

She left the room, returning a moment later with a heavy-looking volume.

"I'll go with you," I promptly said, grabbing on to one end of the book.

"Oh no, you won't," Jo said, tugging the book back. "I hardly think it requires two people to return a single book."

"It's a heavy book," I pointed out, grabbing the end again. "Besides," I added, "remember our pact!"

"It's been a long time since you brought that up," Jo seethed.

"Yeah, well," I said, "we have had a few other things on our minds around here lately."

"Oh, *fine*," Jo said. "We'll go together. But it will look ridiculous if we walk all the way over there with each of us holding on to the end of a single book."

And then she yanked the book out of my grip so swiftly and violently, I swore I suffered book burn.

"Let me do the talking," I whispered as we approached the Laurence household.

"*You?*" Jo said, straining to sound equally hushed but failing. "But this was all *my* idea!"

"I know that," I said, still the voice of cool and quiet reason, "but you're always saying impulsive things, always getting so hotheaded. I know you think you know how to manage Laurie, but really, you only *think* that. I happen to know that if given half the chance you'll louse this whole thing up and make matters worse."

"Harrumph," Jo harrumphed as we jointly knocked on the door. "We'll see about that," she added as the door opened and we stepped over the threshold.

Yes, Laurie's house was big, but it wasn't so big that Laurie could have gotten lost in it. Still, after jointly returning the book to his grandfather, it took us a long time to find him. He finally answered the door to his bedroom when we knocked on our third round through the house.

"I'm thinking of running away," he announced.

"We're sorry we all reacted so strongly," Jo said before I had a chance to get a word in. "We know you didn't mean any harm. You were simply being you."

Oh, there's a way to make someone feel better, I thought, rolling my eyes. Tell them they can't be blamed for being a jerk because it comes naturally to them.

"It's not that." Laurie dismissed her concerns. "Or at least it's not all that."

"What is it then?" I rushed to ask before Jo got the chance to. Hey, I could act concerned too!

Apparently, in addition to being ashamed of what he'd done, Laurie was now upset at something his grandfather had done.

"He could tell something was wrong when I came home," Laurie said. "But when I would not tell him the cause—because I couldn't do that, could I? That would be giving away the secret regarding Mr. Brooke and Meg—he, he, he . . ."

"He what?" Jo prompted. You could see she had no patience for anybody with a speech impediment.

"He *shook* me," Laurie said. "Physically, he *shook* me."

I had to admit, I'd heard of shaken baby syndrome, a form of child abuse back home, but I'd never heard of shaken teenage-boy syndrome before. And I had to further admit, it didn't sound all *that* bad. After all, Mr. Laurence was an old man. How hard could he have shaken Laurie? Surely not hard enough to do any real damage.

What a wuss Laurie was sometimes. An adorable wuss, of course.

"Of course, the shaking wasn't the worst part," Laurie said.

"I see," I said sympathetically, when really I saw nothing. If he wasn't upset about the shaking, then just what was he upset about?

"It's that he always treats me like a child," Laurie said.

Ah, *that* I could understand.

"When I am nearly a man," Laurie said.

Yes, he did look pleasingly masculine when he said that.

"So I am thinking of running away."

And back to being a child again.

Wasn't Laurie seventeen now? What sort of seventeen-year-old boy talks about running away?

I thought about the seventeen-year-olds I knew back home at Wycroft Academy. What would *they* be doing now? Nearly all of them would be driving, most would be thinking about which colleges to go to. Some would have part-time jobs. They'd have girlfriends. They'd have done *a lot* with those girlfriends.

And what was Laurie doing? Whining about getting shaken by his grandfather and talking about running away.

People were soooo *retro* back in this century.

"I'm thinking of going to Washington," Laurie said firmly. The way he puffed out his chest—just like that, I was finding him manly again.

It was amazing sometimes, the seesaw effect Laurie had on my attraction toward him.

"Will you go with me, Jo?" he said.

Jo???

Before I got a chance to say "Don't you mean Emily too?" Jo was already speaking.

"That's the most preposterous thing I've ever heard!" she crowed. Then she at least had the sense to look embarrassed at her outburst. "That is to say, of course I would love to go with you."

What?

"But I'm afraid I cannot," she went on. "It would be such fun to go to Washington with you—such a lark! But I cannot leave Beth and you must not leave your grandfather, not over some silly disagreement. Now then." She headed for the door. "I will go speak to your grandfather and get him to apologize. Would that set everything straight?"

"It would help," Laurie said, still looking bitterly wounded, "but I cannot imagine you will meet with success."

"You'd be surprised how persuasive I can be," Jo said. "Emily?"

"Hmm?"

"Aren't you coming with me?"

"I think you can handle this one yourself," I said. "You're so good at managing people. And anyhow, it's hardly a two-person job, is it? Not like carrying a really heavy book."

I could tell she wanted to remind me of the pact, but she couldn't very well do that in front of Laurie, so she slammed the door and off she went, no doubt fuming all the way.

And then Laurie and I were alone.

Laurie locked the door, causing me to raise an eyebrow at him. He shrugged. "Habit," he said. "I hate it when the servants just barge in."

"Those barging servants can be so annoying," I said, if only for something to say.

"I can't imagine that even Jo can get Grandfather to apologize," Laurie said. "He's never apologized for anything in his life."

"What will you do if he doesn't apologize?"

Laurie squared his shoulders. "I'll run away. To Washington."

"By yourself? Mr. Brooke can't accompany you because he's already in Washington, with Papa, and Jo already said she wouldn't. As for your grandfather, you can't ask him to go with you since there's no point in running away if you take what you're running away from with you."

Laurie looked less sure of himself now, shoulders a little less square. Still . . .

"I'll go by myself then," he said with a forced confidence.

Suddenly a thought occurred to me and with it, a shyness I'd never felt in my life. What if I put myself on the line and got shot down?

"I could go with you," I offered.

"You?"

He looked surprised at my suggestion, but at least he didn't look horrified. That had to be a good sign, right?

"Yes. Me." As I spoke, I grew more confident, more excited at the idea. "I could go see Papa while we're there." I liked the idea of meeting and getting to know this stranger parent for the first time away from the eyes of my sisters. "And it's not as though we'd be away forever."

Although it would give us time to bond without Jo or Amy around, I thought.

What an adventure this could be.

Road trip!

"I can't believe you'd do this for me," Laurie said.

Hmm . . . Stick around here, or go on an adventure to the country's capital with a hot boy who I knew wouldn't put any moves on me I wasn't ready for . . . Such a tough choice to make . . .

I'd been to Washington on a field trip once in eighth grade, but I'd never been there during the American Civil War! Maybe I'd meet Lincoln!

"I don't know what to say," Laurie said softly when I said nothing.

Then he took a step toward me.

"What are you doing?" Without thinking, I took a step back.

He took another step forward.

The way he was looking intently at my eyes . . . "Is there some-thing in my eye?" I wiped at them with my hands as I took another step back.

He took another step forward. "Stand still, please, Emily," he said.

Then he leaned toward me, his face slowly but steadily clos-ing the space between us until his lips were just a breath away from mine and then he closed that space as well.

I don't know how long we stood like that, but it seemed like a very long moment, lips just touching lips, with no other movement.

I can't say it was unpleasant, but it wasn't particularly pleas-ant either. It was just that, two sets of lips touching.

At last, Laurie pulled away.

"Thank you," Laurie said formally. "Ever since that day you, um, threw yourself at me, I have been curious—you know, what that would feel like if I initiated it myself. And then when you said you would go to Washington with me, I was so grateful, it seemed like the perfect opportunity to try it."

I didn't know what to make of this.

"I hope I didn't offend you," Laurie said.

What?

"Oh. No. No. I wasn't offended."

But did I want to do it again? Did *he* want to do it again? I wasn't sure. Because as much as I had thought I *wanted* to kiss Laurie, something had been missing in that kiss, and not just on his part, but on mine as well.

I did think the idea was nice, the idea of kissing someone who probably hadn't already kissed a million other girls before just for the sake of kissing them.

I was standing there wondering if he'd try to kiss me again—perhaps we could both try to put more feeling into it this time?—when there was an insistent pounding at the door, and Jo shouted:

"*Will* you let me in? Oh, very well. I guess I'll shove it under the door."

In the next instant a sheet of paper came flying through the narrow gap between door and floor.

Laurie left me to go to the paper. He picked it up, turned it over, read. Then his face lit up and he unlocked the door, throwing it open wide.

"I can't believe you accomplished this, Jo!" he said. "You really are the most amazing girl! But how did you ever get him to apologize? And in writing!"

Jo launched herself into a long-winded tale of her discussion with Mr. Laurence. I barely caught a word, still too busy thinking about that kiss.

When Jo finally paused long enough to take a breath, I turned to Laurie.

"So," I said, "when do we leave for Washington?"

"Washington?" he echoed.

Odd. They both seemed so far away from me now.

"Yes, Washington," I said. "You know, our trip? Our adventure?"

Laurie looked entirely puzzled by this.

"I'm sorry, Emily," he finally spoke, "but now that Grandfather's apologized, in writing, no less—how *did* you do it, Jo?—there's really no point in my running away, is there?"

That night Jo found some paper covered with Meg's handwriting. She'd written *Mrs. John Brooke* over and over again.

Jo grew extremely angsty over this, worried that the future was being hastened. I didn't even bother trying to comfort her. She'd already loused up enough things for me for one day. And besides, I wondered, when would the future finally "hasten" for me?

Twenty-Two

Christmas won't be Christmas without any presents.

Those were the words that had greeted me in this world, and a full year had passed since I first heard them spoken.

It was Christmas again, only this time there were presents: a soft wrapper for Beth to keep her warm, books by authors no one would care about in another century and a half for Jo, an engraved religious picture for Amy, a silk dress from the Laurences for Meg. Marmee received a brooch made of her and her children's hair: gray, golden, chestnut, brown. As gross as I found the peculiar item, I looked at it closely, having no recollection of being asked to contribute any hair to it. Where was the auburn? But then I glimpsed a single strand. Just one single strand? Oh, well. It wasn't like I wanted to be strongly represented in such a disgusting way. But then I saw something interesting. All the other colors were looped over like the different-colored strands of embroidery floss that comes with a kit. But mine was the strand knotting them together. Mine was the only one touching all the others—coolio!

And wait a second. Where was my present? Hadn't anyone bought me anything?

"Here, Emily," Beth said from her position on the sofa in front of the fire. "I made you this."

I went over to her, took the tiny hand-sewn garment from her fingers. It took me a moment to figure out what it might be.

"A new dress for Joanna?" I guessed.

"Yes," she said, pleased. "Since you and she have become such great friends, I thought you might like something of your own to dress her in."

I held it to my chest and smiled down at Beth. "I'll treasure it always," I said, and I meant it.

And then the others surprised me by having presents for me too!

Meg gave me a pair of white gloves. "For parties," she said. "Soon you'll be going to them too."

Amy gave me a drawing she'd done of herself in which she'd made her nose look seriously smaller.

Jo gave me a large straw hat with a massive brim. "You'll appreciate it come summer. And you know, you do look ridiculous in bonnets."

Even Laurie had something for me, a copy of a book he'd seen me admiring in his library.

"I can't believe you all got me things!" I said, still shocked.

"Of course we all got you things," Jo said. Then she snorted. "What do you think you are, old mutton?"

⚬⚬⚬

Jo and Laurie had been excited all day. Ever since the plan for Laurie and me to run away to Washington had fallen through, he and Jo were tight again.

Right before we were ready to sit down for our big meal—and this year it *was* a big meal, with a turkey and everything—Laurie, having disappeared briefly, poked his head into the parlor. He said he had a big surprise for us. Then he stood out of the way to let two men enter.

One I recognized immediately: it was Mr. Brooke. Leaning on his arm was a tall man all muffled up in scarves. There wasn't much of him that could be seen above the muffling. But when the others ran to him, I instantly knew who he was.

This man was my father.

He raised his head from where it'd been nestled in Marmee's neck, looked at me over her shoulder, a quizzical expression on his face. But before either of us could speak, Beth entered the room, drawn by all the excited noise. She'd barely regained half her strength since her bout with scarlet fever but you'd have never guessed it now as she flew at him and the others parted to allow her flight. And then she was in his arms, happy as I'd never seen her, and then the two huddled in one big chair together, chattering away as if no time had passed, as if no one had nearly died.

Christmas dinner that day was a happy one. Mr. Laurence and Laurie joined us, and so did Mr. Brooke. This last addition didn't please Jo, who leaned over to whisper in my ear at one point.

"Did you see how Mr. Brooke kissed Meg when they first arrived? He hurriedly explained that it was some sort of accident, but I am absolutely positive it was not. And did you see how she blushed?"

I hadn't seen any of that. I'd missed it because my eyes had been fixed on this new addition to the household, wondering if this man who was supposed to be my father recognized the one daughter who hadn't huddled around him, if he even knew who I was.

The Laurences and Mr. Brooke were sensitive enough to leave soon after the meal was done, allowing our family its first night alone together.

As we sat before the cheery fire, and the man who was supposed to be my father and Beth huddled in the big chair once again, Amy urged him to comment on the changes in us girls since he'd last seen us.

He commented first on Meg's hands, saying how they weren't so soft as they used to be but that he liked their rougher state. It proved she understood the need to work hard to make our world go round.

His widest grin was for Jo. He said he'd left behind someone who had more in common with a boy but that now he had before him a young lady, one who would even give away her hair to benefit others.

Beth, he said, was not as shy as she'd once been, but that if possible she seemed even smaller than he remembered her. His face briefly saddened when he spoke that last part, but then his expression lightened again as he turned his attention to Amy.

He said that she seemed to finally be taking the importance of molding her own character seriously and he further observed that she had grown less selfish.

HA! I hadn't seen any less-selfish behavior in Amy!

"What about Emily?" Amy asked. I shot a glance at her

just in time to see a mischievous look briefly pass across her face.

"Emily?" the man who was supposed to be my father said.

"Yes, Emily," Amy said with a chin jut in my direction. "You have not commented on how she has changed since last you saw us."

The man studied me for a long moment.

What would he say? I wondered nervously.

"Emily," he finally said, addressing me directly. "Well, what is there to say really? You are the same as you have always been."

What a bizarre thing to say! All the others had changed, in ways he considered great and significant, while I hadn't? How odd. And how insulting too on another level. It was almost as bad as Marmee's *Wherever you go, dearest Emily, there you are* inscription in that book she'd given me.

I didn't know what to make of it, or him.

A year here. A whole year. I was finally beginning to accept the fact that no matter what I did, I'd never leave.

Twenty-Three

It was the day after Christmas and we were all in the back parlor again. Now that Papa had returned from the war, not dead, and Beth had survived scarlet fever (also not dead), it was time for the family to turn its collective mind to other matters, to matters involving love rather than death:

Meg and Mr. Brooke.

Meg had a dopey, distracted look on her face, while Marmee and Papa studied her with curiosity, Beth looked at her lovingly, and Amy looked at her romantically. As for Jo, she did her usual practical Jo thing: she shook her head angrily at the umbrella in the corner of the room, the umbrella Mr. Brooke had accidentally left behind the night before.

Yeah, shaking her head angrily at an umbrella—that was sure to solve all our problems!

Still wearing her goofy look, Meg drifted out of the room. Jo took off after Meg and I tiptoed after Jo.

Well, I didn't want to miss anything that might turn out to be big excitement, did I?

The three of us wound up in the front room.

"I wish you'd just get it over with," Jo told Meg. Meanwhile, I took up my position as a fly on the wall. "I hate waiting for things. Just do it."

"I can't," Meg said. "It's not proper for me to speak to him about it before he brings it up first. And of course now he won't bring it up since Papa already told him I am too young."

It was obvious from the way she said it that Meg didn't think she was too young.

But seriously, how crazy were these Victorian girls! Meg couldn't talk about something to a guy unless he raised the subject first?

I actually agreed with Papa that Meg was too young to be thinking about getting married, even if that seemed to be all there was to it for these crazy Victorians: Like someone? Marry the person! Me, I couldn't imagine getting married at seventeen. I remembered reading an article once that said people born in the twenty-first century could expect to live as much as one hundred to one hundred and fifty years. So imagine being married at seventeen—you could wind up married to the same person for eight-three to one hundred and thirty-three years! Of course, the Victorians did die a lot sooner. Everyone knew that. But wait a second. Now that I lived here, did that mean *I* would die a lot sooner?

"I'll tell you what I'd say to him if I could." Meg's words cut into my thoughts. "That way, someday when you are in similar circumstances, you will know how to conduct yourself."

"HA!" Jo said. "I will never be in similar circumstances!"

HA! Didn't I know it! With her Peter Pan attitude, she really wouldn't. If Jo had her way, she'd probably spend her entire life span writing bad plays and playing dress-up to act in those plays.

But before Meg could get very far into her speech, there was a knock at the door and then the man himself was among us.

"I came for the umbrella I accidentally left behind yesterday," Mr. Brooke practically stammered. "I came to see how your father is doing."

Well, which one is it? I thought.

I nearly snorted out loud but kept the snort to myself, not wanting to call attention to my presence. Seriously. We all knew why he'd really come over: to see Meg.

Not that that pleased Jo, who flounced off to find the umbrella and Papa.

"Margaret," he said when Jo was gone.

Who was Margaret?

Then I realized. He was talking to Meg.

The blush on her face told me this was the first time he'd called her anything other than Miss March.

As I stood there in my secret corner, he confessed his love to her, asking if she thought that in time she might learn to love him.

Use a girl's first name for the first time and immediately confess your love? Sure, why not. That made sense.

He said he'd wait for her, which I admit did seem incredibly romantic. Meg looked like she thought so too, but then he blew it all by saying he'd been good at teaching her German and that he thought it would be even easier to teach her to love him.

I don't think his self-confidence impressed Meg, who began playing games with him. She even told him that she wanted him to go away. He seemed just on the verge of doing that, hat in discouraged hand, when there came a pounding on the door and Aunt March shouted, "Mar-ga-REET!"

So of course Mr. Brooke did what any self-respecting grown man would do at the sound of Aunt March's voice: he ducked into the nearest closet, pulling the door shut behind him. I can't say I blamed him. As for me, I tried to disappear even farther into the floral wallpaper.

"I'm looking for my nephew!" Aunt March announced, entering.

Her nephew? It took me a moment to realize she meant Papa. But I always assumed they were brother and sister!

"I'll get him," Meg offered, moving to leave the room.

"Actually," Aunt March said, "I wanted to talk to you first. It has come to my attention that an unfortunate . . . *association* has sprung up between you and that man employed by your neighbors. I wish it to stop. In fact, if it does not stop, if you persist in marrying this man, you will not get a single penny from me when I die. Not one."

Five minutes ago, Meg had been ready to send Mr. Brooke packing. Now her normally calm features became enraged and she started to go off on Aunt March. Well, good-bye, Dr. Jekyll, and hello, Mr. Hyde.

Poor Aunt March. Even I could have told her that her plan would backfire. If she didn't want Meg to marry Mr. Brooke, she should have told Meg she *did* want her to marry him!

"Fine," Aunt March said, changing tack. "But you must realize, I am only trying to help. And you must further realize that, as the oldest daughter, it is your duty to marry a rich man so that you can help your family."

What?

I had to put my hand over my mouth in order to stifle the outrage that was dying to pop out.

Aunt March was a lunatic! People should marry the person they wanted. Well, unless the person they wanted was an ax murderer or something. But to marry just for money in order to help the family? What did she think this was, ancient history?

Oh, right. It was.

But again, Meg seemed to have no trouble expressing her outrage.

"This man has nothing," Aunt March persisted. "No money, no position in society, no immediate prospects for changing either circumstance. Surely you must see that."

Well, when she put it like that . . .

"He's marrying you for *my money!*" Aunt March finally cried when all else had failed.

As far as Meg was concerned, that was the last straw. In fact, she came awfully close to using the word *love* to describe what she and Mr. Brooke shared.

It was enough for Aunt March, though, who began her tromp through the room after telling Meg she washed her hands of her.

She paused at the door, turned. Putting her lorgnette to one eye, her gaze swept the room until it at last settled on me.

"E-mi-LY! What are you doing just standing there like a bit of wallpaper? Get over here at once and open this door for me."

My presence had been finally exposed, but once Aunt March was gone and Mr. Brooke had come out of the closet, I had as good as gone back to being wallpaper as they tentatively approached each other as though really seeing each other for the first time.

"Margaret."

"John."

Use each other's names for the first time one moment and the next they're engaged?

Yep. Talk about your crazy Victorians!

It was decided that they would marry in three years' time.

Everyone approved of the plan. Everyone except for Jo, of course, and Aunt March.

Laurie, Jo, and I were all gathered in one corner. Laurie was there to comfort Jo, and I was there because I was nosy, plus I didn't want to leave them alone together.

"It'll be fine, Jo," Laurie said. "We'll still have fun when Meg is gone. Why, I'll be done with college before you know it and then we can go abroad together."

Wait a second here. He'd canceled our Washington trip, but now he was talking about the two of *them* going *abroad*?

"You don't understand," Jo said.

"Maybe he doesn't," I cut in, tired of Jo's attempts to hold Meg back, "but I do."

"*You?*" Jo looked shocked at the very idea.

"Yes, me," I said, trying not to feel offended. "Look, I'll be losing a sister too when she goes." But would I really? I wouldn't be here still in three years . . . would I? I shook the idea off, continued. "You can't go on like this, Jo. If you really care for Meg—"

"Of course I do!" came the outraged interruption.

"Then you have to let her live the life *she* wants to live, not the life *you* want her to live. If you try to hold her back, you'll only push her away. Who knows? You may even lose her."

"Lose her?"

Laurie and Jo both gaped at me, shocked. If I could have, I

would have gaped at myself. Where had *that* bit of wisdom come from?

Apparently I wasn't done yet, though, because when I opened my mouth again, the following words came out:

"If you love something, set it free. If it comes back, it's yours forever. If it doesn't, it never really was."

Jo and Laurie ate it up. It was like I was the Dalai Lama or something.

Seriously. These people were made for Hallmark greeting cards.

Really? *Really?* Three years? Meg and John were supposed to marry in *three years?*

But that made no sense to me. I could have sworn that in the original book they got married not long after being engaged. So how was it possible that—

Twenty-Four

The three years that have passed have brought but few changes to the quiet family.

Three years had passed? Whoa! How the *heck* did that happen? It was like being dropped into this world all over again.

I knew it was three years later because just a few moments before, the others had burst into the parlor where I was sitting and shouted, "Happy birthday!"

"It's my birthday again already?" I said. I couldn't believe it. How had a year passed with me missing it? "I'm sixteen now?"

"Silly Emily." Beth laughed. "You're eighteen now. You know that."

Eighteen. That wasn't possible! I hurried to the first reflective surface I could find, studied my image in it, saw Beth was right: I was taller now, leaner. I looked more like a young woman than a teenage girl. I looked around me. The others, except for Beth, who still looked the same, were visibly older too. Meg looked more proper than ever. Jo, whose hair had been cropped short the last time I saw her, now had hair cascading down her back once more. As for Amy, she looked downright sophisticated. She must be sixteen now. If she lived in my era, she'd be getting her license soon, probably tooling around town in a sports car before long. Amy was definitely the sort of girl who'd be given a sports car as a present on her sixteenth birthday. Not that I was jealous or anything.

Eighteen.

I'd been here four years and somehow I'd missed three of them.

Go with the flow, Emily, I told myself in an effort to calm my anxiety, *just go with the flow.*

Really, I'd been living in Crazy Town for so long now, what was one more stop on the road?

Before long the others tired of celebrating me and said it was time to head over to Dovecote. I had no idea what Dovecote was, but I didn't let on, following along with the other girls and Marmee.

Dovecote turned out to be a small brown house. I wouldn't have thought a brown house could be adorable, but this one was, the interior decorated so cozy it was as though the owners had been living there for years. By remaining quiet and simply listening in on the conversations of the others, I quickly figured that Mr. Brooke—well, John now, as the others called him—had prepared this house for Meg. Were they married then already? So many things I didn't know—talk about story whiplash!

"*Psst*, Beth," I said while the others talked loudly about the furnishings.

Beth turned. "What is it, Emily?" she whispered back.

"I was hoping I could talk to you about something, just the two of us. Is there another room here we might use?"

"Why don't we step outside and get some air?" Beth suggested.

The others didn't notice as we left the house. They were busy yakking about dishes and things.

"What is it, Emily?" Beth asked again as we sat down on the small patch of lawn, arranging our skirts around us. "This is so peculiar. No one ever wants to have a private word with me about anything."

"I was wondering if you could bring me up to date," I said.

"Up to date?" She was puzzled. "How do you mean?"

"I want you to tell me what's been happening the past three years," I said, then added, "with everybody."

"But I don't understand." Now she was even more puzzled. Then she brightened. "I know!" she said. "This is another one of your games! It's like that time when you asked me things that everyone knows just so that I might feel better about my lack of book learning."

"A game!" I snapped my fingers. "That's exactly it! A game. And here's how we'll play: I'll ask you questions and then you answer them."

"All right," Beth said eagerly. "Although I do hope I know all the answers. I shouldn't like to disappoint you with my stupidity."

"You could never do that, Bethie," I assured her. "Okay, first question. Pretend I've lost all memory of the last three years. What's the most important thing that's happened in that time period?"

"I can't believe it." Beth put her hand to her chest, closed her eyes in relief. "I thought this might be difficult, but you're asking me easy questions. I know this one." She opened her eyes. "It's the war ending, right?"

Was she asking me or telling me?

And then it hit me. Wait a second. An entire *war* had gone and ended, and I'd somehow *missed* it?

"And of course you already know," Beth went on, "that Mr. Brooke—that is to say, John—went to war for a year, was wounded, got sent home, and now he has set himself up as an under book-keeper so that he might provide this lovely home for Meg." Beth turned sad for a moment. "Not that I really understand what an under bookkeeper does exactly."

"That's okay, Bethie," I said, recovering from my shock at a whole war ending in my absence, "I don't either. Tell me what Papa's been up to." I hadn't seen him around when I'd come to in the middle of my birthday celebration. Oh, God. I hoped he hadn't died and that I'd just raised a sore subject for Beth that would make her even sadder.

"Papa is the minister in our small parish now."

Whew. He hadn't died.

"Everyone goes to him for advice. He's half a hundred years old, has much gray in his beard, and is considered to be quite the wise old man."

Old at fifty? I mean, half a hundred.

"Oh, I do like this game, Emily!" Beth said. "I know all the answers. Ask me more questions!"

"So Meg is married already?"

"Silly Emily—of course not! She's getting married tomorrow, which is why we are all here today, to help prepare the house.

Marmee has been so busy of late with Meg and all her preparations, she has barely had time to do anything else!"

"And how about Meg—is she happy with this house?"

"You know Meg. When she saw what a fine home Ned Moffat
made for Sallie Gardiner after their wedding, she was a trifle
jealous. But then she remembered how much John loves her and
how hard he worked to make this charming little home for her,
and then everything was all right again."

Ned and Sallie had gotten married? Had I been at the wedding? If I had, I hoped I hadn't made a fool of myself!

"And what about Jo?" I said, my attention turning to my old
nemesis. "What's she been up to?"

"She never went back to Aunt March after my . . . illness.
Aunt March decided she preferred Amy. She even hired a special art teacher to give Amy drawing lessons so that Amy might
be persuaded to stay. So Jo continues in her reading and her
writing for *The Eagle*—did you know they pay her a dollar a col-
umn now? Of course you did, silly Emily—and she is also
working on a book. In between all that, she takes care of me. As
you can see, I am the same as I have always been."

I did see that.

"I've got another question for the game," I said. "I haven't
seen Laurie. What's he been doing?"

"Oh, good—another question I know the answer to! Why,
Laurie has been at college, but he still comes to visit us every
week and sometimes he even brings his college friends. Meg
doesn't pay attention to them, of course—she is too busy with
planning her life with John—and of course I am too shy to even
talk to them. But they like Jo, whom they seem to regard as
another young man. Oh, and they *really* like Amy. In fact, some

have grown quite besotted with her. Amy, as you know, has a way with young men."

Yes, I did know.

"Amy says that Meg should have servants for her house, like Sallie Moffat does, but Meg says she will be quite content with Lotty to run errands for her."

Who was Lotty?

"Amy also teases Laurie when he visits about one Miss Randal."

Who was Miss Randal? I didn't remember any Miss *Randal* from the original book!

"I think you are up to date now," Beth said, "except to tell you that Aunt March, after vowing not to give Meg a penny if she married John, developed a ruse whereby a friend of hers appeared to give Meg elaborate linens for her new home. But of course we all know who was behind it. Oh, and Aunt March is also giving Meg the pearls she promised to the first March bride."

"How generous."

"Yes, everyone is generous to a bride. That is why each of us has done so much to make this a home for Meg and John."

"Each of us?" I echoed. "And what have I contributed?"

Beth's face clouded over with puzzlement, but then it brightened at the sight of a tall guy, at least six feet, vaulting over the fence.

"Laurie!" she cried.

Wow. He looked even hotter than he had three years ago.

"Beth." He raised his hat at her, turned to me. "Emily. My, you're looking even prettier than last time I saw you."

I was? Involuntarily, I raised a hand to my hair. It was pinned up, but it felt thicker somehow, like it must be a lot longer.

"Everyone else in the house?" he asked. "Good, right," he answered his own question. "I've got another present for Meg, so I'll just head on in."

"He's still wonderful." Beth sighed when he was gone. "Of course he always teases Jo. He says he predicts she'll be the next to marry. And of course Jo always says that's absurd, that she will never marry."

She would say that.

Beth sighed again. "Are we finished with the game?" She rose with difficulty from the grass—she was still so frail. "I would like to rejoin the others now."

"Just one more question," I said, "and then the game is over. What have *I* been doing the past three years?"

Beth's face clouded again, even worse than before.

"Oh no," she said. "Finally, a question in the game I can't answer. You know, it's funny, but for some reason, right now I just don't know."

Twenty-Five

"Why don't you do Meg's hair, Emily?" Amy suggested. "I remember when you did mine years ago in le ponytail. If I hadn't gotten into trouble that day in school, I am sure it would have turned into quite the rage."

"That's okay," I said. "You're all doing fine with those, um, braids."

I didn't want them to realize that le ponytail was the only hairstyle I knew. Besides, le ponytail just didn't seem fitting for a wedding.

We were all gathered in the bedroom I still shared with Meg and Jo, helping the bride get ready for her big day. Meg had on a dress she'd sewn herself—she said she wanted the simplest of weddings, nothing like the fuss and bother Sallie and Ned had—and the rest of us were wearing silvery gray dresses with roses in our hair and bosoms. I felt kind of funny wearing flowers in my bosom—I also felt funny calling it my bosom. As for the dresses, I gathered from what the others said that these were our best gowns for the summer, but I'd never seen them before.

It was still troubling me, the idea that three years had somehow passed, that I'd somehow leaped forward in time without having any memories of a single event that had occurred in that time period.

But there was no time to dwell on that now.

We had a wedding to get on with here.

Papa stood with his back to the fireplace, officiating over the wedding of Meg and John.

Meg had said she wanted simple and it was a small crowd, but everyone I knew was there: the immediate family, of course, plus Laurie, Mr. Laurence, Aunt March, Hannah, and Sallie and Ned Moffat. There was one couple I didn't recognize. They were around Marmee and Papa's age and I heard Jo greet them as Uncle and Aunt Carrol.

At one point during the ceremony Papa's voice caught and it was a moment before he could go on. I realized then that he was emotional at the idea of his oldest daughter getting married and leaving the nest. Perhaps he was also thinking that soon all his girls would leave the nest?

As I watched Meg, Jo, Beth, and Amy, noticing the changes of the past three years, I couldn't help but think of Charlotte and Anne. Had they all forgotten about me? And if three more years had passed here, would three years have passed there too? If so, Charlotte would be in college now and Anne would practically be out of high school. What were their lives like now? What were *they* like? Had either one ended up with Jackson?

Jackson.

It'd been so long since I thought about him. Funny. He'd seemed so important to me once. I wondered now why he ever had.

But I didn't get to think any more about that just then because Papa was pronouncing Meg and John husband and wife—Meg was Mrs. John Brooke now!—and the party was about to begin.

I'd thought it promising earlier in the day, when I'd seen Papa pass through the room with a bottle of wine under each arm. After all, I was eighteen now. Wasn't that legal to drink in some places? At least back in the 1800s? But where was the wine now? All I could see was tea, water, and lemonade.

Laurie also noticed the absence of alcoholic beverages, because he commented on it to Meg. Apparently both his grandfather and Aunt March had contributed bottles to the occasion. That's when Meg informed Laurie that Papa was donating most of it to some soldiers' aid society, keeping just a little of it for Beth. Papa only believed in wine for medicinal purposes. Hey, I had medicinal purposes here! I was almost sure of it.

"You know, Laurie," Meg said, "you would do well yourself to give up alcohol."

Laurie looked reluctant.

"In fact," Meg said, "I would consider it a great present to me if you did so."

I knew Laurie liked to go to the saloons. He always said it was so that he'd have people to play billiards with, but anyone with any sense had to figure he drank there too. And I had *some* sense.

No, he didn't look like he wanted to give *that* up. But Meg was the bride, after all, and this was her wedding day.

"I'm sure I'll eventually be grateful to you for this, Mrs. Brooke," he said at last. "Very well. I promise to never drink again."

Wow, I hoped Meg didn't ask *me* to give up anything today!

Hey, wait a second though. This whole thing that had just happened with Meg and Laurie about drinking: Was this the beginning of what would eventually turn into 12-step programs everywhere?

Whatever.

All I knew, as we saw Meg and John off on the short walk to their new life together at Dovecote, was that it had been a lovely day. Perhaps some people, like Sallie and Ned Moffat, needed to have a big wedding to feel their marriage was worthwhile. But Meg and John had proved that it wasn't the money that made marriage worth it and the ceremony celebrating it wonderful. It was the love.

Oh, heck. I was beginning to sound like Marmee!

Someone get me out of here!

But as I lay in bed that night, staring at the ceiling, I knew that no one was going to get me out of there. After all, if it was going to happen, wouldn't it have happened already? I'd been there four years. I'd probably be here forever now.

And that three-year gap between Meg and John announcing their engagement and me basically "coming to"—it was the only phrase I could think of to describe it—the day before their wedding. What did it all mean? Could I only experience things that were part of the original story? And if that was the case . . .

An uneasy thought came to me, something I'd wondered before. When the events of the original *Little Women* ended, what would happen to me? What would my fate be when I ran out of story?

Twenty-Six

It was the beginning of the end.

"What are you doing with that thing?" I shouted at Amy.

"You mean this red-hot poker?" Amy said mildly, waving it in my direction.

"Point that somewhere else, please," I said. "And yes," I added, once she'd moved it away. "That red-hot poker—what are you doing with it?"

"Why, it's for my art, of course." Amy's tone was still unruffled. It occurred to me that over the years Amy had become quite the people person, knowing what to say in order to defuse a situation or to get what she wanted out of others. "I've taken up poker-sketching," she continued. "Basically, you take a red-hot poker and use it to sketch things with on hard surfaces, like wood."

It didn't surprise me that this art form hadn't survived into the twenty-first century—at least, not that I could remember.

The way Amy waved that thing around, sometimes leaving it on surfaces so that some of us feared the house would burn down around our heads—who knew art could be so dangerous?

Now that Aunt March was paying for Amy to take art lessons, Amy had gone from simple pen-and-ink drawings to the poker-sketching. From there, she proceeded on to oils, her paintings shockingly unrealistic; charcoal portraits of family members—was there a reason why only my portrait was so unattractive?; clay and plaster—trying to make a cast of her own foot, she got that foot stuck in a bucket, causing Jo to accidentally cut that foot with a knife when she extricated it, that cut reviving the old tensions between Jo and Amy that had been dormant ever since the manuscript-burning incident.

But all of this—all of Amy's . . . *art*—was a dangerous thing.

The first time I'd read *Little Women*, I remember being charmed by Amy's growing interest as an artist. I hadn't seen it as the beginning of the end, not the way I saw it now. Amy's *art*—it would eventually take her away on a trip, where her newfound sophistication would become impressive, where she would—

Why should Amy end up with the boy?

I had to stop it. I saw that now. I wasn't sure how or when, but when the opportunity arose, I'd stop Amy from taking that trip.

And then I'd take her place.

After the disaster with the clay and plaster foot, Amy turned her artistic attention to nature sketching. *Well, at least there are no red-hot pokers involved with that,* I thought.

But as her special course neared its end, she announced that it might be nice to have some of the girls from her class over for a luncheon, after which she'd take them on a tour of the area so that they might see all the spots that inspired her art, which the girls admired.

Marmee thought this a fine idea.

Until she found out that Amy wanted to invite fourteen girls.

"That does sound like a bit much," Marmee said.

Amy hurried to point out that it was not really "a bit much," because she would use her own money to pay for everything, plus she was certain we would all want to help out with the preparations.

"If I can't have it as I like it, I don't care to have it at all," Amy announced.

Something about the way she said that struck me. I could almost never identify it when my sisters said something word for word in the way they had in the original book—it's not, after all, as though *Little Women* is packed with quotable quotes like "To be or not to be"—but I would have bet my last bonnet that this sentence was uttered exactly as written. It was kind of eerie for some reason, almost as though Amy were repeating a rehearsed line. But I shrugged that off because Jo was busy objecting to having the party at all.

"I just can't see the point of it," Jo said. "You'll work like a dog getting ready for your little luncheon"—I could see Amy wince at that qualifying *little*—"or you'll get the rest of us to work like dogs for you. Then the girls will come or they won't, but whatever the case, they're all wealthy. None of them will be impressed by what you put out and I highly doubt that any of them care about you anyway. So why not save us the bother by not having it at all?"

That's when Amy pointed out, in a surprisingly diplomatic

fashion, that she and Jo had vastly different values. She didn't come out and say that Jo's values were all wrong, but despite Amy's diplomacy, I thought Jo might blow a gasket when Amy detailed what she saw as Jo's values. They involved doing as Jo liked, and not caring what anyone else thought about what she did or said or wore.

But Jo didn't blow a gasket. Instead, she laughed good-naturedly at Amy's comparison between the two of them and even grudgingly agreed to help out as best she could.

And I had to grudgingly admit that I was on the side of Jo's values. Once upon a time, back in my twenty-first-century life, everything that Amy said would have made sense to me: the need to maintain the kind of image that would impress people; the need to be thought cool. But now I saw that Jo's way was the right way.

Jo may have been annoying, Jo may not have cared about dressing fashionably or about what anyone else thought.

But at least Jo was *real*.

The day of the grand luncheon dawned . . .

. . . and then the day passed.

Amy thought she was being smart in telling the girls the event would take place on Monday *or* Tuesday, hedging her bets in case we got a summer storm on Monday. So when Monday turned out to be just slightly drizzly—turning to sunshine by midafternoon—no one showed at the appointed hour. This put Amy into a lobster-finding tizzy, since some of the food she'd had us prepare for Monday was already beginning to spoil, so she went on her own into town in search of live shellfish.

But all of Amy's preparations were wasted, because on Tuesday, a very sunny Tuesday, only one of her invited guests arrived: one Miss Eliot.

Unfortunately the one Miss Eliot couldn't possibly eat all the food Amy had gotten Hannah and Meg and everyone else to put together.

By dinner—our fourth meal in two days of Amy Food— Papa declared enough to be enough.

That was when Amy suggested sending the leftovers to the Hummels, adding that, "Germans like messes."

I still blamed the Hummels for Beth getting scarlet fever, even though I knew in my heart it wasn't really their fault—Beth was so good, they couldn't have stopped her coming to help. But even I would never say anything so obviously rude like "Germans like messes."

Where did Amy come up with this stuff?

No, really: Where did Amy come up with this stuff?

"I look forward to the day I take my place among 'our best society,'" she said that night as we all sat in the parlor. She actually said that phrase, "our best society," as though she didn't even see the irony in the air quotes her tone implied.

She was sketching when she said this, the rest of us occupied with various things.

"What exactly does 'our best society' mean to you?" I asked, fully aware that when *I* put the air quotes in my tone, I intended the irony.

"People with money," she said, "people of position, people who understand fashion."

And just where had this Amy March come from? I noticed for the first time how different she looked from the rest of us:

how much time she put into her appearance and how she did always manage to look fashionable, while we mostly made do with what we had. Honestly, if she weren't living with us in our humble home—what with the way she looked and dressed and spoke now that she'd mostly learned not to mangle the English language—it would be easy to picture her living a *Real Housewives of Victorian New England* kind of life.

I laughed then and, speaking my thoughts aloud, said, "Sometimes, it's almost like you don't come from this family at all!"

"That's because—" Amy started to say, but then stopped herself as she put her pencil aside to stare at me. "What *are* you trying to say, Emily?"

"Only that you're so different from the rest of us." I shrugged, not knowing what was bothering her. "With your interest in 'our best society,' something no one else here is interested in, certainly not Jo"—at this Jo snorted—"you almost seem like you were dropped here from another family. The way you're interested in money, as though you have some sense of what it's like to have money—"

"But of course I do." Amy cut me off. "As you well know, Papa had plenty of money, but he lost it at one point. We used to live a much grander lifestyle than we do now." Blushing, she turned to look at Papa. "Sorry, Papa."

"That's quite all right, Amy," he said.

But wait a second here. I distinctly remembered one time Meg making a big deal about being the only one of us to be old enough to remember the days when the family had been well off and Jo saying she could remember it too, the implication being that the rest of us—including Amy, who was a full three years younger than Jo—weren't old enough to have such memories.

So where did Amy's come from?

When I tried to ask her about it, with what seemed to me to be an innocent enough question, Amy got red in the face and replied with a huff:

"Well, I have heard all the stories, haven't I? I mean, of course that's the only way I could know about it—really, Emily, sometimes I think Jo is right about you!"

Twenty-Seven

One thing Jo should have had right about me was that I was competitive with her where writing was concerned, but she wasn't even aware of that because: 1) I hadn't worked on my book in a long time, and 2) except for that long-ago thing with the *Pickwick Portfolio/Twist Times*, she'd never known about it in the first place.

But that was all about to change . . .

Miss Crocker invited Jo to escort her to a lecture on the Pyramids that was being given as a People's Course.

I couldn't even remember who Miss Crocker was when Jo told us about it, but then, straining memory, I remembered she was the family friend who'd come to dine with us that time Marmee tricked us all into being bored with our leisure, the same day that Jo put salt on the strawberries and Beth's canary, Pip, had died.

Funny thing about living in Marchville. You could meet some-one who was supposed to be a close family friend and then not have them show up again for another four years.

Anyway, Miss Crocker had invited Jo to escort her, Jo had said yes, and Jo was very happy about it.

"It shall be good to do something different for a change," Jo said.

That did sound appealing.

"Can I come too?" I asked.

"No," Jo said, "you weren't invited."

I thought about fighting her on it. It was a free lecture, after all, open to the public—*I* was the public! But—eh—I just wasn't up for all the dramarama.

So I let her go.

I'd planned on ignoring Jo when she got back. After all, if I wasn't welcome, what did I care about the Pyramids anyway? Besides which, the Pyramids were just big sandy triangles in the desert; it's not like there was anything new to say about them.

But when Jo came in, she was bouncing around like a pinball, she was so excited. "Must've been some lecture," I said. "Did some-one discover a fourth Pyramid or something?"

"Oh, who cares about that?" Jo said. Then she pulled some-thing from a pocket of her skirt. It was a crumpled article that she'd torn from a newspaper. Smoothing the creases, she handed it to me. "Read this!"

I read.

The newspaper was sponsoring a contest. The winner would receive a grand prize of one hundred dollars—a small fortune around here. The only thing the winner had to do was write the most sensational story of all those submitted.

"A boy at the lecture gave me the newspaper to read while we were waiting for it to start," Jo went on enthusiastically. "And I had the chance to read one of the stories they regularly print before I even knew about the contest. The story was positively dreadful! I know I could do better than that. But the boy said the author was extremely popular."

"Who was the author?" I asked. If the author was extremely popular, maybe I'd heard of him or her in my previous life. I strained to recall popular authors from the late 1800s, but the only one I could think of at the moment was: "Louisa May Alcott?" I guessed.

"Who?" Jo's puzzled expression quickly turned to typical annoyance as she shook her head at me. "No, it was Mrs. S.L.A.N.G. Northbury."

"Of course," I said, as though I'd known all along. It was crazy the strange names people came up with around here. Mrs. Northbury's first name was as bad as Blank Hospital when Papa was sick down in Washington. But then I realized that Evelina Massachusetts, the pseudonym I'd chosen to be published under in *The Eagle* that one time, was right up there.

"You can't possibly have ever heard of Mrs. Northbury," Jo began to object, "when *I* have never even heard of her before tonight!" She shook her head again. "But never mind that now. I am going to enter this contest *and* I am going to win it."

"Oh?" I asked innocently. "And have you decided yet what your winning sensational story is going to be about?"

"*Yes.*" Jo's eyes shone. "It will be about romance and despair, there will be an earthquake, *and*"—here she paused dramatically as though waiting for an invisible drummer to add a roll—"it will all take place in . . . *Lisbon.*"

"My, that does sound sensational," I said.

But inside I was thinking:

Bring. It. On.

Jo completed her sensational story about romance, despair, an earthquake, and Lisbon, and sent it off with a prayer. Meanwhile I brushed off "A Woman from the Future"—the story I'd originally written for *The Eagle*—adding to the original story about a teenager who time travels from the twenty-first century to the 1800s. Then I sent mine off too, and I even used my real name this time, but without the prayer.

I figured I didn't need it because I had the most sensational story going.

We waited six long weeks to hear the results of the contest. Jo waited loudly, because everyone knew she'd entered—even the milkman had to listen to her go on about it!—while I waited in silence, because no one knew I had.

At last, after we'd both given up on winning—Jo loudly, I silently—an envelope arrived.

"*Emily* won the writing contest?" Amy all but shrieked.

I couldn't believe it—my story chosen as the best! It was the most excited I'd felt about anything in a long time. One hundred dollars? Around here, I could probably buy my own house for that kind of money!

"Here," Amy said as the others gathered around, "let me see that story."

She read, moving her lips, as the others read over her shoulder, not moving theirs at all.

"But this is that story that appeared in *The Eagle* years ago!" Amy all but shrieked again. "*You* were Evelina Massachusetts?"

I nodded modestly.

"You never should have done this," Amy said, thrusting the sheets back at me.

"Ex*cuse* me?"

"Writing about time travel, giving people all sorts of crazy ideas—it's dangerous."

What an odd thing to say. "What are you talking about?" I demanded.

"Never mind that now," Jo said, her face solemn as she took a step toward me. "Congratulations, Emily," she said, thrusting her hand out. "I didn't even know that you *could* write, but apparently the best woman won. And that's as it should be." Her expression turned to sad puzzlement then. "Funny, though. I was almost certain I would win."

That's because you were supposed to, I was tempted to say, remembering how it went down in the book.

I took Jo's hand then and gave it a firm shake, but all the excitement at winning had gone out of my body. Somehow I'd altered the story of *Little Women* just enough to steal victory from her.

I should never have won that stupid contest.

Jo should have.

Once the moment had passed and everyone had congratulated me, people wanted to know what I would do with my winnings.

Everyone had ideas.

Me, I wasn't so sure. There were so many possibilities!

"New things for my wardrobe so that I can be more fashionable like Amy?" I mused aloud, completely forgetting my earlier conclusion that Jo's attitude was the superior one, that surfaces didn't matter. Then I grew really excited. "I could buy a lot of new books!"

"New books would be wonderful," Jo said, but for once she didn't sound enthusiastic, even though books were usually her favorite material thing in the world.

"Well, what would you've done with the money if you'd won?" I asked.

She didn't even have to think about it, which told me she'd already thought this out in advance. "I'd give the money to Beth and Marmee so that they could go to the seaside for a month or two. It would do them both a world of good."

Beth and Marmee immediately made noises about how they couldn't possibly accept such a thing, even though Jo had no financial power to offer it, but I saw Jo was right. I may have interfered with who won the contest, but the same good stuff could still come from the winnings.

"Yes," I said. "That's exactly the thing to do with the money."

"I'm giving up writing," Jo announced as Beth and Marmee packed the next day. Back home, going on vacation took some real planning, but here, apparently, you could decide you were going away and—poof!—you were gone.

Too bad it didn't work that way for time travel.

"What do you mean, give up writing?" I said in a more scornful voice than I'd intended. "You can't give up writing. You're Jo March. It's who you are! It's what you do!"

"It's who I *was* and what I *did*," Jo said. "But not anymore. Why, if I can't even win a simple contest against *you* . . ."

Any other time, I would have been offended. But not then. She was serious. And I couldn't let her give up writing. Jo and her writing—it was one of the best things about the story.

"It wasn't a *simple* contest, Jo," I said. "It was a *stupid* contest."

"What are you talking about?"

"It was a stupid contest," I said again. "Why do you think I was able to beat you? I only did because it was a stupid contest, challenging writers to come up with the most outlandish thing they could come up with. And let's face it, I'm pretty outlandish!"

"What are you saying?"

"I'm saying that you're better than that contest, Jo. Someday you'll write something far superior to your story about romance, despair, an earthquake, and Lisbon—you'll even write something superior to my story—but only if you don't quit."

When Beth and Marmee returned from the seaside, Beth didn't look as perfectly healthy as we'd hoped for, but she did look better. As for Marmee, everyone agreed she looked at least ten years younger.

As everyone else continued to greet and exclaim over them, I turned to Jo.

"Beth looks good," I said, "better than she has in a long time."

"She does," Jo agreed.

"This is all your doing."

"*My* doing? But you won. It was *your* money."

"Maybe. But it was your idea."

First encouraging her to keep writing and now this, giving

her credit for a good idea—Jo looked at me as though seeing me for the first time. Well, maybe she was.

Jo didn't stop writing.

In fact, she'd gone back to her manuscript right after Beth and Marmee left for the seaside. She'd copied it out four times until she had it the way she wanted it—oh, what these Victorian writers had to go through for their art!—and then she'd submitted it to three publishers. And now that Beth and Marmee were back? Jo had gotten a positive response from one publisher, saying that yes, they would publish her book, but only if she trimmed it by a third and cut all her favorite parts.

The house was divided on what Jo should do, with opinions varying from Beth's, that not a single word should be changed, to Amy's practical advice to cut it up and sell it, further saying that when Jo made her fame and fortune, *then* she could "afford to digress, and have philosophical and metaphysical people in your novels."

It was easy enough for any of us to imagine Amy using the word *philosophical* because it was a word Papa used with some regularity. But *metaphysical?* Jo shrugged it off, even joking that Amy must have meant to say *mysterious* or some other word but had stumbled over *metaphysical* first. But I wasn't so sure. I knew that *metaphysical* meant something to do with a reality beyond what is perceptible to the senses—or, to put it shortly, the supernatural.

What was Amy doing with such a word in her vocabulary?

"That's what I'll do!" Jo announced, cutting off my train of thought. "I'll hack my book to shreds and then I'll sell it!"

Which is exactly what she did.

She cut the book. Then she sold it to one Mr. Allen for the sum of three hundred dollars and he published it to equal parts praise and scorn from the general public.

Jo was on her way to where she was always meant to be.

Twenty-Eight

"Where's everyone going?" I shouted.

First Jo had raced by me, followed by Amy, Marmee, Papa, Hannah, and finally Beth.

Beth turned, already half out of breath, and stopped long enough to answer.

"Didn't you hear Lotty?" She paused to breathe again and then gasped out with, "Meg's had her baby!"

"Her *baby*? When was Meg even *pregnant*?"

"Silly Emily. Always playing fun games with me. Everyone knew Meg was pregnant." She laughed. "Where have you been the last nine months?"

Here we go again . . .

Yes, theoretically, I knew at least a few more months had passed since Meg got married, what with the contest, Beth and Marmee going away to the seaside, and Jo selling and publishing a book and all. But *nine* of them?

And it had to be at least nine, since Meg and John would never have done anything, er, *baby-producing* before they got married.

But how had this happened to me again? First I'd lost three years between their engagement and wedding, and now I'd gone and basically lost another nine months?

I shook my fist at the ceiling.

Darn you, book!

"Emily, why did you just do that?" Beth wondered.

"Hmm . . . ?"

"Shake your hand at the ceiling like that."

"Oh. Sorry." Suddenly I had to know how much time I'd lost. "How old am I, Beth?"

"Silly Emily." She laughed what had become my favorite laugh in the world; she was so sweet. "Once again you pay me the favor of asking me a question to which I know the answer. You are eighteen. You have been eighteen since the day before Meg and John's wedding, it is now ten months later, so you will be nineteen in a few more months."

Nineteen in a few more months? At this rate, I'd be old and dead in another few chapters!

"Excuse me," Beth said, visibly struggling to control her impatience, "but do you think we might join the others at Dovecote now? You know, to see the babies?"

"Babies? But you said 'baby' before. I would swear on my life that you did."

Babies? Had another nine months or more already passed just in the time I'd been speaking with Beth, and Meg had already had a second child?

Oh dear. If that was the case I was going to need some smelling salts and a fainting couch over here.

Beth laughed again. "I'm sorry if I confused you. Meg had

twins. But I was so surprised at that news myself, I keep saying 'baby' when I mean to say 'babies.'"

Thank God for that, I thought, feeling some small relief as I rose to join her on the walk to Dovecote. At least I wasn't totally losing my mind. Or sense of time.

"Meg had a boy and a girl," Beth chattered happily as we strolled together. "Lotty said they are to be called John and Margaret, after their parents, which I do think might get awfully confusing."

There were three words I hadn't spoken aloud together in years, not since before I came to this strange new world. In fact, the last time I said them, it had probably been to my parents back home, but I felt moved for some reason to say them now.

"I love you, Beth," I said impulsively.

Beth stopped in her tracks, turned to look at me in surprise.

"Why, what a lovely thing to say, Emily! I'm sure it's something we all feel for one another and yet, oddly, we never speak the words out loud." She paused before adding shyly, "And I love you, too."

It felt good to hear that. I hadn't realized until that moment how much I'd missed hearing someone, anyone, say those words to me.

Upon arriving at Dovecote and meeting the new additions to the family, I learned that baby Margaret was to be nicknamed Daisy, while baby John, at Laurie's suggestion, was to be named Demijohn. Or Demi for short.

Demijohn?

Were these people for real?

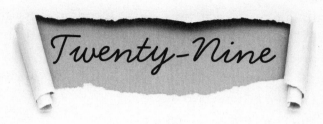

Twenty-Nine

Jo, Amy, and I were at Aunt March's visiting with Aunt March and Aunt Carrol.

Aunt Carrol.

It reminded me of that Miss Crocker woman, the one who was supposed to be such a close family friend when she appeared for dinner the night Pip died, only to turn up again much later to have Jo escort her to that People's Course on the Pyramids. Similarly, I'd never heard of Aunt Carrol until she showed up at Meg's wedding, and now here she was again at Aunt March's.

If I didn't know any better I'd swear these barely seen women were some sort of literary contrivance.

And how had we gotten here—Jo, Amy, and me—visiting Aunt March and Aunt Carrol?

It had started a few hours earlier . . .

"But, Jo, you *promised!*" Amy all but whined. "You said that if I did that picture of Beth for you, you'd go on six calls with me today!"

Okay, she actually did whine.

"I'm sure I said nothing of the sort," Jo said. "I hate going on calls."

Calls, apparently, were visits paid to friends in the neighborhood. Certainly it had nothing to do with having a telephone.

I missed having my own phone.

Gee, I wondered if I'd still be stuck here in 1876 when Alexander Graham Bell invented his.

"You did so promise," Amy said.

Apparently calls were something people regularly did in the 1800s and yet this was the first I heard of anyone in our family going on a round of them since being here.

"You promised, you promised, you promised," Amy insisted.

"*Fine*," Jo said irritably. "I'll go with you on your stupid calls . . ." She paused dramatically before adding, "But only if Emily goes with us."

"*Emily?*" Amy was clearly both shocked and displeased at this.

Emily? Me, I was just shocked.

"Yes," Jo said coolly. "If Emily comes along, I might find the idea of paying calls on people I couldn't care a fig about just barely bearable."

Since when had *I* become Jo's go-to person for companionship?

Wow, when I talked her back into being a writer again, it must have made quite an impression.

✦

"It's important we make a good impression on people," said Amy, adjusting her gloves so that the bows were in the exact same position on each hand as she strolled along. "You never know who might be someone who can do you a favor later."

"Oh, absolutely," Jo and I said simultaneously, breaking into simultaneous giggles as we trailed along behind Amy.

"It's bad enough she made us change into better clothes," Jo whispered to me, although Jo's voice was always so loud regularly, her idea of whispering could probably be overheard by the object of our discussion.

"I know, right?" I agreed. "And now she expects us to behave properly on top of that?"

We broke into peals of laughter.

"What *is* so funny?" Amy spoke sternly, wheeling on us.

"Emily said something uproarious," Jo said, punching me in the shoulder in a friendly way as she tried to stop laughing.

"I only did that because Jo did it first," I said, giving Jo a friendly shoulder jab right back.

"Yes, I can see something is funny," Amy said in exasperation, "but what exactly?" Before either of us could answer, she shook her head.

"Never mind that now. We are at our first stop, the Chesters'. And do please refrain from punching each other when we are inside. It is so unladylike."

Amy may have made a good impression at our first stop, what with her ability to make lame small talk, but Jo and I didn't. The need to behave had been so ingrained in us by Amy that we remained stiff the whole time. I'm sure the Chesters thought we were totally boring.

The second stop, the Lambs', was even worse, but in reverse. We were *too* chatty there, with Jo telling embarrassing stories about Amy as a young girl, and me adding embellishments, leaving the Lambs to conclude we were "great fun," while Amy just glared at us.

At the third stop—I didn't catch the people's name, which made it very difficult to speak politely to them—Jo had yet more fun, and I had fun with her, talking to a bunch of guys our age. With the exception of that time Laurie had taken us picnicking with his English friends, had I spoken with any guys close to my own age? Funny, I couldn't remember. While we talked to the group of guys, Amy focused her attention on just one: a Mr. Tudor, whose uncle had married an English lady who was third cousin to a real live lord. I couldn't see anything great about him, but Amy, being in love with the idea of royalty however far removed, did. Well, Amy would.

At the fourth stop, the Kings', no one was home so we left a card.

At the fifth stop, the young ladies of the house were home but otherwise engaged—too busy to see *us*? But we were so cool! So again we left more cards.

Finally, we arrived at the last stop, Aunt March's.

Which was how we had arrived at Aunt March's to visit with her and Aunt Carrol.

Aunt Carrol: who was this mysterious new relative, really?

She looked like a troublemaker to me.

Jo hadn't even wanted to go inside, claiming she'd rather

risk her life for someone else than be pleasant to people when she didn't feel like it. Remembering the rude parrot, Polly, I'd agreed, but Amy shot us down.

And now we were here.

Jo and I, restless with all these visits, kept popping up from our seats to look at books in the bookcases or pace the room like caged animals. While we did that, Amy sat on the sofa with her back ramrod straight, close to this Aunt Carrol person.

Suck-up came the uncharitable thought.

Even though I was enjoying looking at books and stretching my legs with Jo, far more than I would have sitting with Amy and the aunts, after a while I began to develop a strange sensation of something going on beneath the surface. I turned just in time to see Aunt March and Aunt Carrol exchange a series of meaningful glances: first at Jo, then to each other, to Amy, and to each other again.

What was going on here?

It was immediately obvious that whatever the aunts were trying to figure out, Jo was suffering from the comparison. Well, of course *they* would prefer Amy, with her perfect clothes and her suck-up manners.

Blech.

"Do you speak French?" Aunt Carrol asked Amy, out of the blue.

"Oh yes," Amy replied enthusiastically. "I speak it quite well. Ever since the time I stayed here when Beth was ill, and during my subsequent visits since Aunt March arranged for art lessons for me, I have been able to practice with Esther, her maid. Esther is French, you know."

"And how about you, Josephine?" Aunt Carrol turned her

attention to my restlessly strolling sister. "How are you getting on with languages?"

A chill went up my spine at her words. I don't know what came over me then. I only knew I had to stop Jo from answering. The aunts were testing Jo and Amy, and I suddenly knew that whatever impulsive, brash thing Jo said next would cause her to flunk that test.

"Isn't it lovely out this time of year?" I began chattering just as Jo opened her mouth to speak. "I love everything about"—*what month and season was this?* my mind screamed—"whatever month this is. Why, whenever I hear the birds or see the"—what kind of flowers would be out now?—"*general* flowers blooming, I am always reminded of"—gosh, what could they remind me of? I spied a book on the shelves—"the part in Shakespeare where—"

"Emily, what *are* you talking about?" Jo said, cutting me off when I was really doing so well. "Not knowing what month it is, *general* flowers blooming—and what does Shakespeare have to do with anything?" She shook her head at me, annoyed, before turning to Aunt Carrol. "Don't have any other languages. I've got English and that's plenty for me, the only one I have any use for."

Oh, Jo.

She was always her own worst enemy.

I tried to tell myself it didn't mean anything, the rapid meaningful glances that once again passed between the aunts. As the visit wore on—and on and on—I continued to tell myself that everything was going to be fine, that I'd simply been imagining things. By the end of the visit, I'd almost convinced myself of that.

But as we finally left I felt an impulse to go back, and used the excuse of wanting to borrow that Shakespeare volume from Aunt March.

It was as I stood outside the parlor door that I heard Aunt March say to Aunt Carrol, "You'd better do it"; and Aunt Carrol say ominously in reply, "I certainly will, if her mother and father consent."

NOOOOOOOOOOOOOOOOOOOOOOOOOOOO!!!

Thirty

Soon after our visit with Aunt March, a letter arrived addressed to Marmee from Aunt Carrol, fallout from that fateful day.

Marmee read the letter silently, a smile spreading across her face as she read. When she was finished, she announced the following news:

"Aunt Carrol writes that she is leaving in a month to go abroad and she wants to take—"

"Me!" Jo crowed, cutting her off as she began to prance around the room.

"Amy," Marmee finished her original sentence.

"*Amy?*" Jo said in shocked disgust, ceasing her prancing.

"Yes, Amy," Marmee said as the March girl whose name she just mentioned preened in personal delight and satisfaction. "Apparently the last time you were at Aunt March's you each said things revealing that Amy would make the superior travel companion. And of course Aunt March is paying for the trip."

"Oh, me and my big mouth," Jo said. "But I've wanted to go abroad forever!"

"So have I," Amy said.

And so have I, I thought. This was wrong, on so many levels. But I saw something now that I'd never seen before, not when I was thinking only of myself.

I had to do something.

"Summon Aunt March here," I said with authority.

The others looked at me as though I'd gone mad. Well, maybe I had.

"I don't care how you get her here," I went on. "Someone borrow the carriage from Mr. Laurence, I don't care, but Aunt March must be made to answer for this."

"Emily!" Marmee was shocked.

"I'm sorry, Marmee," I said evenly, realizing as I said it that it was the only time I'd ever actually called her "Marmee" out loud, "but it's only the truth. That old bat throws her money around just to get everyone else to dance to her tune. It isn't right and she must be stopped."

That's what I told them, but it was about more than just putting Aunt March in her place. It was also about keeping Amy from going to Europe. It was about changing the story so it would go the way it *should* have gone all along.

Amy had her hands on her hips as she moved right up into my personal space. "Just who do you think you are to interfere so?" she said.

"I know exactly who I am," I said, hands-on-hipsing her right back as I straightened to my full lack of height. "*I* am the Middle March."

As we waited—*and waited*—for Aunt March to arrive, I had some time to think.

Yes, I was the Middle March, here and back home, but what did that really mean?

I'd always been in the middle, not just in birth order but in the middle of everything, on the fence—scared to say what I really wanted, scared to even *know* what I wanted!

And I'd also always been so down on myself, always looking to others to define my place in the world, wherever that world might be. I'd even accepted it when the others here told me things like "You don't like to garden, Emily" or whatever else they said about me. Instead of resisting, I'd just taken it and walked away.

Who am I? I wondered. *Who have I ever been?*

I'd let myself be so defined by the opinions of others, it was almost impossible to answer that question. But I did know one thing, and that was who I wanted to be now:

I want, I told myself, *to be the kind of person who stands up for what's right.*

Aunt March tromped in with her stupid cane and her stupid lorgnette. Thank God she'd left the stupid parrot at home.

"What *is* the meaning of this?" she demanded.

Who did she think she was, demanding anything? Honestly, we'd been waiting for her there for over two hours. It was a good thing my temper hadn't worn off.

"Don't take that tone with me," I said. "What I'd like to know is: What is the meaning of *you* sending Amy abroad with Aunt Carrol when it's Jo who should go?"

"Josephine?" Aunt March was so shocked at my outburst,

she forgot to turn the last syllable of Jo's name into one long shriek.

"Yes, Josephine. Josephine's the one who took care of you for years and years. The only reason Amy even entered into your world was because she'd never had scarlet fever. You may have fallen in love with Amy's pretty ways, but Jo's the one who deserves a reward. Why, at times she may be the most annoying person who ever lived, but when she's not doing that, she's always sacrificing for other people. She sold her own hair during the war so we'd have money when we needed it. And when she won a hundred dollars in that writing contest, she spent it all so that Beth and Marmee might go to the seaside." I paused. *Oops, wrong plot, Emily! That happened in the original story!* "Okay, so maybe I did that, but it was Jo's idea that inspired me."

I paused to breathe and into the silence of that moment Jo's voice fell with a stunned:

"Emily, I never knew you cared."

"Yeah, well." I brushed her off, like a hand on the forehead when one isn't sick. I had no time for any of that now as I continued:

"If you send Amy abroad instead of Jo, why, it's as bad as what happened to Great-Aunt Louise. She's the one who had to leave school and go to work to help the family during the Depression while her sisters got educated, always getting everything. She's the one who took care of all the older relatives as they died one by one. And what was there for her? No husband, no kids, she never even got out of the country, and the most amazing thing was, she never resented anyone else."

Someone had been tapping me on the shoulder for that whole last sentence. Finally, I turned, saw it was Beth.

"Excuse me. Emily? I hate to interrupt you, but who is Great-Aunt Louise? I've never heard of her before."

I looked around the room, saw the others were all looking at me with equally puzzled expressions on their faces.

Shoot. Of course they'd never heard of Great-Aunt Louise. She was *my* great-aunt from back home. I'd never met her—she'd died too soon—but my real mother had told me all the stories about her.

"Okay," I said quickly, "so I made that part up. But it doesn't matter, because what Aunt March is doing is wrong and it's Jo who should—"

"You know, Emily," Aunt March cut me off, "I never really could see the point of you before today, but now I'm seeing there might be possibilities in you after all. Perhaps I have been hasty in my decision. Perhaps I should send *you* abroad with Aunt Carrol."

Me? Was it really that easy—all I had to do was stand up to Aunt March and Europe was mine? I had to admit, if I had to be stuck in the story forever, it would be a lot more bearable if I could finally see Europe. Once there I could—

Amy's shout cut into my daydreams.

"*You!*" Amy shouted, pointing an accusing finger in my direction. "You . . . *interloper*. You stop interfering right this second. I knew you were going to be trouble from the moment you showed up here."

What did she mean by that?

"Amy," Papa said sternly, "be careful what you say here."

"What do you mean," Marmee said, perplexed, "from the moment Emily showed up here?"

Amy blushed.

And a realization hit me as Amy grabbed on to my elbow

with a muttered "Excuse us for a moment, please" to the others as she practically dragged me from the room:

All those stray things Amy'd said that had struck me as odd since coming here—somehow, Amy had known all along that I'd never really belonged in the story in the first place.

"How long have you known?" I asked, needing to make sure, once we were safely out of hearing.

"Ever since the moment you showed up in front of the fire that time and Jo was saying how it wouldn't be Christmas without presents."

Of course. That was the moment I'd arrived here. But . . .

"How did you know?"

"As Beth would say: Silly Emily!" Amy laughed her tinkling laugh. "I knew because I wasn't in the original story either!"

What???

"What???"

"How else could I know? Like you, I came here from a different time, like that time traveler in that stupid story you wrote." Her expression turned to an admonishing one. "You know, it was very irresponsible of you to write that. Who knows what might happen to us if the others ever guessed we don't really belong here?"

"Wait a second." This was too much for me. "I know how I got here. I'm from the twenty-first century. I was working on some paper on *Little Women* for school in 2011 and—*WHOOSH!*—I got sucked into the book. But how did you get here?"

"2011? Fascinating. You know, I'd always wondered what year you came from, but of course I could never ask *that* question!"

This was incredible: the idea that the book I thought I'd known so well hadn't always been the book I knew.

"Are we the only ones?" I asked.

"Yes, the only ones I've ever seen here. Well, except for Papa."

"*Papa!*"

"Yes, he's really only *my* papa, although he's never minded that the rest of you call him that—not even *you*, Emily, and of course he also knows you don't belong here."

"Well, you don't either," I said heatedly.

"Perhaps not. But *I* got here first."

"When did you and . . . *Papa* come?"

"1881," she answered promptly. "The year after *Little Women* was finally published in one volume."

"One volume?"

"Yes. Originally, it was divided into two separate books. See how little you know?" She shook her pretty head at my stupidity. "I'd read it first when it was two books, so I already knew the story. Anyway, Papa had bought me a copy of the new one-volume book, we were reading it side by side, I was saying I didn't like certain parts of it, he was agreeing and, as you say— *WHOOSH!*—we got sucked right in."

How well I knew that *WHOOSH!*

"You know," Amy went on, "before *we* got here, it was just a story about a mother and her three daughters during the Civil War. The husband is fighting down South but then he dies. Very sad."

"Wait a second. There were only *three* girls in the original version?"

But Amy waved off my question and was speaking again.

"You know, having you around was just barely tolerable when

you were doing nice things like trying to save me that day on the ice—what a surprise that was to me! I was expecting Jo to come to my rescue, because she always does at that point in the story. But then you stalled us at the house and I began wondering how the scene would play out. I have to say, it was a treat to see it go so differently for a change. You know, when you've lived through a story as many times as I've lived through this one, a surprise can be a beautiful thing. But never mind that now. It's no longer tolerable if you're going to try to change things like who goes abroad."

"But haven't *you* ever tried to change anything?"

"Oh yes," Amy said. "I change things all the time. Usually just little things. Like that part where I invite the other art students over? That wasn't in the original. I added it because I thought it would be fun to have a luncheon centered all around me." She frowned. "It's too bad it didn't work out so well." Then she brightened. "Oh! And I also added the incident with the limes. That accomplished two things for me: it got me lots of sympathy, plus I was sick of going to that wretched school with Mr. Davis. Being the only March girl to have to go to some stuffy school? I should think not!"

"Little things," I said, understanding, "like I changed things with Beth, making it so she won't die. Well, I know that wasn't a *little* thing."

"You think you've kept Beth from dying?" Now Amy looked sad.

I nodded. "Of course I did. I think it was when I invented penicillin."

"Penicillin? What's that?" She shook her own puzzlement away before I could answer her. "No, you didn't," she said, still sad. "You only postponed the inevitable. But you can't stop Beth from dying. Believe me, I tried everything I could think of to stop it. One time, I even went to the Hummels' in her place, but it didn't change anything. She snuck out when I wasn't looking and went to see them by herself. Beth dying—it was always the one thing I hated about the book. In fact, it was the thing Papa and I were complaining about when we got sucked into the story, how unbelievably sad it was. But it never can be stopped. Beth always dies in the end."

"You mean, then . . . ?"

"Yes, she'll die this time too. It's just a matter of time."

Wait a second. I'd thought my purpose here was to keep Beth from dying. But if there was nothing I could do to prevent that, how was I ever going to get out of here? Then I thought of the reality of what Amy'd said—*Beth dying*—and worries about my own problems disappeared for the moment.

"Now I'd like to ask you some questions," Amy said, intruding on my thoughts.

"Such as?"

"What's the future like?" she asked eagerly. "I've been dying to know, ever since you got here, but of course I couldn't ask you before today."

"The future?"

"Yes! What are the fashions like? What are people like? What is *life* like?"

Up to this point, I'd felt kind of like I was conducting an interview with her, trying to learn as much as I could because there was finally someone to answer my questions. But she'd turned the tables on me and now it was *her* interviewing *me*.

"Fashions?" I echoed. Typical Amy. That would be the first thing she'd ask about. "Well, people no longer wear long dresses unless they're going to a prom or something."

"What is a prom?"

"A prom is . . ." I stopped myself. It would take too much to answer that. "Dresses are much shorter, but girls like us wear mostly pants or even shorts."

"And shorts are?"

"Really short pants."

Amy's eyes opened wide. "You mean girls show their *legs*?"

"All the time."

Amy thought about this. "Oh, I would love that. I have very nice legs, but no one ever gets to see them. Tell me more! How else are things different?"

"Well, there are skyscrapers, tall buildings that are sometimes over one hundred stories tall."

"One hundred stories tall? You are lying!"

"No, I'm not. And there are phones, devices for talking to people in other places. Instead of horses and carriages, people drive their own cars, which are motorized vehicles. Oh, and they fly in planes too."

"People *fly*?"

"No, the people don't fly. The planes fly and the people fly in the planes."

"Oh my. The future does sound very different indeed."

"It is different, but some things are exactly the same. We still have sibling rivalry."

Amy wrinkled her nose. "What's that?"

"It's what makes you want Laurie instead of letting Jo have him. I think it's what made me want him too."

"I don't feel like talking about Laurie right now." Amy wrinkled her nose again. "There will be plenty of time for him later. Now tell me, I know Louisa Alcott wrote a sequel to *Little Women* called *Little Men* and—"

"She wrote two," I said. "There was another called *Jo's Boys*."

"*Two* sequels? Oh my! The second must have come out after I got stuck in here. At any rate, I never read the one I know about and I obviously never read the one I didn't know about, and I've been positively *dying* to know for ages: Am *I* in those books too? What do I do? What is my hair like? What—"

"Never mind all that now!" OMG, was there ever a creature more vain than Amy March? "Getting back to these 'little changes' you say you're always making—don't readers notice? When you originally changed the story in 1881, by joining it, didn't anyone notice?"

"How should I know what readers noticed or not?" Now she was disgusted. "I wasn't out there with them, was I? I was stuck in here!"

"Haven't you ever tried to get out?"

"Yes. At first I thought there must be a rabbit hole somewhere—you know, like *Alice in Wonderland*?—but if there is, I haven't found it. You'd think if there was a way in, there must be a way out, wouldn't you? Then Papa got the idea of apologizing to the book. Papa's not usually given to such..." She paused as though struggling to find the right word. "... *whimsical* thoughts, but he was feeling pretty desperate that day. It can be tough being Papa in a book like *Little Women*. As it stands, he doesn't get to do much except be talked about a lot when he's in the war and then come back and officiate over Meg's wedding. At least I have my big skating scene. At any rate, Papa's idea was that since we got drawn into the book by criticizing it, perhaps the way out would be through apologizing for that criticism. So we tried that. 'Oh, Book, we apologize for saying anything bad about you.' 'Oh, *Little Women*, we are sorry if we have offended thee.'"

Wow, there's something I'd never thought of—talking to the book!

"But that didn't work," Amy said. "And really, we did feel silly. Eventually, we began to accept that we'd be stuck here forever. It can get dull at times—so much sameness year after year!—but it seems there's always new things to discover, even if they're just small things, and it beats dying."

"But what happens when you get to the end of the story? When the book ends?"

"Why, we just go back to the very beginning, of course. What else would happen?"

Go back to the very beginning? If I couldn't get out of here, I'd be doomed to live through this book over and over again throughout all of eternity? I couldn't let that happen! If that happened, I'd wind up as crazy and silly as Amy!

"The original book," I said urgently, "the *real* original, you've read it—how did it end?"

"Oh. That."

"Yes. That."

Now she looked uncomfortable as she twisted her hands together. "Well, Jo goes abroad with Aunt Carrol and there she eventually meets up with Laurie—you know, he goes to comfort her after Beth dies—and then of course they get married in the end."

They *what?* Amy had claimed that she'd only ever been able to change "little things," but changing the person who goes abroad with Aunt Carrol—and the person who winds up with Laurie—was no little thing!

I started from the room, but Amy grabbed my arm, hard.

"What are you planning to do now?" she demanded. "You

can't interfere any more. Don't you understand? Do you have any idea how difficult it was for me getting used to the hardships of the 1860s when I came here used to the modern conveniences of the 1880s? If I have to live through the story, I'm going to wind up with Laurie."

Talk about an interloper!

I shook her hand off and marched out of the room.

Reentering the parlor, with Amy scampering behind me still trying to stop me, I walked right up to Jo.

I grabbed Jo by the biceps with both hands—*man,* she had well-developed biceps!—and gave her a good shake. I didn't care that everyone else was looking, what they were thinking.

It was time I did the right thing. It was time I became a better person.

"I don't care how you do it," I warned Jo, "but you must be the one to go abroad. If you don't, Amy will go. She'll go to London, she'll go to Paris, she'll go to Heidelberg." I stopped. Heidelberg—where had that come from? I'd never even heard of Heidelberg! I shrugged the thought off, barreled on. "And she'll go to Nice. Eventually, Laurie will find her there to comfort her about"—I shook my head, shook the sadness away—"something really sad, but never mind that now. The point is, he will find her and eventually they will get married."

"Amy and Teddy married?" Jo laughed, as did everyone else except for Amy.

"I know," I said, "it's a real laugh riot, right? Except it isn't, because that is exactly what will happen if you don't go abroad. Meanwhile, while Amy's larking around Europe on *your* trip with *your* Teddy, you'll go to New York to live in a boarding-house. You'll meet an old German guy with a beard and you'll agree to become his wife one day when you come across him walking in the rain with a parcel under his arm and he shares his umbrella with you."

"New *York*? An old German *guy*? An *umbrella*?" Jo wrenched one of her arms from my grasp, placed her hand on my forehead.

Now, *that* was still annoying.

"Are you feeling all right?" Jo's voice was full of concern. "Is this just one of your castle-in-the-air stories like before with Great-Aunt Louise?"

How was I ever going to persuade her?

"So what *if* it is?" I sighed. "I'm telling the truth." I paused. "Think about the bread, Jo," I said meaningfully. "Think about the moldy bread."

Jo looked sharp at me then and I knew she was remembering. Maybe it was wrong of me to use that, since I knew now that the bread hadn't saved Beth, wouldn't save Beth. But maybe it would at least make Jo listen to me.

"I know things," I said, and I did, even if I didn't know how to save Beth. "You may not realize it now, but you love Laurie. You're in love with him. Maybe you're too blind to see it, but he certainly knows he's in love with you."

It was so true, all of it. I saw that now.

"Everyone knows you two belong together," I finished some-what lamely.

Jo was puzzled now.

"But I thought," she said, "you wanted Laurie for yourself."

"No. Maybe. I don't know. I thought I did, once."

It struck me then, how for so long I'd *thought* I wanted Laurie, but it was only ever the *idea* of him—the idea of having something that was really meant for one of my sisters. It was the whole Jackson thing all over again. And now I saw that there had been signs all along that I didn't really *like him* like him—starting with the fact that I felt nothing when we kissed—but *I'd* been the one who'd been too blind to see the truth.

"It doesn't matter anymore," I told Jo, "what I once thought I wanted. Now I want him for you. Anyone who's ever seen the two of you together knows you belong together." I paused before adding, "It's the way the story was always meant to be."

V-ROOM!

What was that sound?

It sounded like a vacuum cleaner.

Wait a second, I told myself. No one had a vacuum cleaner in the 1800s!

But the sound didn't stop. Instead, it grew in volume and suddenly I felt myself spinning in circles rapidly, spinning and spinning until . . .

WHOOSH!

Epilogue

Talk about getting sucked out of a good book!

I sit at the desk staring at a piece of paper without even seeing what's on it.

Okay, *what* just happened here?

Really, *what* just happened?

I get out of my chair and rush to the floor-length mirror in the corner of the room. The reflection looking back is me. No more gowns and boots. No more hair piled on top of my head in pins. It's me, in my regular clothes with my regular hair. I move a little from side to side—hey, I don't have a corset anymore! I reach into the neck of my shirt and snap the thin strap on my shoulder. Yup, I got my bra back.

I turn away from the mirror and look around my room—*my room*—and see all my familiar things, familiar even though it feels like forever since I've seen them. I touch my iPod and my computer like I'm greeting old friends and it hits me: I'm not in the March house anymore. Or at least not *that* March house.

What happened?

Did I bump my head? Did I fall asleep at my desk and have the longest dream ever? Is this like *The Wizard of Oz*, with me as Dorothy, certain I've had the most amazing adventure ever while everyone around me is trying to convince me it was all just a dream?

Did any of that really happen at all?

"Emily!" Charlotte calls, and a moment later there's a knock at my door. "Emily. Mom says it's time for dinner."

Charlotte! Mom!

I throw the door open and throw my arms around Charlotte's neck. I've missed her so much without even realizing it.

"Um, Emily?" she says, stiff in my arms. "What are you doing?"

"Sorry," I say, letting her go.

"It's okay," she says hurriedly. "I just didn't understand. I think it's been over four years since you hugged me."

Four years? That's the amount of time I was away!

"What year is this?" I ask.

"It's the same year it was when you woke up this morning, you know that. What's gotten into you?"

I can't believe it. I feel like I've been away forever, and yet I haven't?

I go to my desk, look down at the date on the paper there, the one I was looking at without really seeing it before. It's my outline for the paper for Mr. Ochocinco's class. The date on it? Let's just say it is *not* in the 1860s.

I feel like so much has happened to me, like so much has changed in my life, and yet nothing here has changed at all?

Suddenly I hear a voice in my head, my *own* voice:

It's the way the story was always meant to be.

Maybe Charlotte and me have never been close, and maybe I always blamed *her* for that. But I see now that while I'll never be able to control anyone else's behavior or choices, I *can* control what *I* bring to my relationships.

I go to Charlotte, grab her by the shoulders.

"You have to let Jackson know you like him, Charlotte. If you don't, eventually—maybe not tomorrow, maybe not until next year, but eventually he'll wind up with Anne."

"*Anne?* What are you talking about? Have you bumped your head?"

Maybe I have. Mentally, I gotta give Charlotte credit though. At least *she* doesn't put her hand to my forehead to see if I've got a fever.

"Never mind about me," I say. "I know what I'm telling you may sound crazy. But you have to believe me. I do know what I'm talking about."

"But why would I tell Jackson I like him? And why would Jackson ever go for Anne? You two are always together. He clearly likes you."

I swallow my guilt. Not only does Jackson not know that Charlotte likes him, but Charlotte has no clue that Jackson likes her.

I do what I should have done all along.

I tell Charlotte the truth.

It's the way the story was always meant to be.

After dinner, even though the rest of the weekend is still ahead of me and even though the assignment for Monday is just for the outline, with the paper not due until the following Monday, I sit down to write my paper.

Might as well get this over with while my thoughts are still fresh in my head.

But first, I really want a shower.

I go to the bathroom, thrilled with what I find there: a real live twenty-first-century bathroom. Do people who live in the present even know how lucky they are?

After about an hour of hot water and conditioner, I return to my paper.

> *When you first gave us this assignment, to change one thing in a favorite book, I knew which book I wanted to write about,* Little Women. *But deciding on just one thing proved harder than I thought. You see, as I'm sure most readers would agree, there are two things wrong with* Little Women: *Beth dying and Laurie winding up with Amy instead of Jo.*
>
> *Let's face it: everyone hates it when Beth dies. It's just so sad!*
>
> *So for a long time, that's what I thought needed changing: Beth dying. But then I finally came to realize: Beth's dying can't be changed. It's written in the cards the first moment she goes to see the Hummel family. From then on, it's just a matter of time. I realize now that you can change a lot of things in life, but you can't change death. You can't stop it. Death will come, whether you want it to or not.*
>
> *Louisa May Alcott was right to have Beth die, sad as it is.*
>
> *But she was wrong about Laurie and Amy!*
>
> *It's Laurie and Jo who belong together. Anyone with eyes in their head and a brain to read knows that!*

So that's the one thing, the only thing, I would change about Little Women.

Laurie and Jo should wind up together, because while you can't stop death, love should always, always be allowed to grow where it's meant to be.

On Monday, even though the paper's not due for another week, I hand it to Mr. Ochocinco at the end of class. And, because my paper's short, he sits and reads it while I wait.

While I wait, I think about how since Friday night I've come to realize that whatever I may have thought had happened to me—time travel? really? what was I thinking?—it had all been in my head.

Mr. Ochocinco finishes my paper, hands it back to me.

"Aren't you going to grade it?" I ask.

"It's a fine piece of writing, Emily, and under normal circumstances I would give you an A. But I can't even grade this paper. You'll have to do it over again."

"*What?* Why?"

"Because you obviously haven't read the book. Or if you did, you never finished it."

"What are you talking about?"

What is he talking about? Never even read the book? I feel like I practically *lived* that book!

"You say right here that Laurie winds up with Amy in the end," he says. "But that's wrong. If you'd bothered to finish *Little Women*, you'd remember that Laurie winds up with Jo."

"No, he doesn't," I insist.

"Yes, he does." Mr. Ochocinco swivels his chair, plucks a

volume from the bookcase behind him. Turning, he hands me a copy of *Little Women*, the same volume I have with the woodcut illustrations.

"See for yourself," he says. "Turn to the last chapter where the three remaining sisters are picnicking with their families."

See for myself. See for himself! Is this man on drugs? I'll show him, I think, paging through the book.

I quickly scan the text.

Wait a second here. I don't even see Professor Bhaer's name mentioned. But that's Jo's husband!

I scan through again.

There's something about Meg and John and their kids. Next Jo's name is linked with Laurie's. And Amy—her name is linked with someone I've never even heard of before.

I study the final woodcut at the end of the book, a scene that depicts the three remaining girls clearly paired off with their spouses: Meg and John; Jo and Laurie; Amy with some other guy. Wait a second. Instinctively, I know that guy—he's the red-haired guy that Jo didn't want to dance with one time at a party!

I'll tell you one thing. In that picture, Amy does *not* look happy. In fact, she almost looks as though she's scowling directly at me.

I hand him back the book, stunned.

"So you see, Emily," he says, "you'll just have to rewrite your paper. Choose something else to change about *Little Women*. Or better yet, choose another book, preferably one you know better."

"Yes, I do see," I say vaguely.

I can't believe this. OMG, did *I* change *Little Women*? Did everything I thought was a dream really happen?

Still feeling dazed, I head toward the door.

"Emily?" Mr. Ochocinco calls after me.

I turn.

"You dropped something from your notebook," he says. Bending, he picks something up from the ground, hands it to me.

I look at the thing in my hand. It's a paper crown, with the initials "P.C." on it.

The Pickwick Club, I mouth the words silently.

But how . . . ?

OMG, it all really did happen. I *lived* in *Little Women*, and I changed the ending!

As I close the door to Mr. Ochocinco's room behind me, I see Jackson and Charlotte pass by in the hallway, holding hands.

After I told Charlotte about Jackson liking her on Friday night, and after we finished eating dinner, she got up the nerve to call him while I worked on my paper—the paper I'll now have to rewrite.

Oh, well.

So Jo wound up with Laurie, and Charlotte is winding up with Jackson. Me, I wound up with neither Jackson nor Laurie. But that's as it should be. It's the way the story was always meant to go. Someday, I'll have my own guy. He won't be either Jackson or Laurie. He'll be some guy I genuinely like for who he is, and who likes me for who I am.

I have *got* to find Kendra—I *need* to tell her everything that's happened!

But then I realize: I'll never be able to tell anyone what's happened to me, what I've seen, where I've been, and how I changed the story even as it changed me—who would ever believe me?

And suddenly I miss my family, my *other* family: starchy Meg, annoying Jo, sweet Beth, and even Amy, the interloper.

I finger the paper crown in my hand as words come to me, words that I instinctively know are the last bit of dialogue Beth speaks before she dies, saying, "... for love is the only thing we can carry with us when we go; and it makes the end so easy."

Yes, Beth, I think. *Yes, it does.*

Author's Note

[Author's Note about the Author's Note: Please don't read this if you haven't finished the book!]

When I was younger, I read *Little Women* more times than I can count. I loved the world Louisa May Alcott created, although I did have two major issues with it: I always hated it when Beth died, and I really hated that Laurie wound up with Amy instead of the person I'd have him end up with if I were in charge of the world, Jo. There are some books you first encounter when you're younger—*Jane Eyre* and *The Great Gatsby* immediately spring to mind—that you read again as you get older, but *Little Women* had never been that way for me. Once I reached a certain age, it became a book I no longer reread, the Marches existing instead in fond memory and movie adaptations.

But then, a few years ago, my daughter, Jackie, and her best friend discovered *Little Women* for the first time, and I began really thinking about the book once more. We discussed how sad it is that Beth dies, how even Joey on *Friends* is so upset about it that he makes Rachel hide the book in the freezer! And we discussed how wrong we all thought it was that Laurie winds up with Amy instead of Jo.

That's when I had the kind of moment that drives so much of my writing: *What if?* In this case, what if a contemporary teen somehow found herself inside the world of *Little Women*, her mission there being to change one of the two problems readers traditionally have with the book? So I sat down and wrote the prologue to *Little Women and Me*, in which Emily is literally sucked into the story. And then I pulled out a copy of *Little Women* and set about writing the rest of my book.

Normally, when writing a book, I might do all of my research first, which in this case would have meant rereading all of *Little Women* before writing my own version. But I didn't do that. Instead, I'd read one chapter of Alcott's book and then write my own version, keeping the plot points and whatever else I wanted from hers, while inserting Emily into the story and adding my own twists. This chapter-by-chapter correspondence goes on through Chapter 30. Alcott's *Little Women* continues for another seventeen chapters while my version veers off there into the epilogue. I leave the story before Beth dies, although the reader now knows that eventually she will, that no matter what Emily did, she couldn't stop that.

Here's the most surprising thing I found while rereading *Little Women*, something I never noticed when I was younger, but that Emily comments on several times during her journey through the book—it's all so random! Sure, there's a plotline, but family members and friends and even events enter the story from out of the blue, like the meeting of the Pickwick Club. The March sisters have been seemingly meeting regularly to put together their own newspaper, but no mention is made of the club before or after the chapter in which that one meeting takes place.

So if readers of my book occasionally think, "Wow! That thing that just happened was so random!" chances are the original book was random first.

One thing that may surprise readers is how I came up with the ending. Most of the time when I write a book, I know how it's going to end practically from the beginning. Not so with *Little Women and Me*. Louisa May Alcott wrote her book in episodic fashion, and so it was with me and mine. But about two-thirds of the way through, I had one of those epiphanies that sometimes happen while writing a book, and I realized: Whoa! Emily's not the only time traveler in the book—Amy's a time traveler too . . . and Papa! That's when I knew how the book would end: Emily and Amy would confront each other, and eventually Emily would "fix" the story, making it so that Jo would wind up with Laurie, thereby earning her way back to her own life.

It was while I was writing the epilogue that another moment of inspiration struck. Earlier, I mentioned the Pickwick Club. In my chapter about that unusual writing society, just as in the original version, the March sisters wear badges with the initials "P.C." on them wrapped around their heads like crowns. There's a great book on writing by Christopher Vogler called *The Writer's Journey*. It primarily discusses writing for film, but a lot of it can be used for writing novels as well. It breaks down a story's structure into twelve parts, and one of the parts near the end is called "the return with the elixir"—think of the elixir as some tangible item that the hero or heroine brings back like a reward for their successful journey or, in Emily's case, proof that the journey even happened. In the epilogue, after Emily talks to her teacher about her paper, she's still stunned by everything that's happened, still unsure if it was all a dream or if it was real. Then the paper crown with "P.C." on it falls out of her notebook—the elixir Emily didn't know she brought back with her—and the truth finally hits: she time traveled into *Little Women* and she changed the ending.

I hope you enjoyed *Little Women and Me* even half as much as I enjoyed writing it. Thanks for reading!

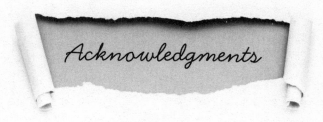

Acknowledgments

Thanks to Pamela Harty and everyone at The Knight Agency for superior representation.

Thanks to Melanie Cecka and everyone at Bloomsbury USA for superior publishing.

Thanks to writers who helped this particular book on its way—Lauren Catherine, Andrea Schicke Hirsch, Greg Logsted, and Rob Mayette—for superior help.

Thanks to Lucille Baratz for being a superior mother, Greg Logsted for being a superior husband, and Jackie Logsted for being the most superior of daughters.

Thanks to booksellers, librarians, and readers everywhere—superlative beings, one and all.

Imitation is the sincerest form of flattery . . .
until it becomes a deadly obsession.

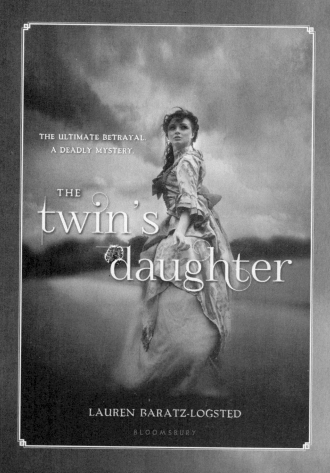

THE ULTIMATE BETRAYAL.
A DEADLY MYSTERY.

THE
twin's
daughter

LAUREN BARATZ-LOGSTED

BLOOMSBURY

Read on for a selection of **LAUREN BARATZ-LOGSTED**'s
engrossing gothic mystery of a long-lost twin, jealousy, and
a murder that will keep you guessing to the last page.

I was thirteen the year everything changed with a single knock at the door.

It was a strong door, sturdy oak, the kind designed to keep the worst of the world's elements outside while keeping safe the occupants on the inside. My mother was making the rounds of the neighborhood, as she often did on weekdays, preferring the use of her own feet to the carriage, while my father was no doubt at his club, regaling his friends with stories concerning the progress of the latest novel he was writing; born into great wealth, my father could afford to treat his career with leisure.

I don't know where the servants were when that knock came. For surely it should have been one of *their* jobs to answer it. But as I sat on the floor of the back parlor, in front of the fire, my long skirts all about me on the carpet with the drawings I was working on spread out along the perimeters of those skirts, the knock came again, more insistent this time. I thought to ignore it—the self-portrait I was working on, showing my long dark hair off to best advantage, was really coming along too nicely to be disturbed! It was probably just one of my mother's friends. Or perhaps it was one of the beggars who occasionally found their way to our front steps, quickly made short shrift of by Cook providing food we no longer wanted at the back. But then the thought occurred to me: what if it was something—however improbable—important?

With reluctance, I set down my charcoal pencil. Brushing off my skirts to straighten them as I rose, I made my way to the source of the knocking, opening the door just in time to see the caller turning away.

The caller's back to me, from behind I made out the tall figure of a woman, so painfully thin as to make me want to feed her, her long gray dress bearing the stains of the elements we usually tried to keep out. Her hair, also glimpsed only from behind, was a naggingly familiar thick hank of gold that no amount of living hard could tarnish, nor could it be kept completely under control by the pins that sought to bind it up in a twist; the tendrils would escape, wisping their way onto the air. Both hands were gloveless despite the frigid day, and in one she carried a thread-bare carpetbag.

"Can I help you?" I asked, catching her attention before she started away.

She turned slowly. At first, her eyes were downcast, but as she moved them upward to meet mine, there came a shock of recognition as I took in the familiar bright blue of her eyes and knew where I had seen that hair before. It was the same place I had seen that porcelain skin, although, I must confess, I had never seen it quite like this: with soot smudges on it. It was as though she had been cleaning out fireplaces herself and hadn't a looking glass to consult before leaving her home.

I couldn't prevent a gasp from escaping my body. "Mother?" I said, reaching a hand out to her. "What has happened to you?"

. . . . .

Of course, as it turned out, it wasn't my mother who had come knocking on the door. Does not a child recognize her own mother?

"Is Aliese Sexton at home?" she asked, speaking in an accent reflective of her lower class attire, naming my mother and ignoring my gasp and what I'd said.

"No, she is not," I said.

"I hope you won't mind, then," she said, slithering around me and into the entryway without so much as a by-your-leave, "if I wait inside."

Shutting the door behind her—it felt good to shut out the cold—I turned just in time to catch sight of the surprise and surprising visitor taking in our vestibule. She nodded as her eyes swept across the soaring height of the ceiling, as though approving it, nodding a second time at the pink marble floor, a third time at the ornate hat rack with its mirrored back and bench seat.

I started to offer to take her cloak, as I would that of any visitor arriving in the winter—or as my parents or the servants would—but then I stopped myself short. Of course, she hadn't a cloak.

"Would you like to leave that here?" I said, indicating the carpetbag she still clutched and pointing at the bench.

"If it's all the same to you," she said coolly, "I prefer to keep it close to my person."

"Of course," I said, trying to smile, trying to appear natural, trying to behave as I thought the adults I knew might behave in similar circumstances . . . as if there ever *could* be similar circumstances. "I don't think Mother will be much longer," I said. With a hand I gestured toward the front parlor. My drawing things, which I was missing now with that longing you have for safe objects when the world has turned confusing, were in the back parlor, but I couldn't bring her there. That cozy room was for family, while the front parlor was for more formal visitors and was surely where my parents or the servants would have shown this woman. "Perhaps you would like to wait in here?"

She followed the direction of my hand, seating herself on one of the white silk sofas, her back ramrod straight, hands tightly clasped in her lap, her carpetbag so close to her legs it touched against the ankle of one of her worn boots. She did not change her position even when I called a servant to bring tea and the tray arrived, the servant barely containing her shock at the appearance of my guest. For my part, it surprised me that the woman did not take any refreshment, since I would have thought she would have accepted a cup, if only to hold something warm in her hands, which I could see now were chapped and raw.

I sat with my own teacup and saucer balanced in my lap, my legs delicately crossed at the ankle beneath my skirts, and it occurred to me for the first time: I didn't even know her name! And yet how do you ask that of someone *after* you have invited them into your home and *after* you have offered them tea and a comfy seat in the front parlor? Do you say, "Oh, by the way, and what are you called and who might you be?" Just as odd, when I stopped to think about it, she hadn't asked my name at the appropriate juncture either, and so that time had passed.

"I don't think Mother will be much longer," I said again, striving for a bright tone, while inside I was hoping my father would arrive first. My father, even if he had been drinking with his friends, would still be better equipped than Mother to deal with whatever . . . *this* was.

"I can wait," the woman said. "I have waited for a very long time."

And so that is what we did: waited, waited, waited in silence as the ornamental clock above the fireplace ticked away the seconds and minutes, eventually striking a new hour.

We both started at the sound of the front door opening, followed by heels tapping on the pink marble floor. I knew from the quality of the tapping that I had not been granted my wish; it was not my father's step.

"Lucy?" I heard my mother's voice call out, and I could picture her removing her gloves, followed by her wrap and finally the pins from her hat, which she would toss blithely at the rack, laughing if she missed the hook. I heard that laugh. "Where are you?" I heard her call to me. "I have missed you." I could hear her step growing closer to the doorway, and I rose from my seat thinking to go to her, to warn her somehow first—although warn her of what exactly, I couldn't say—but her energetic glide was too quick for me and as she blew into the room, the woman who had been seated across from me rose as well.

I stood between them looking from one to the other: the one who was dressed and coiffed in a way that showed she had every advantage in the world—my beautiful, *gorgeous* mother—and her mirror image, but dressed and coiffed far differently. I can say with near certainty that I am the only child in the world who can claim she was there the first time her mother met her twin.

My mother fainted dead away.

Lauren Baratz-Logsted is the author of more than twenty books for adults, teens, and young readers, including *The Twin's Daughter*, *The Education of Bet*, and *Crazy Beautiful*, as well as The Sisters 8 series, which she cowrites with her husband and daughter. She lives in Connecticut.

www.laurenbaratzlogsted.com
@LaurenBaratzL

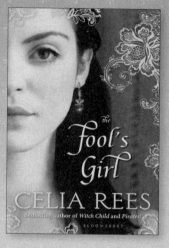
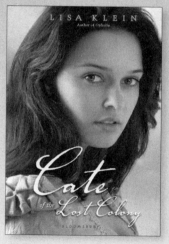

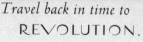

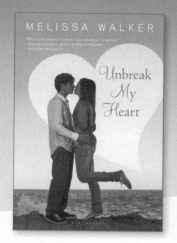

Looking for more
real-life drama?

GIRLS LIKE YOU.
PROBLEMS YOU TOTALLY GET.
ROMANCE ALMOST TOO GOOD TO BE TRUE.

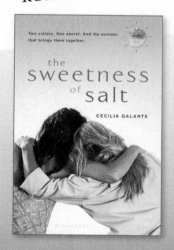